# HIT
# COUNT

# HIT COUNT

BY

## CHRIS LYNCH

ALGONQUIN 2015

Published by

Algonquin Young Readers

an imprint of Algonquin Books of Chapel Hill

Post Office Box 2225

Chapel Hill, North Carolina 27515-2225


a division of

Workman Publishing

225 Varick Street

New York, New York 10014

LIBRARY OF CONGRESS CATALOGING-IN-PUBLICATION DATA

Lynch, Chris, [date]

Hit count : a novel / by Chris Lynch.—First edition.

pages cm

Summary: Arlo Brodie loves being at the heart of the action on the football field, and while his dad cheers him on, his mother quotes head injury statistics and refuses to watch, but Arlo's winning plays, the cheering crowds, and the adrenaline rush are enough to convince him that everything is OK, in spite of the pain, the pounding, the dizziness, and the confusion.

ISBN 978-1-61620-250-7

[1. Football.—Fiction. 2. Sports injuries.—Fiction.] I. Title.

PZ7.L979739Hi 2015

[Fic]—dc23

2014043009


10 9 8 7 6 5 4 3 2 1

First Edition

# HIT
# COUNT

# FRESHMAN YEAR

# THE DRILL

"All I ever wanted to do was hit people, is that so bad? Does that make me a bad guy?"

That would have been funny if Lloyd was trying to be funny but he wasn't.

"That's not so bad, Lloyd," I told him, "And you are not a bad guy. I think you should stop that, though."

We were walking home from football practice. Early days, my freshman year, Lloyd's senior. It was that ships-passing-in-the-night moment Lloyd and me were floating through, at least as far as football was concerned. See, he had made the junior varsity as a sophomore and had every reason to expect to move up from there. But he plateaued, physically and developmentally, and even if no one else was, he was shocked to find himself on the jayvee again as a junior, and flat-out humiliated about being a junior varsity senior student.

He was already giving off sparks when my making that very same jayvee team pissed gasoline all over him. Me, his baby brother. Who he pounded regularly in our backyard.

And then that day's mess.

Lloyd had been sticking guys pretty good all afternoon, like usual. His area, across the middle of the field in dink-and-dunk territory just beyond the linebackers, was becoming a place only the stupidest and bravest receivers ventured. Lloyd's maniacal style of play was disrupting everything, causing nervous players to drop passes without him even having to hit them. And then of course he'd hit them anyway.

He wasn't making friends anywhere, but that's not the kind of thing he cared about. He wouldn't pause to consider that he was an unimportant player on a team he should have outgrown by then, and he was running around breaking the wills and bruising the bones of offensive players who were ultimately going to be on the same side once the games started.

You could sense that something was going to be done about it, something by design.

I had a fleeting moment when I thought I was going to try and talk to him about it. I decided not to, though. Because if he knew, he'd have laughed, and started acting even worse. And probably gone after me, too, if he could.

It may not have mattered anyway. As the play rolled out, it looked like a lot of other plays had. Small slot receiver darted from the right side, across the middle, but the quarterback dumped him the ball almost immediately. Seeing the ballcarrier coming into his zone from so far away, you could sense Lloyd's excitement as he gathered himself into his compact, low-down torpedo approach. Then, just as he was about to lay the mother of all annihilations on the guy, the massive tight end beat him to it.

Lloyd took the blindside hit with the tight end's shoulder pad crashing right into his jaw. At the same instant, the blocking back—who had been following the tight end like they were two cars of the same train—slammed into Lloyd before he could even finish falling. He nailed Lloyd at just the right angle to snap Lloyd's torso grotesquely backward before planting his spine in the turf.

They might as well have pistol-whipped him. Not the tight end. Not the blocking back. Not even the coach but an assistant coach who, I would bet, never got above the jayvee level himself. The guy was giving Lloyd the usual rigmarole of do-you-know-where-you-are-and-what-day-it-is questions to test his mental function, and flicking the flashlight back and forth to check for any delay in eye movement in order to gauge the severity of the impact of Lloyd's last collision.

Which was stupid, and the reason the assistant nobody coach would always be that and nothing more, because all you had to do to assess that hit was to watch the damn thing.

Anyway, it wasn't even that that finished off Lloyd once and for all.

"A career jayvee might want to consider whether this is even worth it." Those were the words that did it. "Career jayvee."

Suddenly Lloyd's instincts and reactions were as sharp as they have ever been.

"Career?" he yelled, snatching the flashlight out of the guy's hand. He got up off the bench carrying his helmet in one hand and the flashlight in the other. The assistant went silent, backing up until Lloyd jammed his helmet on top of the guy's head. The force caused the assistant to tumble backward and land on his back. Lloyd dropped to his knees, straddling the guy, and flashing the light in his eyes. "Career's all yours, pal. Except for all the fear I'm seein' in those eyes, I'm sure you'll do great," he said as a couple of players wrestled him away. "Cause I quit!"

* * *

"Shut up and take a sip, I don't like the way you're looking at me," Lloyd said as we shuffled down the sidewalk toward home, in the evening cool.

"Thanks, no, Lloyd," I said, trying to grab the squat flat whiskey bottle. He slapped my hand away.

"Fine," he said, tipping the bottle way back.

"You *heard* the trainer," I said.

"No, I did not hear the trainer."

"Yes, you did. I heard him myself. You might have a concussion, and glugging a whole pint of whiskey down within minutes of getting clocked is a terrible idea."

He stared deadeye at me. Then he drained the bottle, let it drop from his hand while his head was still thrown back. The glass shattered on the pavement.

"For your snot-faced information, I only drank half a pint just there, little boy. I drank the other half *before* practice."

The thought made me gag, as if I had drunk the stuff down myself. How could anybody do that to themselves?

"Well, I guess that's telling me, huh? Proud of yourself? Proud, Lloyd?"

He didn't even look when he snapped out a big backhand right across my nose bridge and forehead, with his big tennis racket hand and his gnarly knuckles.

He'd given me worse. The backhand barely even registered with either of us.

"What do they want from me? Huh? What do they want? I play the damn safety position the way it is supposed to be played, the way *they* showed me, and then when people start paying too close attention it's like, oh no, we cannot have that dangerous barbarian soiling our lovely field and our lovely boys with their lovely squishy brains all tucked nice in their lovely eggshell skulls."

"I don't have a concussion anyway," he went on. "That's just stupid."

"How would you know?"

"How would I *not* know?" he said, pointing at his own skull. "I'm the one who's in here. I'm the one who knows what it's like. Concussion, hell. I got my bell rung. Every defensive back knows the drill. Every single back on that field has had his bell rung plenty of times. It's part of the job and we understand that, we like it. That's why we're defensive backs. *Especially* safeties. Safeties have their ears ringing all the time. At this point I'd get lonely without it. Just like big giant tight ends have to get used to twisted and mangled ankles because how else are we supposed to stop them once they get up a head of steam. Right, get their ankles, and work 'em all day long. Chop 'em and twist 'em till they're flopping around like fish. Wrench the foot right off 'em if you can. Then who cares how big they are, right? *Just like they taught us.*"

There were whole weeks when Lloyd didn't say this many words to me. Maybe the bash in the head was spilling them all out.

"Coaches never taught you that, Lloyd, c'mon."

He stopped, so I stopped. He grabbed his forehead with one big hand and started massaging out the rapidly rising tension. "Are you calling me a liar?"

"Absolutely not." I watched the hand carefully to make sure it stayed on his head.

"What do you mean, then? What exactly, possibly could you mean?" He continued the massaging, limbering up the hand as much as soothing the head.

"What I meant, ah, was they really haven't taught me anything yet. Coaches not talking much to the freshmen yet at all, actually, was what I meant. So just wondering, when are they gonna start teaching me stuff."

He broke right back into stride. I could see he was glad he was in on a secret I didn't know about.

"You won't hear that kind of thing from the coaches. Not in so many words anyway. You'll hear it from the upperclassmen. You'll hear it on the field, not on the sideline, not in the locker room. You'll hear it and you'll feel it. Then one day, you'll just *have*"—he pointed at his temple—"without even totally realizing or remembering where and when you got it.

"Like it came outta nowhere."

"Right," I said, "kind of like a secret s—"

The air blew out of me as he stopped short and landed a sharp elbow perfectly in my solar plexus.

8

"Kind of like that," he said, walking along as I hunched over, struggling for breath.

* * *

"Good," Ma said, with uncommon force.

Lloyd had just stormed through the front door, with me in his slipstream, announcing his retirement from football. Ma thinking this was good was not a shock.

"No, not good," Lloyd answered, as if it wasn't even his idea, as if Ma was the one who'd removed him from the team.

"Yes, yes. This is good," she said. She liked things to be good. And quite some time ago she had decided football wasn't good at all. "Very good. Great, even."

"Ah, go to hell, Ma," he said.

"Lloyd!" I barked.

"It's okay, Arlo," she said serenely, knowing things were going her way. "I will go to hell, Lloyd, if that is what you wish. Happily to hell, as long as you're not going to football. Let's shake on it."

"No!" he said, actually shrinking from her offered hand. He looked almost like a kid, hiding the hand behind his back. Somehow she could still make him like this. She was the only one who could.

"What am I hearing?" Dad said, coming in from the kitchen. He had his apron on. Which meant we were having steak. It was the only thing he could cook. If you could call the curious things he did to meat cooking.

9

"I don't know what you're hearing there, master chef, but here's what I'm hearing: NO MORE FOOTBALL. Lloyd left the team."

Dad did not share Ma's distaste for the finest of all sports.

"You quit? You actually just quit?" he said with a combination of bafflement and disgust pinching his features. "Are you joking?"

"Do I ever joke with you, Dad?" Lloyd snapped. "Anyway, I didn't quit. I retired."

Dad turned away, muttering to himself, as if Lloyd wasn't even worth addressing. "Fine. No football, no steak."

Lloyd just let his snort follow Dad back out.

Ma had walked up close enough to get a whiff of the snort. "You've been drinking," she said.

"Yes, Mother, of course I've been drinking. Wouldn't *you* be drinking if you were thrown off the football team?"

"No, I wouldn't. And neither should you—I don't care what excuse you have. Anyway, I thought you said you quit the team?" she asked, hands now on her hips.

If it were me caught drinking—though it never would be me— I'd be pretty humble at this point. But Lloyd just made a big show of not caring. He toggled his head around, rolled his eyes, and made a blah-blah-blah gesture, his hand opening and closing like a quacking duck's beak.

I loathed it when he did that to me. But when he did it to Ma, my blood boiled.

"And you started drinking before you even got to practice, so that doesn't really make sense," I blurted, because I just had to say something to knock him off his horse.

The room emptied of anything—people, furniture, air—that was not me and him. I had never seen him angrier than this. I had seen him *precisely* this angry a couple of thousand times before, however. He was seething, his face purple, his teeth grinding, and his eyes were pumping like they were desperate to launch and get first shot at me.

I braced.

"Lloyd!" Ma screamed, running toward us.

Luckily, he passed out cold before he could manage to drop me.

**\* \* \***

"Knock it off, I'm fine."

"You were unconscious, Lloyd," Ma said, holding a cold face-cloth to his forehead as he sat slumped against an ottoman.

"I was never unconscious. I was aware of everything, I just couldn't move. Must have been a stress thing."

"Yeah," I said, because what could he do to me now? "The stress of a pint of whiskey and a concussion."

"Concussion?" Ma gasped.

He glared up at me as best he could. "Kicking me while I'm down? Hooray for you, big man. You think I won't remember this, Arlo?"

Still feeling fairly secure and upper handy, I said, "Under the circumstances, I think there's a pretty good chance of that."

He kept his head down, to keep his strength up.

"Pray for it, my brother. You better pray for it."

Weak, pathetic, on his ass, nursed by his mommy, and still scary as all holy hell.

# THE FILE

And so, I inherited *The File*.

"Oh, Ma," I said, "is that what I think it is?"

She had caught me mid-sit-up on the floor of my bedroom. I stopped right there, and held the very tough half-up position as I stared at The File in her hands.

"If what you think it is is valuable information and good common sense, then yes, you are correct."

"Ah," I said, falling back flat on the floor. "That's what I was afraid of."

The File was something my loving mother had been compiling for quite some time. From about the time the brain injury center at Boston University started popping up in the news almost as often as the weather forecast. It was like a little bomb went off in her own head, blowing out most of the regular motherly stuff like buying me shirts I would never wear and deciding whether raisins really belong in meatballs. Those things were replaced by an obsession with the subject of head injuries. In that File was one graphic horror story after another, clipped from newspapers and magazines, downloaded from seriously unhelpful do-gooder websites, possibly even whipped up with her own desktop publishing skills for all I knew, all on the subject of brain trauma. Most of them about sports-related brain trauma.

"I don't want to interrupt your sit-ups," she said, taking a seat at my desk. "So why don't I just read to you while you work out. Wouldn't that be nice? It's been so long since I read to you, and you used to love that, remember? Shall I just start at the beginning?"

I was, of course, already well familiar with the contents of The File, which was generally in Lloyd's room collecting dust unless he and I were ridiculing it. I should have realized that with Lloyd now out of the game, she was free to turn her powers on me. The weak stray, isolated from the herd.

"That's okay, Ma. I'll have a look at it later. You can just leave it there on the desk."

"Here's a fascinating thing," she said, emphatically *not* leaving it there on the desk. "It's from that wonderful woman who runs the Center." The Center. Officially, it's the Center for the Study of Traumatic Encephalopathy, but they're on a first-name basis. "She says, 'The biggest problem isn't concussions, actually. It's the subconcussive hits that mount up every single time these guys line up.' Huh. That's something, isn't it?"

My extra grunty sit-ups weren't fooling her and weren't deterring her.

"I say, that's something, Arlo, isn't it?"

With one last operatic grunt I sat straight up and addressed her more like the polite son I actually was most of the time.

13

"Well, Ma, I'm not sure it is something, actually. It sounds like it's exactly *not* something because what is a subconcussive hit? Sounds like it's everything that isn't a concussion, which is practically everything. I mean, there, I just got another subconcussive. There's another one. Oops, you just got one, too."

She nodded graciously, smiled generously. It was good for us that it was never a struggle locating each other's humor zone.

"Clever boy," she said.

"Thanks," I said.

Then she busily shuffled through The File. "Here, let me show you a picture of a brain slice from another clever boy. Well, former clever boy, obviously . . ."

Arrgghh.

"Tell you what, Ma, if I lop off a slice of my brain for you to examine, will you go look at it in another room?"

"If I did have a slice of your beautiful brain, I'd show it to everyone I met. Like people do with grandchildren photos. Which I also want to show off someday, by the way, so if you can't take care of yourself for yourself or for myself, could you at least do it for them?"

"I'll look at The File, Ma. If you just let me finish what I'm doing here in peace, I promise I'll have a look."

"Well then," she said all huffy mock-offended. In reality, she was kind of elated with this small progression. "I can tell when I'm not wanted. Should I just leave it here on the desk, then?"

I was already back in mid-sit-up when she laid that on me, and

I fell back flat again with the laughing. "Yeah, Ma, that sounds like an excellent idea."

I was hard at work again as she floated out of the room, dropping last words on me like a post TD spike. "You promised, Arlo."

Ah, hell. I did not lie to my mother. And when she snapped my name on the end there in just that way she had, it was like signing a pact in blood.

I was sweaty and winded sometime later when I finally could not outwork, outrun, outsmart my promise.

The File was patiently, smugly lying there when I dropped into the chair at my desk.

I opened it.

I said I would, and I did. There.

I closed it again with a *thwap.*

What the hell was that? What happened there? Okay, it was brain slices, as promised, so what?

What was I, a coward all of a sudden? This was moronic.

I opened The File again, held my stare on the slices for a full eight-count. One sample had what looked like diarrhea seeping out from between brain folds, while another had large crusty black patches like from frostbite. Still another one was covered all over with scars, growths, as if the lucky owner of that brain got to walk around with mushrooms and maggots filling up his head. Then the next page showing brains, some like shriveled apples, some like old milky pumpkins, some of them like they'd had a whole party of cigarettes stubbed out in them. Others looking like—

I slapped it shut again. I had not lied to my mother; I had not folded to the fear.

And I was not one of those guys in the pictures. Never would be. No disrespect, but you had to be a certain type of athlete to wind up in that state, a certain type of *person*. Fine, maybe Lloyd's brain did look like that, a little. In spots. Because he played like a maniac, like he wanted to be hurt. But I was not that type of person. I played hard, but I played controlled, and I played smart. Football is a hard game that rewards smart. A guy does not get a brain like that if he uses it correctly in the first place.

"Hey!" was the shout right in my ear, with the slap across the back of my head. "There it is. What are you doing with my file, ass?"

Lloyd grabbed The File off my desk like the big winnings off a poker table and glared at me as he walked out of the room.

Lloyd wanting The File? Well. That certainly was an occurrence on the WTF side of unexpected.

I had wondered if he might get a little freaky without football. But already he was showing enough unrecognizable weird to be worrisome.

# THE GOOD LIFE

I had been aware of Sandy for some time before we got to high school. We didn't go to the same junior high, but hers wasn't far from mine and our circles were not far off from each other's and she was deadly cute and I was big. So we knew each other, like "Hey" when we passed on the street. Just like that, "Hey" with the smiles, and at some point she added a little sort of military salute wave and that did it, gaffed me with a giant fishhook.

So when we got to high school, there was more of that, and more often and in the same hallways, so we were getting there.

But there wasn't *there* until football took us all the way there.

I was on the team already, the jayvee as a freshman, which brings some cachet with it, and we were on the field for preseason practice.

And she was there for cheerleader tryouts.

Not as an applicant. As a protester.

Like everybody else on the field, I was paying at least as much attention to cheerleader tryouts as I was to the business of football. Guys were missing tackles, missing blocks, dropping passes or throwing them to places miles away from where they could be caught. If it weren't so dangerous, it would have been funny. It was funny anyway.

After a while I saw her, there in the stands close to where the head cheerleader was screaming at the new recruits, holding up a sign that said: YOU MUST BE JOKING, GIRLS.

I was torn big time now. Concentrate on the football. Pay attention to the jumping, cartwheeling, lovely go-teamers flying around in my peripheral vision. Or laugh at the adorable little radical trying to mess up the wholesome sideline tradition that had been in place for generations and was quite possibly the key to America's uniquely successful breeding program for producing better and better athletes.

I managed to do all three, because I was always a gifted multitasker.

But when the cheerleaders started yelling things at Sandy, and Sandy started yelling things back, my laughter won out over both football and legs.

It was the kind of thing that made Sandy stand out. She could have easily been mistaken for another good-looking girl going out for the squad, while she was just determined to tell the squad where to jump.

"Why would somebody do that kind of thing?" I said as I trailed her home that afternoon.

"I don't know," she said, walking on without looking at me. "Why would a girl with even a scattering of brain fragments allow herself to be thrown high in the air by other girls and let the whole football team gawp at her little panties under her little skirt?"

I was closing the distance between us on the sidewalk.

"Nobody gawped," I said.

"Everybody gawped. That's what the spectacle is all about. You gawped."

"I never gawped."

"You gawped."

"How would you know if I gawped? Unless you were gawping at me."

"I never gawped at you."

"Maybe you should. Would you like to?"

Like a receiver with great footwork losing a defensive back, she took a quick cut down a side street I was almost certain was not hers. I stood there on the corner watching her walk away.

"Go home and gawp yourself," she said without turning her head.

"Oh-ho," I said, laughing, admiring her work, then quickly looking around to see if anybody had witnessed it.

* * *

"So what have you got against football?" I said to her the next time I saw her, by which time I had had a lot of practice pretending she was already my girlfriend.

"I love football," she said, staring at the large café mocha I had placed on the spot right next to her, on the low wall that ran along the front of the school grounds. She looked at the coffee for a fairly long time, contemplating it, and I was anxious about it because I had seen this on TV when the male penguin brings a stone to the female penguin, to try and formalize their relationship. If she takes it to the nest, they're good. If she stares at it and then just walks away in front of the whole colony, then he might as well just go throw himself in front of a speeding orca. There were hundreds of other students around.

"What's this?" she said finally, waving at the cup with one of her flippers.

"It's, I don't know, a gesture." The penguin surely didn't have to deal with a discussion about the gesture.

"What are you, a penguin?"

She'd even watched the same program. Please, Lord, let her take the coffee.

After letting the clock tick down to almost zero, she lifted the cup. I practically threw myself onto the wall next to her.

"How do you know I even drink coffee?" she said, peeling the lid off and drinking the coffee.

"You didn't seem like somebody who did not drink coffee," I said.

That must have accomplished something, right there, because she turned my way, looked right into my close, gawping face. She smiled just short of softly and breathed me all mocha right down to my toes.

# MUSCLE MEMORY

I didn't take it seriously enough.

All before high school, sports, and especially contact sports, were a cinch. I was big and I was dedicated, and by the time I made the jayvee as a freshman, I thought everything would just be waiting for me along the road to success, all I had to do was scoop it up as I went along like a video game character gathering up coins or zombies while hopping on to each next level.

But there was a difference. There was an important *difference*.

I watched from the sidelines for the first two and a half games, but because I was a freshman with respect and patience and knew my place, that was all fine. Except that we lost the first two and were well on our way to losing the third, so maybe patience would have its limit. The game looked a little faster, a little tougher than what I had known in Pop Warner, but no more than I had expected. I had grown up getting belted around by Lloyd, and so I was conditioned to expect the other guy to be stronger, faster, meaner than me. But one thing I learned from watching this team was that all that training had done the job. I was as good as the other linebackers we had. That wasn't bragging, it was just a fact. I knew my time was coming and so did they.

Coach finally got fed up and put me in late in the third quarter of that third game when the cause was already lost. I knew my stuff, knew the positioning and the schemes, and so I did not embarrass myself when I got my chance. I was nearly in on the play, first play, second play, both short-gain end runs where I made no tackles, little contact but no mistakes.

After the opposition got the first down, they went back to the running game. This time, though, I saw the patterns emerging, saw the play unfolding, got into my spot. And it was the right spot. Their offensive line made our defensive line look like an open gate, spreading a lane for their big running back to burst through. However, he was bursting right my way, and this was going to be the end of this nonsense.

I lined up, planted, and drove like a bull, timing it perfectly.

But the tight end came across from my right side and *nailed* me an instant before the ballcarrier arrived, and I heard the great embarrassing *oooff* come out of me as my rib cage collapsed around my internal organs like a crunchy cartilage shrink-wrap.

For take-that and remember-this good measure, the running back veered slightly off his course to stomp over me, stepping right on the side of my helmet on his way to a big, big gain while I lay on my side watching and covering up. I had, immediately, a kind of headache I had never had before, never knew existed before. It was all on the right side, started near where the spine meets the skull, and shot forward like a net of piercing electric shocks beneath the scalp. It pulsated, *jolt-jolt-jolt*, and caused just the right eye to twitch in rhythm with it.

That was the instant. That was when I learned the difference. I had never in my sports life experienced being blown away, being stomped, being punished, being *nullified* like that before. I had received many beatings, courtesy of Lloyd, but nobody else ever *beat* me until then.

No more kid stuff. Raise your game, Arlo Brodie, or get out of the way.

No way was I getting out of the way.

* * *

Conditioning.

"You're out of shape, dude" was the first sentence of this particular lesson.

"Shut up, *duuude*" was my response.

It wasn't the greatest of starts, but it wasn't the best of circumstances, either.

The other guy, a sophomore called Dinos, whom I only recognized because he had a weirdly big head, was beside me, panting and sweating as we drove as hard as we could into a tandem tackling sled. Standing on the back of that sled and pouring disgust all over our effort was the junior varsity coach, Mr. Kasperian. After the end of that depressing third straight loss to begin the season, Mr. K kept the most underachieving units of the team on the field for some punishing remedial drill work.

"Brodie!" Mr. K screamed in my ear. "Look at you, Brodie! The quarterback is running in circles and doing backflips while some stupid fat left guard twirls you around like you're in your little tutu on top of a damn music box."

"No kidding, dude," Dinos said, close enough that I could hear him over all the guys laughing at me. "You've got a lot of work to do."

Both Dinos and the coach had every right to be doing this to me. Despite my best effort, the sled kept doing doughnuts, carving one bog circle in the turf as Dinos outmuscled, outdug, and outplayed me worse as every second passed and my stamina faded well ahead of his.

I was ready to request the firing squad when I finally made the tiniest progress. The sled started going less circular, more like a sweeping sickle pattern, as I started gaining on Dinos's effort. Then it got even straighter, and the coach made a vaguely positive screamy noise, and then we were even, and we stayed exactly even as we drove exactly evenly for ten, then fifteen yards upfield.

He was easing up to make me look better. "Cut it out or I'll kill you," I growled at him.

"Don't you ever want to go home?" he growled back.

So I gathered what I had, and I *hit* that sled with fury and desperation.

Caught Dinos off guard, which was satisfying as the sled started circling in his direction for a change.

"Good, Brodie, good!" the coach screamed. "That's more like it—dig deep, find the will!"

I did, and so did Dinos, and it probably served as inspiration that the two of us were looking right at each other and bellowing as we drove that sled and that coach right off the edge of the field and onto the old cinder running track that circled it.

The two of us were panting so heavily it was almost like some ancient religious chanting thing. We were both bent at the waist, hands on hips, when the coach came up to us.

"Better," he said, sounding so controlled and different from the sled-riding guy I had to look up and be sure it was him. "More like it, guys."

"Thanks," Dinos said, and I noticed that his wind was coming back to him much quicker than mine was.

"Now," Mr. K said, "over there with the footwork group."

"Ah, Coach . . . ," I moaned.

Mr. K nodded slowly. "Fair enough," he said. "Wind sprints it is, gentlemen."

When the coach had gone, Dinos turned to me. "The only reason I'm not going to kick your ass is that I know this is gonna hurt you a lot more than it does me."

He was right, too.

# DINOS

Stamina.

Before jayvee I never thought endurance was a big deal for athletes who weren't marathoners. And I frankly never thought of marathoners as athletes so much as skinny masochists with lots of time and no real skills.

It would not have dawned on me that a defensive lineman or a fullback, whose job involved a lot of individual, intense moments, separated by huddles, would have any use for distance training. As long as you had good balance, explosiveness, and muscle, you had all the ingredients for excellence.

Higher-level football straightened me out on that. If you are competing with everything you have, colliding with packs of guys who are as fast and strong and ferocious as you are, you find something out after about the third down from scrimmage. Huddles are not rests, and if you don't train for endurance you're not going to last.

I wondered if Lloyd ever got that. If maybe he flatlined as a player when he failed to recognize that just being a ferocious hitter wasn't going to be good enough.

After the embarrassment of another loss, Mr. K stepped up the punishment of postgame drills on Monday. He forced us to be committed to every block, every tackle, every sprint. The energy level was nuts. The bellowing and barking made the field sound like a zoo. Things were going to be different for this team. They were going to be different for me. Even if I was close to puking.

Finally Mr. K seemed almost satisfied and called it a day. I was following him off the field when a runner on the track jabbed my back with his elbow as he passed.

It was Dinos, and in a few seconds he was thirty yards on down the track.

I turned my head and saw that the coach was watching from the locker room door. I looked back at Dinos.

I started running. Broke out fast, to make up ground, while he continued around the quarter-mile oval at a medium jog. The crunch of the track made it impossible to sneak up on anybody, so by the time I had come up to him he was ready for me.

"Are you lonely or something?" he said as our strides fell in sync.

"No," I said. "But you looked like you were." Night was starting to come down. The sound of us just emphasized the absence of anyone else around.

"I appreciate that. But I'm sure you must be exhausted. I'll be fine, so feel free to peel off when we circle around by the locker room."

I responded by running along with him as we chugged past the locker room again. And again.

"Okay, I'm impressed," Dinos said when we passed the mile mark of our run together.

"Well, that's all I need," I panted through shorter breaths, "'cause that's what I'm here for, to impress you."

"Ha, very good," he said smoothly. "At least what you lack in stamina you make up for with good sense."

He shifted down a gear, then another, and we started walking the last half lap.

"I'm not out of shape," I said.

"Well, you're out of a certain kind of shape, and you know it. But because you now know it, you'll be fine soon enough. Better than most of the guys around you, that's for sure." We had turned off the track and were walking into the locker room, where every last guy had cleared out.

"I don't know. Did you see the way that practice went today? Guys are getting it now, don't you think?"

He shook his head. "You could tell that some of them meant it. But I bet the fire goes out of most of those slugs before the week is over."

"Not me," I said, quick and defensive.

"No, probably not," he said, grinning at my enthusiasm. "And anyway, I figure it's to my advantage the way it's going. I wasn't going to get a whole lot of playing time based on natural ability. Now, I'm confident I can *train* my way right up the depth chart." Instead of heading to his locker, he went to the door that led to the weight room.

I found it impossible not to admire the guy's approach.

"Do you need a workout partner?" I blurted just before the

weight room door could shut behind him. Lloyd and I had planned to work out together after I made jayvee, but I figured that wasn't going to happen now.

He poked his substantial head back around the door.

"I was right the first time," he said, "you are lonely."

"I am *not* lonely," I said, losing that exchange just by answering.

"Ha," he said. "Okay, sure. As long as you can keep up. Go home, eat well, and get some extra sleep, and maybe your stamina will improve overnight. We'll talk about a program tomorrow."

He yanked the door closed behind him this time, assuring himself the last word.

I glared at the door thinking he might make me a better football player just by *antagonizing* me to greatness.

\* \* \*

We started extra weight room sessions before school started on Monday, Wednesday, and Friday mornings, and extra laps on the track after practice on Tuesday and Thursday afternoons. I was already at it when he walked in that first Wednesday, standing in front of the mirrored wall watching myself do shoulder presses.

"Your technique sucks," he said for "good morning."

He timed it well, catching me midpress. I laughed, struggled, and failed to get the weight up. I dropped the bar to the floor.

"Good morning to you, too, jackass," I said.

"Hey, Arlo," he said. "In all seriousness, though, your balance is kind of iffy. You look like you're trying to put a boulder up on a high shelf. Didn't anybody ever show you proper technique?"

"Well, yeah," I said, "my brother did. But I guess that was mostly with lighter weights we had at home. And half of that time was spent with me dodging weights that he threw at me. Heavier stuff I've mainly worked on the machines at the Y."

"Machines are fine, man, but you have to mix in the free weights because the machines are already balanced for you and you're always going to have to keep your balance work a priority. Take it from a guy with kitten mittens where his feet are supposed to be—"

"And a planet where his head is supposed to be . . ."

"Yeah, thanks for that, I almost forgot. But it's more to do with the fact that I have the upper body of a hog farmer and the lower body of a rock guitarist."

"Sounds like a career to me."

"What? I'm a science guy. Now be quiet and pay attention."

Dinos reached down and picked up the bar I had been using. Moving deliberately, he set his little hooves just slightly wider than shoulder width apart. He breathed in deeply, hoisted the bar to his chin, then up over his head. He began a series of shoulder presses so precise and fluid, it was like there was no stress on his joints at all.

I watched and watched and watched as he effortlessly pumped the weights up and down behind his head until he appeared to stop because of nothing but boredom. It was easily twice as many reps as I could have done.

I retreated to the safety of the wonderfully self-balancing weight machines and flattened myself out on the bench press. I knew I could press as much as him, on the machine. I started right in pumping as he walked over toward me.

"That's not bad," he said. I drew big breath in as I lowered the weight and blew hard out as I pushed it up again.

"Yeah," I blew.

"Still, though," he said, looking toward the ceiling and leaning with one hand on the weight I was trying to press.

"Dinos!"

"Oh, sorry, man," he said. "I was just thinking about your balance problems again."

I lowered the weight, slid out, and sat up. He immediately sat next to me on the bench but facing the other way.

"Oh yeah?" I said. "Well, I'm starting to think you might have your own special kind of balance problem." I started banging the great sidewall of his head with my middle finger like a woodpecker at the side of a barn.

"Ha!" he said, then reached back around, hooked me around the waist, and flipped me backward onto the floor with himself landing on top of me.

A couple of our running backs, Tyrone and McCallum, came in as we were wrestling.

"See," McCallum said, "I told you, it's always the linebackers."

"Jealous!" Dinos yelled at them as I pinned him with a lot of effort that should have been saved for the weights.

But a guy has to assert himself sometimes.

* * *

"What you going to school so early for?" Lloyd asked as he opened the refrigerator door and I headed for the back door. It was Friday, the last day of the first week of the new exercise schedule, and my crying muscles were letting me know about it.

"I think the more obvious question is what on earth are *you* doing starting the day this early?"

He straightened up, to give me a look. "Don't be stupid, stupid. I didn't just get up. This might be the start of your sad little today, but my awesome yesterday hasn't ended yet. So there's my answer, now what's yours?"

He turned his interest again to the contents of the refrigerator. As if he had no interest in the answer to his own question.

"I'm hitting the weight room before classes," I said. "Some of the guys on the team are putting in extra workout sessions. We've got to get better."

He grabbed the orange juice out of the refrigerator, snapped the door shut sharply. He took a big swig from the carton, knowing I would not be able to touch the juice after that.

"Some of the *guys on the team*, huh? Whatever happened to working out with me? Am I beneath you now that I'm not one of the *guys on the team*?"

"Not at all, Lloyd. You know it's not like that." Or maybe it was. I couldn't even visualize a workout with him now, and it pained me that I had to spare his feelings.

"So how come you don't ask me to come work out with you?"

Because you haven't done a lick of exercise since the day you finished with organized football, for a start.

I almost sighed.

"Sure, Lloyd. You want to come? Come on, but you need to be quick."

"What, now? I don't want to come *now*. But I just might one of these times."

"Sure," I said, backing out the door. "Excellent. Anytime. See you later. Use a glass."

"Use my—" he snapped back, but I slammed the door and cut off the undoubtedly clever ending.

* * *

As Dinos predicted, you could tell after the first few days that the novelty of consistent effort had already worn off for some guys. But our extra-credit workouts had the surprise benefit of leaving me feeling like I had *more* energy when Saturday game time rolled around.

"You know," I said to Dinos as we did our stretching along the sidelines before kickoff, "I was afraid I was leaving too much in the gym and not saving enough for the game. But I feel like I could play two games today."

"Easy there, big fella," he said, laughing, as we went through the ritual of slamming each other's shoulder pads. *Bam.* "Sometimes you can waste your energy just by being too excited." *Bam-bam.*

"I know that," I said even though it was something I'd never really considered before. *Bam-bam.* "You don't have to tell me every damn thing, Dinos. You are only *one* year ahead of me." *Bam-bam-bam.* "And, if I might point out, you are still on the same junior varsity team that I am."

33

*BAM!* Dinos the Elder came down on my pads with a two-handed hammer that was powerful enough to buckle my knees. Which made us even.

"First, kid," he said as the whistle blew for teams to hit the field, "you will notice that only one of us is *starting.*"

"Okay, gramps, you win," I said. "Get on out there."

"And second," he said over his shoulder as he started his way onto the field, "if I had fifty percent of your natural talent, I'd be on varsity this year. *And* starting."

Varsity, sophomore, starter. Yeah, right.

What if, though. Didn't hurt to have goals, did it?

We lost the toss, and kicked off. Big D was on special teams for the kickoff. He did little more than trot downfield after the kick, but he didn't do anything to hurt our cause, either.

And then he was there to line up with our first-string defense.

The opposition, the vocational-technical high school, was a well-known and reliable operation. Much like the focus of the school's educational specialty, the football team followed a practical, sound, feet-on-the-ground approach. They ran on almost every play. This was excellent news for my friend Dinos, who was a run specialist. You could say run defense was Dinos's vocational-technical specialty. So the V-T and the Big D were made for each other on this fine fall football afternoon.

Dinos meant what he said when he talked about seizing the opportunity to outwork everybody else. The first three plays V-T ran from scrimmage were all runs to his side of the field, as if they didn't respect him even against the run. He read the first

34

one as if he had a copy of their playbook. The quarterback rolled right, faked a pass that nobody believed, then pitched wide to his halfback, who took the ball right up the sideline. The kid was fast, and ate up ground quicker than the first defenders figured. He left them lunging at his shadow until Dinos came rumbling over and caught him after a five-yard gain, right in front of where I stood.

*Ca-raaack!*

Dinos had driven the guy two feet up off the ground and then six feet hard right down into it.

I was close enough to smell the sparks off that collision, and feel the thud in the ground beneath my feet. Best—*Bam!*—start to the game you could ask for.

Second play the quarterback faked the pitch and bootlegged it himself. I definitely heard the roar come from Dinos as he sniffed the play out way early and had such a clear run at the overmatched QB that they were both screaming at the time of impact and a two-yard loss.

Third down and three to go for a first down. Nobody could have been figuring they would come at our left side again, which must have been their clever ploy because come they did, without a fake this time. The halfback slipped through a neat seam between their guard and tackle and was bulleting for the sideline and the first down marker when Dino launched himself at that sideline marker, lifting right off his little feet like a big meaty torpedo.

It looked like the back was having that first down as he reached ahead with the ball, and just about made it. Until the crunch, the almighty *crack-bang-crunch* of all of Dinos's and his equipment, landed with all its force on that boy's shoulder and arm and back and pounded him into just one more layer of the turf itself, and the ball popped out of his possession and wobbled away as if it had no intention of coming back.

The modest smattering of spectators made a stadium full of noise, and as I looked down at a smiling Dinos right there at my feet it felt like a great day was unavoidable.

"That was all for your benefit, rook," he said, remaining coolly on his back. "Learn from the master."

I helped the master to his feet. "Pace yourself there, Master. Could be a long afternoon."

Dino snorted. "I made three consecutive tackles. First three plays of the game. Did you see that? Did you see? At this rate I could make every single tackle the entire game." He had so much adrenaline pumping now, it was coming off him like a mist, and I was breathing it.

He slapped the side of my helmet. "Stamina," he said, "is the key to all things."

*　*　*

Dinos did not, actually, make every play single-handedly. Not that he didn't try to, but each tackle seemed harder to get as the game wore on. We got a touchdown, then missed the extra point, and a lot of points after.

"What's going on?" I said to a panting, slouching Dinos as the first quarter ended 6–0.

"He's testing us," Dinos said, bent way over with his hands on his knees. He was hard to hear, so I bent down alongside him.

"Who's testing us?" I said.

"Mr. K. He's throwing the starters into the fire. To see. Who took last week's message seriously."

I looked around me and noticed there were more players hunched over like Dinos than there were straight-up ones.

I couldn't believe Coach would be willing to lose the game to prove his point, but there was no time to debate it because we punted and Dinos was humping his way back onto the field.

It was painful to watch, but Dinos was running down noticeably in the second quarter. He did *not* have unlimited stamina after all. He was gritty and smart and well conditioned, but he was flailing at plays now, arriving a little too late, or a lot, or getting faked entirely and winding up on the wrong side of the field. The defensive unit looked like a panting herd of buffalo.

When the whistle blew for halftime, the team gathered around Coach, who spoke loudly but with none of the wildness he showed at last week's loss. None of the frustration that a 20–6 deficit would seem to warrant.

"You, and you, and you, and you, you're off," he said, in one stroke removing two of our starting linebackers and two down linemen. "You, you're moving to left defensive end." That was Dinos. "You and you and you," he said, "you're in." I was the last "you."

I was determined to take advantage of this, but I would not burn myself out by being overeager. I would be aggressive, but I would be smart.

Do your job.

Be where you are supposed to be.

Follow the play, follow through, and finish.

"Finish your tackles, Brodie!" Coach screamed at me two minutes later when I had the ballcarrier all lined up and then grazed him with a weak attempt at an arm tackle. He bounced off me, scooted away, and gave me a long look at his backside as he glided into the end zone.

"That was awful!" Coach screamed at me on the sidelines as the opposing kicker nailed the point after. "Brodie, Brodie, that should *never* happen to you. Look at you," he said, knocking on my chest like it was a door. "Look at you," he said again, jamming his hands up under my arms and squeezing my lats. "What in the *hell* does somebody like you want to go *arm* tackling for? Never again, Brodie!"

"Never again, Coach!"

"Never!"

"Never!"

Never, goddammit. Never.

As our offense made some progress in trying to regain points I had given away, I stood next to Dinos, still reverberating from the coach's one real outburst of the day.

"I think he likes you, Arlo," he said.

"You might be joking," I said, "but I think he does."

"The little muscle-squeeze thing? Was that what did it?"

"No. The fact that he said my name more times just there than all the other times put together."

"You could be right," Dinos said. "There may be times to come when you wish he hadn't learned your name, however . . ."

That thought would not trouble me. All I wanted was to be on the field. I didn't care that the more I was on the field, the more that meant the game was out of hand. I didn't care about our offense. The game was already out of hand, and that didn't matter.

All I wanted to do was finish the tackles.

When I was younger and Lloyd couldn't get a neighborhood game going, he would come home and ask if I wanted to play tackle.

"Yeah!" I would say every time, too pumped with excitement at the invitation to remember, or care, that I got slaughtered every time.

Not here. Finish the tackles. Show Coach what I could do.

This was now a simplified thing, a game of tackle, not football.

Coach signaled for me to blitz on a second-down play in the third quarter, and I thought I might squirt myself with joy. I almost gave the plan away as I hopped in place before the snap. But as soon as we were in motion, there was only one way this was ever going to end. There were maybe two players on the field as far as I could tell, and I don't know if anybody even tried to block me, but it didn't matter because I was in their backfield so quick I might as well have lined up there in the first place. My heartbeat erupted like popping corn when I saw that quarterback go into full panic mode, looking over his shoulder and scrambling away from me as if his life depended on it. I had seen enough tiger-zebra encounters on TV to think that maybe it did.

It was something close to mercy when I did finish the guy off. Except that I was merciless. I hit him so hard, the clash of helmets and pads sounded like gunshot across the field. I crushed him with the hit, held on to him, and crushed him again when I slammed him into the ground.

I got up from that tackle howling at the sky, and I assumed everybody else was, too, because the noise in my head was deafening.

And it was so good, Coach called the same play again. And again, I torpedoed straight through and slaughtered the quarterback.

I had arrived. This was what I had been looking forward to, forever, and there would be no stopping me now. I sprinted back to every huddle, every formation, because I couldn't wait for more. I was a monster.

I heard Dinos laugh at the beginning of the fourth quarter when, on one play, I knocked him down, ran right over him, after I'd sniffed out a double reverse and slammed the poor stunned receiver so brutally backward I'm sure he saw his life pass before his eyes in reverse. He fumbled the ball, too, and though I was the closest guy to it I made no real effort to get possession because I didn't want to hand the field back to our pathetic offense.

"That was not team football," Dinos said as he pulled me by the arm back to the huddle.

"Sorry," I said.

"No, you're not." He laughed.

"No, I'm not." I laughed.

We gave up no points in the fourth quarter and we scored seven, which left us, as the whistle sounded to end the game, comfortably on the losing end. But you could say it was a quality loss. We were the better team on that field at the end. We were a superior team to the one we had been an hour earlier. And I realized I actually could play another game, immediately. And better.

"Get over here, you!" Coach Fisk barked at me before we reached the locker room entrance. He was the coach of the varsity, so it seemed like a good idea to answer when he called.

"Yes, sir, Coach," I said.

"What was all that about?" he yelled, but I knew it was a good thing because he was shaking my hand as he yelled it.

"It was all about football, Coach," I said.

"It sure was. What did you make, like ten tackles in the second half?"

It was fourteen.

"Don't know, Coach. I wasn't counting."

"And the majority of them unassisted, kid. That's some nose for the ball you've developed."

The ones that were assisted, I didn't really need any assistance.

"It's a team game, Coach. Everybody's a contributor. Just happy to be on the field doing my part." Fingers crossed that he didn't see me decline to collect that fumble.

He ignored the BS. "Listen, you put some muscle on that frame of yours during the off-season, you could be looking at big things around here next year."

I heard what he was saying. I was too small.

"And one more thing. I noticed a few times there, you *bringing* guys down on some plays."

"Yes, sir, that's my job. Bring 'em down."

"Yeah," he said, nodding, nodding. Then he made a fist, and thumped me in the middle of the chest just loud enough to make a noticeable noise. Varsity coaches knock harder than jayvee ones. "But from here on, don't bring anybody down, on any plays."

"No?"

"No. Knock them down. Smack them down. Drill them down. *Break* them down. You want them to remember you, and to flinch whenever they do. Much of the game of football happens here," he said, reaching up and tapping my skull. "You want to get in *there* on the other guy. Then your job gets a lot easier. Understand what I'm saying?"

"Yes, sir, Coach. I absolutely do."

"Great, then. Four games left this season. I'll be watching. Play hard, have fun, and do your off-season work. Then who knows, right?"

I knew, that was who. I was always a quick learner, and so I didn't need that lecture twice.

I had to get bigger.

And I had to get nastier.

# EVERYTHING IS A COMPETITION

"I shaved off another ten!" I shouted into my phone without even saying hello first.

"Ooo. Did it hurt?"

"Not at all," I said, still thinking we were sharing the same wholesome conversation. "That's the best thing. I tore another ten seconds right off my four-mile time, and it felt like I was just cruising. You'd think I'd start to feel a bit of burn, but not at all."

Sandy was getting used to these sweaty excitable phone calls from me.

"Are you all sweaty?"

"What? Yeah, you *know* I am. You know I'm too fired up to shower before I call you when I have results like this."

I heard a breathy, muffled huffing sound on her end.

"Are you laughing, Sandy?"

"Don't get upset, Arlo. It's the right kind of laughing. Just yesterday I was comparing notes with Jenna, and the sweaty excitable phone calls she's been getting from Dinos are a verrry different thing from these."

"You compare . . . What? Sandy?"

"Don't worry, she and I each felt we were getting the better deal."

"I'm not sure how I feel about the comparison thing," I said.

"Relax, it's not a competition."

Everything is a competition. How else do you know how you're doing?

"Sure, of course, you're right. Are you not impressed at all with my four-mile time?"

She started giggling again, but it felt less troubling since she didn't try to hide it from me.

"I'm incredibly impressed. You are very fast. Who's a fast boy then? Huh? Who's a fast boy?"

"See, Sandy, now that to me sounds like something way different from impressed."

"Oh stop, ya big baby. I am crazy impressed. And I'm even more impressed that you have to phone in your results to me before you can even get in the shower."

"Don't make me sound lame."

"I didn't. I made you sound lovely."

"Lovely. Now I'm lovely. Great, that's just lame wearing a dress."

"Ha. That was a good one, Arlo. Now I have something juicy to say back to Jenna. Nobody's going to want to see *her* boyfriend in a dress, that's for sure."

I got caught up short then. Despite all the frustrating stuff in there, the dress thing and all, I ran right into the word. *Boyfriend.* I had been too shy to talk about anything as openly as that and had been spending my Sandy time instead clumsily trying to maneuver her into saying the word. I was wickedly unsuccessful, so much so you could possibly conclude she was on to me.

She said it right there, though. She did.

"Arlo?" she said after some time that had gotten away from me.

First the ten seconds, then this.

"Okay, if you're going to keep being weird, I'll just go now. I do have other boyfriends I need to talk to, you know."

And I was just about to say something really nice, too.

"Witch," I said, still trying to decide how I meant it.

"Bwa-ha-ha . . ." she erupted, releasing that full and goofy laugh that was the least girly thing about her and also irresistible.

"All right, all right," I said, joining in the laughter finally. "I have to go take my shower now."

"Yes, stinko. I can smell you through the phone."

"See ya, then," I said.

I lay there flat on my bed, on top of the bedspread and spread eagle, shirtless. Smiling. Allowing life to be this good.

"Yo, Lovely," Lloyd yelped, causing me to jackknife right up off the bed and halfway to the ceiling.

"Jesus, Lloyd," I said, whipping my sweaty shirt at him in the doorway. It hit him right in the face because he couldn't get his hands up quick enough to stop it. This was a guy who was re-nowned as a defender with superb reflexes and great hands. But as he bent to collect the sweatshirt off the floor and throw it back, it took him three grabs to even get hold of it.

"What, are you phoning your times in to the papers now?" he said as it landed a foot or so from where I sat. "Nobody cares, y'know."

"Ass," I said, going to my dresser to get fresh socks and underwear for after my shower. "What are you doing, hovering there through my whole conversation?"

"I wasn't hovering. I was just about to go out for a run, and ask you to come along. But then you spoiled everything by going out without me."

Even though he was standing there in his leather vest, baggy jeans, and mechanic boots, he was seriously expecting me to believe that he was just about to go out for a run. More alarmingly, he looked like he believed it himself.

"I'm sorry, Lloyd," I said, and in a way I really meant it. I was sorry we couldn't go running together, sorry that he looked like a run might actually kill him, sorry he was so oblivious to it all. I tried to push past him to get to the shower, but he blocked me with a hand on my chest.

"You're not leaving me," he said. I paused there, allowing his hand to hold me in place even though I didn't need to do that. "You're not leaving me in your dust, if that's what you're thinking."

I gave him several more seconds, respectful seconds, with his hand pressed against my chest.

"I wasn't thinking that at all, brother," I said. "That was the furthest thing from my mind."

**46**

We both looked at his hand there for a few seconds, then he let it drop and looked up at me, nodding.

I nodded back. Then I continued on to my shower.

I wasn't thinking that at all, Lloyd, because I've already left you in the dust.

# HIT LIST

I always knew I was good, because I always was. Every sport, even the ones I was crap at, I was good at.

But something changed. People started *telling* me I was good. Then I really believed it. It was right about that time it occurred to me that writing down some long-term goals might be a help in keeping me locked in on what really mattered.

Maybe it would be fun to start at the end and work backward. But what would that be? The NFL? Sure. But as long as you can get to that level, you might as well keep going for it. It would make no sense to just make it, get drafted by the Patriots maybe, and then relax. Since you are there, why not keep doing what got you there, and go for great. Shoot for the top.

Canton, Ohio? Pro Football Hall of Fame?

Okay, so starting at the end could get quickly out of hand. Start at the beginning.

### HIT LIST
#1. Go for Great.

* * *

"Ah, do my eyes deceive me, or are the four of us in the same place at the same time?" Ma said as I walked through the door, late. She was just laying a massive lasagna in the middle of the table. My first thought was that it reminded me of a football field, the shape and the way the pasta sheets made a grid pattern. That was the kind of thing Ma had done for our birthdays when we were little, but now my even thinking it was nuts.

"*That* looks amazing, Ma," I said. "I'm starving. Hey, Dad. Hey, Lloyd."

Lloyd just glared at me. I could tell he was fuming about something. Maybe that I was coming in late and he was forced to sit at the table and wait, like a little kid. He looked like he hadn't showered in a week. Maybe he hadn't.

"Of course you're starving," Dad said while he parceled out some lasagna onto Ma's plate, then his own. "You must be burning something like ten thousand calories a day, the way you're going at it."

"More like five to six, Dad," I said, waiting for Lloyd to pass me the second spatula. He was doing a deliberate slowdown.

"Here," Dad said, handing me the one he'd been using and giving Lloyd a look.

I loaded my plate with a slab roughly the size of a chessboard, plus garlic bread and Caesar salad for six.

"Oh, Arlo," Ma huffed. "Really?"

"You know I won't waste a single bite, Ma."

She loved feeding us, so this was a bit of a conflict for her. Then she zeroed in on her main thought. "Come on, though, is all this

**49**

really necessary? The crazy long hours, mornings, evenings, on top of practice. It seems a little excessive."

I had just taken a big bite of salad, followed by a big bite of bread, so my first move was to hold out pleading hands like I was disputing a penalty call. "Ma, I want to compete—"

"Please, Arlo, close your mouth, chew and swallow first. I'll still be here when you're ready. You're even starting to eat like a big brute."

Dad stepped in for me while I got a handle on my good manners.

"Go easy, Emma," he said, lightly punching her arm. "He's just doing what he needs to do to be the best."

Lloyd gave a half snort, half cough, and Ma's eyes sliced Dad a look that had him pulling that fist away as if she were made of hot lava.

"I said," I said, wanting to get this over with and return to my food in peace because it was so much more interesting than anything else on Earth right now, "that I want to compete. At every level, with everybody. That means outlifting, outrunning, outthinking, and outeating all the other guys, which will pay me back when I'm on the field."

I quickly popped some more of Ma's fine cuisine into my mouth and gave a sincere moan of appreciation.

"You have to agree, hon," Dad said to her, starting to sound like my agent, "that if he is going to be on the field, you want him in peak physical condition. You probably want that more than anyone when you think about it."

This was making Ma tense. She held her lips too tight and got all eye-shifty again with Dad. If Dad was going to be my agent, he'd have to play it cooler when he was pressing an advantage.

"All this wasn't necessary when Lloyd played," Ma blurted. "And Lloyd was always in terrific shape."

The obvious answer, of course, was that I had bigger things in mind, literally and otherwise, than Lloyd ever had, and that I was going to work for them. We all stared at our plates, trying not to acknowledge that Lloyd was sitting there, an almost ghost, with Ma talking about him as though he wasn't there.

I found myself feeling sorry for him. And for that I hated both of us.

"Well, as it happens," Lloyd said loudly, "Arlo has invited me to join his little workout group."

"I did *what*?" I said, showing everybody the food in my big gaping manga mouth.

"Arlo," Ma chided.

"Just the other day," Lloyd said. "The morning when you were heading out early, and I had to remind you to use a glass for your juice . . ."

"Jeez, Arlo," Dad said, "again? No way I can drink that now."

I gave Lloyd a small sneer. The saintliness of the smile I got in return was like an end-zone touchdown dance only I could see.

"Well . . . that's nice," Ma said, tripping on another conflict of her interests.

"But I thought you didn't want him getting all hulked up like me," I said, now completely frustrated. "I thought Lloyd and his terrific shape were being held up as the better model?"

"I wouldn't hold—" Dad started.

"This is true," Ma cut him off, "but that doesn't mean you can't do some training together. It's been a long time since you two spent time with each other." Ma was straining mightily to sound casual about it, but her eyes were pleading eyes, needy eyes, eyes I never want to have to see.

"Please, Arlo," the eyes were saying. "Please be there for your brother, who could really use it right now, your brother who is a Lost Soul."

"Of course," I said to Ma, then turned to repeat it in Lloyd's direction, "Of course. We've always been a team, and we always will be. My brother is welcome wherever I go."

He shot me an expert chilling grin, the kind that said he knew exactly what I thought about it all. Pretty powerful stuff for a lost soul.

We were washing the dishes together when dinner was done. Meaning, Lloyd pawed around in the cupboards and freezer for something to satisfy his wicked sweet tooth, while I washed and repeatedly reminded him to finish clearing up and start drying.

When he finally sidled up beside me and slapped the lasagna pan on the counter next to the sink, I asked him, "You don't really want to come and work out with us, do you?"

"Nah," he said, like he'd been dying for me to ask.

"So why the show?"

"I don't know," he said. "Bored? Something to do? A sad cry for attention?"

"What are you doing with your free time these days anyway?" It sure wasn't homework, given how little time he spent at home in the evenings.

He shrugged.

"Does that mean you're doing nothing?"

"No."

"Does it mean you are doing something?"

"I've got irons in a few fires," he said with so much deliberate mystery it made me lose all interest.

"I thought you were going to fix up your motorcycle? Now would seem to be the perfect time."

"Yeah," he said, pushing off me abruptly.

As he passed through the living room I could hear my father asking him where he was going.

"Out," he snapped, and the front door slammed shut. There was silence after that.

# GIVE THANKS

It was my first Thanksgiving Day with meaningful football. It was Lloyd's first without it.

It was also the day Sandy would properly meet the whole family.

Thanksgiving is football, after all. And Thanksgiving is family.

"Are you sure about this?" I said to Ma when she first encouraged me to invite Sandy for the big day. I couldn't remember our ever having anybody over for any dinner before, never mind a big holiday do, so the possibilities for social calamity were pretty real.

"Of course, of course," she said, and I could see it right there on her face, her calculation face, which meant she was already adding special somethings to the menu and I would be leaning into a mighty gale if I tried to fight it. It was like it was her own personal Super Bowl Sunday.

"Are you sure about this?" I said to Sandy after she made it clear that there was nothing stopping her from attending.

"My dad always goes to his college's Turkey Day game with his old buddies. And my mom compensates by volunteering at the soup kitchen, which she has to book like six months in advance because there are so many selfless do-gooders trying to do all their good on the same day that there's no room for you if you aren't way prebooked. Which means I normally go to my sister's house and spend the first half of the day babysitting her two kids while she and her husband cook the dinner and marinate themselves in red wine, and then I babysit my sister and her husband until their friends come over, and then I hide. So, sure, let's give your people a shot."

Which made me think about my people.

"You'll be really spotlighted. Lloyd's never brought a girl anywhere near the place. And, well, obviously, I've never—"

"Strict household, I'm impressed. It'll be an honor, then. I'll try and make it an experience they will want to repeat."

Obviously, this was going ahead.

"Let's hope we all will," I said.

* * *

First order of business was the football. The dangerous stuff could wait.

Ma was never going to attend. Dad always was, and Sandy always was.

The wild card was, naturally, Lloyd. I figured he would want to be as far away from the scene as possible, but with Lloyd you never knew.

There was a knock on the door to my room as I was finishing getting ready. It was Lloyd, which was a surprise since he considered knocking to be a sign of weakness.

I opened the door to find him looking like he had the wrong address.

"Hey, man, what's up?" I said warily.

"Are you ready, or what?" he answered. "We don't want to be late."

He remained stuck there, his hands clasped in front of him, and fidgeting. He was trying hard. I got it now. This explained his lost look, because this was a place none of us had ever been before, a place where my older brother was learning to be *my* supporter, on *my* day.

"You're coming to my game?" I said, appreciative.

He looked back down at his feet, then came up.

"Ah, man," I said, reaching out and tugging on his shirt sleeve, "it's still a little early. Come in here, will ya?"

I kept tugging, and he came in.

"Nice place you got here," he said, looking around before sitting himself at my desk.

"Thanks. Now, you gonna give me advice, like a good big brother?"

He looked a little startled but recovered admirably. "Advice? You want advice, from me? The chick, you mean? Well, as soon as the parents go in to wash the dishes—"

"Ah, thanks for that, Lloyd. But I meant football. Football advice, and big game stuff. Tell you the truth, I'm more than a little bit nervous. A lot of people show up. I know they're there for the varsity, but some of them will be watching us, too. Hey, this is the first time I'll have you or Dad watching me play jayvee, and that's enough to give me the shakes."

This pleased him noticeably. And loosened him up.

"Okay," he said, getting up and closing the door before starting, then speaking and pacing like some Hollywood version of a big-game coach. "Here's the main thing. . . ."

I knew exactly what he was going to tell me to do. I was already doing it. Ever since the pep talk from Coach Fisk, I was getting and going. I played clean, but I played to crush bones. Anybody who came across my area of responsibility paid for it, and if somebody was carrying the ball into a zone of responsibility that was within my reach, he likewise paid for it. Dearly. Receivers were hearing footsteps before I arrived if I was in pass coverage; running backs altered their routes to avoid me; quarterbacks lost their composure and their effectiveness.

It's not that I was suddenly mad talented. I wasn't. I was good, but only as good as a lot of other guys.

But now I was fierce. I was menacing, and I was a threat to my own teammates in practice. I knew Monday I was already ready for this game. McCallum took a casual run in my direction after a lazy handoff because our offense thought our defense wasn't taking things seriously.

If I have pads and a helmet on, I'm taking it seriously, so you'd better take *me* seriously.

When McCallum popped through the line and *smiled* at me as he came my way, I felt the roar come up from my guts. I flattened him. I drilled him right in the numbers, exploded through him, planted him flat on his back and continued running right over him.

I kept running down the field, bellowing, smacking myself on the helmet, jumping in the air. I wanted the game to start right then and to go on forever, even after I finally reversed field and saw that McCallum remained on his back for a few minutes before getting very slowly up.

When I blasted the competition with the perfect violence of a vicious clean tackle like that, it altered the offense's game plan. And it altered me, made me better, stronger. My head exploded with the impact, because of the physical jolt and because of the crazy rush of power that came over me. Lining a ballcarrier up and knocking him out of his shoes with precise timing and malice only made me want to do it again, right away.

And I knew well whose game I got it from.

". . . and a lot of times, if you add a little loud growlin' and snarlin' to your business just before you make contact, it'll give 'em the yips somethin' awful, and they'll become gradually useless over time. And the harder you hit, the stronger you get, physically. Hit big and you're invincible—be tentative and watch how quick you get injured. Or even better than all that, you get up from the best kind of punishing tackle and you feel like your feet aren't even touching turf. You're high, is the truth of it. Honestly, wickedly, high, the best feeling in the world."

It was hard to tell even what Lloyd was looking at as he stomped and pumped around my room throughout his motivational speech. Glassy-eyed but clear at the same time, he looked at the floor, the ceiling, the middle distance and someplace way beyond that until he had said what he had to say, and he slowed himself like a jet's engines powering down. Then, a little sweatier and breathier than when he had started, he gazed over to me as I sat on my bed, looking hard back at him. The talk left me unsurprised and mesmerized.

"Like that," he said. "Do it like that, and you'll be all right, Arlo."

I knew what he was looking at, off in that distance. He was looking at the game he would have been playing, that *we* would have been playing, the Brodie Brothers mowing down the world together.

"I will," I said, standing and slapping his shoulder hard enough to make him arch-brow me. "I will do it exactly like that."

* * *

I was keenly aware of the full stands, the biggest crowd I had yet played in front of, and of my people being up there among the fans. My girl. My dad, who had never seen me play jayvee. My brother. I got onto the field, but it was like I left half of my brain up there in the stands. I couldn't get my rhythm. I was floundering when the playing field, the gridiron, was supposed to be mine.

The other guys were a famously free-passing team, loving the aerial game. But there is a big difference between knowing that fact and knowing what to do about it. Our whole unit was a step behind, a yard wide of making the plays we needed to make. They scored two of their first three possessions, both on deep throws after pump-faking our defensive backs into thinking short. And

I was right there, in coverage, watching the beautiful spirals their all-conference quarterback was known for drift high over my head.

"Come on, Arlo, head's up!" Dinos yelled. I glared in his direction, *on the sideline* because he was useless at defending the pass.

"Pass-pass-run, or run-run-pass!" Coach hollered after our offense chased us halfway back into the game. "It's the stupidest damn thing I have ever seen in a game, and I feel so insulted I want to run right over to the other sideline and punch that coach right in the face. And I want to punch you guys right in the face because you're too stupid to realize what they're doing. But since I am not allowed to do that by the state's interscholastic sports competition rules—and I know that because I checked last week—I need you guys to do basically the same thing, *on the field!*"

This was embarrassing, and loud enough that I actually felt compelled to swivel around and check up in the stands to see if Sandy was watching this too closely. Or worse, if Lloyd was getting disgusted enough that he was coming to drag me out of the game by my face mask.

"Hey!" Coach said, rapping on my helmet about fifty times before I even had a chance to answer the door. "Listen, Ferdinand the gentle bull! If you are that interested in whoever is up there in the stands, you are free to go and join them. Because for all the good you're doing, you could just as well wave at those touchdowns from up there."

A couple of guys were bold or stupid enough to laugh but stifled it when Coach whipped round on them.

"Pass-pass-run! Run-run-pass. Know what that means? It

means, at the very least, you boys know what *every* play is gonna be on the second down. Right?"

"Right, Coach!" we yelled together.

"Right! So, feel 'em out on first down. Flex defense, bend-don't-break. Then, second down we drop the hammer. Pass rushers, linebackers, deep backs, you will *know* where to be. Be there! And MOW THEM DOWN!"

The entire defensive unit howled out a wordless Neanderthal roar, and the stands gave it back to us twentyfold. Lord, this was it. I could feel this, under my feet and inside my ribcage. The intoxication athletes always say they get from a raucous home crowd. It was the best thing I ever felt, and I wanted it to go on and on.

After the first play from scrimmage, they got a five-yard gain off left tackle, but it didn't mean anything and we knew it. At the snap, we packed the line, our linemen standing their linemen straight up, just powering straight like plow horses while the linebackers all rushed in to catch the run coming right tackle. The three of us rammed into the running back all at once, blasting him and ourselves back through that line, on his ass, coughing back up half of those yards they had just gained.

Then we knew the pass was coming. Our strong-side safety, like he was told in advance, was running so hard, to the spot, he could have had his eyes closed, and he and ball and unfortunate receiver reached the exact same spot in the angry universe at exactly the same time.

They started going with the run again, and on second down I was first man in. Since we were so clued in, it became purely a race, of speed and power and ruthlessness, and suddenly I was the man. Popped that running back so hard I went right over him, blasted him. *Ka-blam!* It was like an explosion of humanity. It was *just* like Lloyd used to do it. The other guy never even knew what hit him. His arms and legs just stopped working, his knees gave out, and he dropped on the spot like a rag doll.

I kept right on in a somersault that left me in the backfield where I hopped to my feet and met the quarterback face mask to face mask.

"Hello," I said, smiling right into him. I could not stop smiling.

And right there he showed me. In his expression, in his blinking. He showed me what he really never should have showed me.

When we lined up for the pass, I kept looking over to Coach for the sign that I could blitz. I looked, looked, looked again until I did everything but fold my hands *please*.

And then he gave it to me.

At the snap I was gone as if there were no football game in front of me at all but just wind sprints I was running alone on the track. I was vaguely aware of maybe a hand brushing my arm or something, but that was it as I came barreling in weak side and absolutely crushing my new QB pal, belting him square in the middle of the number eleven on his back before he could even get his feet set. I even carried him a couple of extra yards into the backfield, feeling a rush of power and strength that surely had no limit now, before I slammed him to the ground.

While the crowd roared crazy, I rolled him over, and could feel myself smiling again, and I said it again.

"Hello again."

"Yeah, hi," he said, wincing.

This was already the greatest day of my life.

It became muscle memory then. I didn't think, I just knew without knowing. I was everywhere the ball was, appearing for all the world to be the fastest, hardest, smartest thing that had ever played, because the game was making total sense to me, and it was getting so easy. I hit everything in sight, some things I didn't even see. I hit running backs and receivers, tight ends and offensive linemen. I found out I *loved* hitting offensive linemen. They were big but not much stronger than me, and had no chance of getting up the same head of steam a charging linebacker could. A couple of times I had a straight shot at the ballcarrier, but I veered slightly to barrel down his blocking lineman anyway, just to be inclusive.

I wound up on my back, or on my front, with my face mask full of dirt like I was cutting turf cookies. I got sandwich-blocked by two very angry linemen. My hand was stepped on when I was at the bottom of a pile. The backup quarterback drilled me in the side of the head with a throw, and it was too hard and too precise in the vicinity of no open receivers to have been an accident.

I loved every single down of it.

Deep in the game, under two minutes to go, they were lined up in our end, third and goal and four yards out. They lined up one of their defensive linemen at fullback. He was an absolute beastmaster of a guy who had done his fair share of terrorizing our offense all afternoon, which was the main reason I even bothered to watch when our offense was on the field.

**63**

The snap, the handoff, the crush of bodies, the line partially opening up and partially just getting stamped down by the guy like they were so many weeds in his footpath.

Middle linebacker, he was my responsibility.

I turned on the jets like it was my life on the line and not just four yards.

Three yards.

Two.

The behemoth and I were formally introduced at the one-and-a-half-yard line. A pleasure to meet you, I have admired your work. Same to you.

The almighty crack was a gunshot cutting silence, a clash of equipment and muscle and physics blasting through the din of a thousand crazies.

My everything hit his everything, his everything my everything, shoulder and shoulder and shoulder and shoulder and helmet and helmet and scream and crunch and *down* like the last two dinosaurs.

At the two-yard line.

The stop.

I had dreamed about a stop like that. Everybody who plays linebacker dreams about a stop like that, and as I jumped up and over the great beast—and I think guys were slapping and pounding on me—I felt it, *it, it* high like high like no drugs could possibly fake, just like Lloyd said. I floated as I sucked up the crowd roar and spurted adrenaline sweat like a lawn sprinkler and I screamed until my lungs emptied and my feet were *not even there.*

Somebody, whoever, grabbed me by the shirt as I continued down the field toward whatever, who cared, and over to the proper sideline and off the field.

Time passed quickly, in spurts, like somebody was alternating between stomping on my accelerator pedal and my brake as I showered and changed and smiled and we made way for the varsity and Coach Fisk said things and pointed at me with both hands and everybody thanked Thanksgiving and out we drifted—some of us to watch the varsity game, others to find our people in the parking lot or to be found by them.

Sandy grabbed me just as I was leaving the locker room.

"Did you see me?" I said to Sandy, who was around my big neck like a lilac-scented boa constrictor.

"Are you okay?" she said, leaning back to look at me.

"Amazing," I said. "Incredibly amazing." Words were not sufficient to explain.

We walked to the parking lot, me a thousand feet high. Suddenly Lloyd had me, I didn't even know how. He stole me and now I was his, his hands gripping my shoulders.

"I could hardly believe my eyes," he said, both solemn and elated.

"Believe 'em," I said, rising up on the toes of where my feet should have been to look down on him.

"What are you so giddy about?" Dad said, verging on dampening the holiday spirit. "You lost."

"What?" I said, still grinning because I couldn't help it.

"You lost," Dad repeated, though straining to hold his stern

**65**

face. Team game or no—won, lost, or whatever—he couldn't hide how proud and excited he was about what he had seen of *me*. Of *his* boy. His brute of a boy. "The field goal? Last minute? You lost." He was chuckling at this point.

"So that's funny now, is it?" Lloyd said, cutting an icy chill through the heart of the conversation.

"What?" Dad snapped back.

"You never seemed to think it was funny when my teams lost. Whatever happened to 'A loss is a loss is a loss'? Huh, Dad? Must have taken you a whole weekend to come up with that gem. Or the one you basically stole from Bill Parcells, 'You are exactly what your record says you are.' You thought I was too stupid to even know you didn't make that up."

"Right, Lloyd, can you not spoil the day for everybody?" Dad said.

I turned from him to Lloyd, who was shrugging and nodding in a petulant, aggressive way. Then to Sandy, who was shimmering.

"Anyway, I'm not the one doing the spoiling," Lloyd said. "It was Arlo who lost."

"Maybe *they* did," I said, "but I didn't."

And that was exactly how I felt.

"That's right," Sandy chirped, the sound of her tone pulling all the menfolk happily away from the football talk.

"Aren't you going to introduce us?" Lloyd said. He was looking at Sandy in a way that instantly suggested a world of unfortunate possibilities.

"A pleasure," Dad said, shaking her hand with both vigor and delicacy like she was kind of robust royalty. He was never a naturally sociable creature, and it could seem like every time he met a new person he had to relearn the whole process all over again. I feared he might be odd, and he was, but kind of charmingly so. Good start.

"Pleasu'." Lloyd's speech was garbled because he had something in his mouth, and that something was the back of Sandy's hand. Specifically, the knuckle of her left index finger.

"Lloyd," I snapped.

"Shows you what you know about these things," he said to me. "A gentleman is *supposed* to kiss a lady's hand."

"Teeth don't play any part in hand kissing," Dad said.

I turned to Sandy, mortified. She was laughing. I opened the car door and pushed her into the back and climbed in after her, just to make sure Lloyd didn't. He and my father got in and we eased our way out of the crowded parking lot.

"Your brother is *sooo* funny," Sandy said as she leaned in close. She said it very softly, so Lloyd wouldn't hear her from the front.

"He is?" I said. "Well, I know he can be. I mean, I'm glad he was."

"What was I?" he said, whipping around and laying his old devil grin on us.

"Who says we were talking about you?" I said.

"Pffft. Who else would you be talking about, *him*?" He gestured dismissively toward the driver.

"Don't be nasty, Lloydo. I think your father is a lovely and very interesting man as a matter of fact."

Lloydo. Miraculous. How can women achieve things like that, well, easy intimacy I guess, accomplishing in an hour what guys can almost never manage?

He turned around and beamed at her.

"Yeah, Lloydo," I said.

And again, how does the same head, with the same lips and teeth and eyebrows, change expression comprehensively without seeming to flicker?

"Right, fine," I said, hands up, "no Lloydo. Anyway, shouldn't we be talking about me?"

"Yes" was Dad's first word of the drive.

"Yes," Sandy said, matching his tone.

Lloyd didn't say anything. His silence said a lot.

"I had no idea," Dad said. "I mean, I knew when they put you on the junior varsity instead of the freshman team . . . and then when you said they made you a starter. But, I guess you have to see something like this in the flesh to fully appreciate the scale of it. You're a very good player, son."

My dad was a very understated man. So this meant something.

"Thanks, Dad," I said, and felt my head getting a little hot with embarrassment.

Sandy squeezed my arm.

Lloyd stared at the side of our father's head.

"You weren't bad, little brother. Not bad at all. Once you stopped sucking," he added. Dad shifted in his seat like he was about to say something, but Lloyd barreled on. "You really sucked on those first two touchdowns. There was a loud sucking sound you made on

**68**

those plays that was so loud people were talking about it in the stands. Sucked the hats right off a whole section of people sitting at the fifty-yard line. That happened, didn't it, Sandra?"

"Sucked. Sucked the whole section of hats off. People scrambling around, climbing over each other to get the hats back."

"See," Lloyd said triumphantly, gesturing at Sandy as irrefutable proof of my suckiness.

"Her name is Sandrine," I said flatly.

"Even sweeter," Lloyd said to her.

"Have we changed the subject?" I asked.

"You were outstanding," Sandy said, laughing and banging into me with her shoulder. "A little unnecessarily violent perhaps. . . ."

"Yes! Unnecessarily violent. Exactly," Lloyd shouted violently close to Dad's ear. My father's restraint is sometimes a thing to marvel at. "That is the thing you need to keep up. It's what separates the men from the boys, the greats from the scrubs."

"And the sociopath from the productive citizen," Dad said as he pulled the car sharply into the driveway. He stuck the car into park and got out so abruptly that Lloyd was left burning eyeholes into his headrest.

"And he claims to love football," Lloyd said, shaking his head in mock disbelief as he got out the passenger side and followed Dad into the house.

Alone with Sandy for the first time that day, I kind of felt like this moment in the backseat in the parked car was going to stand as one of the non-sports-related high points of this Thanksgiving Day. Except I couldn't help asking.

"You didn't really think I was unnecessarily violent, did you?"

She paused, blinked a few times to let her butterfly lashes sweep away any bad airs.

"Maybe it just takes time to figure out how much of it is necessary and how much isn't. You'll probably be an even better player when you don't feel like you have to dismember people to get your job done."

"Ha," I said back to her, thinking how much I loved the way she never didn't have an answer if you gave her a few seconds to ponder anything. "That's what you figure, huh?"

"That's what I figure."

* * *

"Bup, bup, bup," Ma said, accompanied by a two-finger no-no wave and a forty-five-degree turn of her head. This was her way of letting you know she did not care to hear what you were about to say. "I already have all the information I need. You are here, walking upright like all the other great apes and superficially unscarred. And you are physically capable of feeding yourself, I assume." As she said the last part, she reached out and lifted my top lip with both hands, examining my teeth like she was buying a horse.

"'A, ith thith not thorta wude?" I said, trying to somehow not be embarrassed in front of my guest.

"Sandy," Ma said anxiously, wiping traces of me off her hands and onto her apron. "Sandy, it is so lovely to meet you. Please, you have to forgive me, but I do get a little demented when there is a game on and I think all the worst until I get him back in one piece."

"Not at all," Sandy answered, offering a polite hand until Ma seized her in a hug. "And you had nothing to worry about from what I saw."

"On the other hand, the mothers of all the boys he played against had plenty—" Lloyd started.

"Bup, bup, bup," Ma said, fingers no-ing, head turning that-away. "It's done, it's nice you all went, now let's get dinner ready."

Dad headed off to the living room to watch the Lions-Bears game, and Lloyd headed off to his bedroom to do the same. That left Sandy and me on kitchen duty. It was all weirdly normal. Ma lightheartedly grilled Sandy about her family as I whaled away at a pot full of helpless potatoes.

"I think they're mashed," Sandy said after a while. I stared down at the spuds, which looked like they had been put through the food processor. I had lost track of time, thinking about the game.

"They just won't need any milk, is all," I said.

"Right, salt and butter them," Ma said, taking her bird out of the oven for its final roundup. "And focus this time. Too much salt and the entire day is a failure."

"No pressure then," Sandy said, applying her own laser focus to the gravy chemistry. This was a serious leap of faith for Ma, ceding a pivotal job like gravying to a complete unknown.

"Is it ready already?" Lloyd appeared in the doorway. "I'm starving."

"Lloydo!" Sandy called far more brightly than anyone else would have.

"Lloydo," Ma said. "I might have to adopt that."

"Well, you can't," he said. "That's a thing, just between me and Sandra."

"Oh, how proprietary," Ma said, then turned to Sandy. "Can I call you Sandra?"

"Sure you can," she said.

"Except that her name is Sandrine," I said.

Ma stopped, offering open palms to the heavens like, Is this my birthday or what? "That," she said to Sandy, "is the name I was going to give Arlo if he was a girl. Spooky, huh? Or fate, or kismet, or something?"

"Or something. That something being nonsense," I said. "You were going to name me Audrey if I turned out to be a girl. You told me that a hundred times. Arlo or Audrey, Audrey or Arlo. It kind of makes sense, like in the way that Arlo or *Sandrine* doesn't."

My mother had, really, two modes, deeply serious and silly. I envied her silly. I lacked a capacity for it. But I could not recall one single TV interview with a great athlete who seemed like he was really just a goofy guy in his off hours. If the greats didn't have time for silliness, why should I?

"Come on, Sandra," Lloyd said, holding his hand out in the manner of a guy who's about to take a girl ice-skating. "These people are a little bit nutty, but I hope that doesn't put you off."

"Oh no, I have a pretty high threshold for nutty," she said, skipping along with him. "I'm not certain, but I think somehow that's why I'm here."

The kitchen went quiet as I pressed my mental ear, my whole self to the wall of the rest of the house to hear where they were going. I should have been more self-confident than that, but I just wasn't. She was there for me, and I had had my best day in front of her and everybody. Lloyd's time with the likes of Sandy was already past, not to mention that Lloyd's time with the likes of Sandy never was.

And yet. My older brother, Lloyd. He was him, and I was me, and Sandy was elsewhere, and *Your brother is sooo funny. . . .*

"She makes it like a family, practically," said my dad, suddenly filling the doorway. He never helped out, so this was a stunning development. It certainly was a unique kind of day.

"You mean Sandy?" I said, holding out the pot of mashed potatoes to him.

He dipped a finger in. "Salty," he said, lapping around at the air with his tongue like a lizard.

My shoulders sank, my head sank. He adored perfect potatoes. He wanted satisfying and simple dishes and clean, crisp tackles.

"I will go get milk, and butter, and—"

"But mostly butter, right? Cause the milk will just insipidize everything at this point."

"*Insipidize*, eh, Louis?" Ma said, She was sharp at pinpointing the moments when his criticism could tip into day spoilers. She took the pot of mashed potatoes from me and shooed us into the dining room with the turkey and green beans.

We set the platters down. "I'll go get Sandy—whose name is Sandrine—and Dad, you will sit right there and wait. Save this seat— this seat right here," I said, slapping the chair to his left loudly. "And I will sit next to her and it will be a family, practically."

73

To my mild horror I found Sandy in Lloyd's Lair, the two of them huddled next to his old oak bookcase. That's what he called it, Lloyd's Lair. My alarm rose further when I smelled the place.

"Lloyd?" I said in a big whisper. "What are you smoking in here?"

They both turned toward me. Sandy was holding one of my brother's old trophies from his Pop Warner days, when *he* was the undisputed star. That was when I first witnessed football played by someone so crazy in love with it and crazy good at it that spending time on almost anything else didn't make any sense.

He was showing her his awards.

"That smell was here when I got here," she said, grinning.

"Hey, I did it for Ma," he said righteously. "She did all that cooking, and I wasn't hungry. Now I am."

"He's very gallant," she said.

He concurred. "I'm gallant."

I formed my hands into a kind of bullhorn, and called out in a police negotiator kind of style, "Miss Sandrine, put the little shiny man down, and walk slowly away from the big shiny knight. You may be in danger, and dinner is served."

Sandy placed the trophy back on the shelf. "Those are some pretty good reasons," she said to Lloyd, patting him on the chest and walking my way.

I did a little bow and "after you" gesture, and as she passed she said, "He's really just a sweet and harmless creature."

"Yeah, people say the same thing about the poison dart frog. Until he gets all poisony on them."

I was still in scrape-and-bow posture as the boy himself passed through. "Hey, I think my charisma's working," he said, giving my head a little hammer of exclamation. "I just might get lucky here."

"Great, good luck with that," I said as I straightened up quickly to catch up. Too quickly, as my head went swimmy for a second.

But then again, not quickly enough. Sandy was already trapped between Dad and the usurper, an unholy Sandy sandwich.

"Would anyone like a little glass of festive holiday wine?" Ma asked, standing by the table with a bottle of white wine in one hand and a bottle of pale ginger ale in the other. "Which for you youngsters means a wine spritzer, of course," she said directly to Sandy and me.

"No," Lloyd snapped, drawing stunned looks all around. Then, after a good comedic pause, "I want a really *big* glass."

Ma and Dad looked at one another sort of helplessly. Lloyd knew exactly what he was doing and that they were going to shrink from any risk of serious disruption to our special day with a special guest.

And we all knew that Lloyd was a serious risk of serious disruption at any given moment.

Sandy took a little spritz, and so I took a little spritz. Dad and Lloyd took white wine, and Ma finally took her seat.

And there she would remain for the duration of the meal. She always front loaded the effort, took care of every detail, laid out the whole thing for everyone to self-serve, and then, plunk. A militant immobility, she said, was one of the great rewards.

"Let's tell stories," Ma said brightly as she passed around the dark-meat tray.

"Let's not," I said quickly, sounding too alarmed to have done myself any good.

"We never have stuffing in this house," Dad said after shooting down his glass of wine briskly. He was sounding almost effusive under the influence of wine and possibly Sandy, who was looking around from person to person to person with such smiling energy she was powering up the whole room.

"Oh, jeez, man," Lloyd said, making short work of his own wine.

"The reason we can never have stuffing is that Lloyd had a big chubby rabbit that died," Dad continued. "And his name was Stuffing, and Lloyd gets all weepy if he's around stuffing."

Sandy made the isn't-that-just-darling brand of an "Oh" sound, and Ma and I joined in as if we hadn't ever heard it all before.

"That's a story," Ma said.

Lloyd calmly—on the outside, at least—refilled his glass and said, "Here's another story. Dad killed Stuffing."

"I did no such thing," Dad said, trying to sound light but not succeeding. "Someone didn't lock his cage, and he ran away and got into the road. That happens."

"What was all that mess on your tire then, huh?"

"Come to think of it," I jumped in fast, "it looked a lot like sausage stuffing."

Sandy burst out laughing, slapped her hand over her mouth quickly, then wide-eyeballed the room.

76

"Was I not supposed to laugh?" she said from behind her hand.

"Oh no, hon, you're fine," Ma said.

"Yeah," Dad said, "it comes out different every Thanksgiving. Sometimes nobody laughs, sometimes we all laugh."

"Except Lloyd," I said. "He's pretty consistent."

After that we all fell into our traditional pattern of fitting short questions and comments in between chewing bird and swallowing mushy stuff, clattering silverware, and clinking glasses. The food was impeccable as always, and I did believe that the improved gender balance had an undeniably positive effect on the holiday meal.

Well into the meal when the tryptophan from the turkey must have been felling my mother, the conversation was allowed to turn to my football game. Dad, in particular, got so animated I thought he might start reenacting plays right there in the dining room.

". . . he was a mammoth guy, Emma, just a colossal specimen. And when they met, the clack of it sounded like a gunshot. Everybody in the place caught their breath. Full contact, I mean, full-on, chests and arms and helmets and—*Bang!* Something. I know . . . but you couldn't have helped being proud, even you."

Ma had that telltale shock-horror-rapture look of somebody who can't stand the rough stuff and can't manage to look away, either. She really had loved the game in the early days, before our injuries started mounting up, coming closer together, and most worryingly, traveling north.

Lloyd was a freshman when ankle sprain became knee tweak became charley horse became hip pointer became rib crack became partially separated shoulder became eye-gouge scratched retina.

Became head trauma. Possible first concussion.

It turned out never to even be a confirmed diagnosis. And it wasn't even a result of playing the dangerous game too hard, because the touchdown had been scored, and Lloyd had been beaten by a receiver who then went on to celebrate that fact possibly a little too enthusiastically. Until Lloyd lost it and charged him and the receiver ducked at the very moment Lloyd lunged. So it was not the fault of the grand game of football played sideline-to-sideline that my brother lost his temper and that the league could not afford padding for everything at that time, and that the other guy was smart and slick and my brother slow and stupid as he rammed himself right into the base of the goalpost and right out of consciousness.

That was the *no mas* moment for Ma and The File was started.

"It was really, really something special," Dad concluded with a big gulp of wine.

I squirmed and waited for him to say something negative like he always did, something to make sure I wouldn't turn into a diva. But he didn't say another word, just held up his glass like he was toasting me.

Lloyd got up and walked off to his room. With his third glass of wine.

"What's he doing?" Sandy asked.

"What he always does," I answered, "whatever he feels like."

"Probably off for his nap," Ma said. The sound of hope speaking for itself.

But no such luck. Five minutes later he was back with us,

clutching his wine goblet—empty and upside down. He also smelled a little more like his room.

"We missed you, Lloydo," Sandy said into the sudden silence as he scraped back his chair and sat down.

"Missed you, too, Saundra," he said, possibly rewriting her name again, possibly just sludging it. "Now, where were we? Right, Dad's admiration for our all-pro here. Hey, Dadmiration. Look at that. Dadmiration, for ArlPro. Too perfect, huh? It's like that thing, where they say a sculpture has been there inside the marble all the time, just waiting to be discovered. Those words were clearly just waiting for this minute to emerge into the world for this occasion. Awesome."

There are moments when it's a real blessing to have an alien person at the table, who can choose to miss all the unhappy undercurrents family can't.

"Very good, Lloydo," Sandy said. "You're a natural words—"

"Shush," he said to her.

"Hey," I barked.

He turned to me . . . turned *on* me, more like. "Shush," he said again with his Doberman smile and a snarl.

"*Llllloyd,*" Ma growled.

He had never been able to put up much resistance when she rolled out the extra *l*'s in his name. So he stopped, but not before he gave her a modified, more modest edition of his snarly smile. Which was a whole new development. And she let it go. Gave up.

I didn't believe, then, that there were many links left in his leash. Not even for her.

"Sorry, everybody. Anyway, I interrupted. Father, I believe you were going on about Arlo and his sporting awesomeness and how you were very proud of him."

"Yes," Dad said, defiant on the witness stand. "Yes, I certainly was."

"Can we change the subject, please?" I said.

"That would be nice," Ma said.

Lloyd wasn't relinquishing the floor yet. "I used to play football, Saundra. Did you know that?"

"Yes, you showed me your—"

"You weren't supposed to tell anybody about *that....*"

"Trophies," she said sternly. But I was disappointed to notice she was also fighting down a grin.

"Oh yes, my trophies. Thank you for bringing that up. Too modest myself. Yeah, I was good. Until I had to give it up when that old injury flared up again. Knee, or brain or something, I can't remember."

"I bet you were good," Sandy said.

"He was a fine athlete," Ma chirped.

"Taught this lump everything he knows," he said, ignoring that past tense, lucky for the rest of us, and pointing with Uncle Sam certainty at the lump of me.

"Pretty much," I said.

"Want to see some pictures, Saundra?" he said. "Some family pictures?" Lloyd's mind lately, postfootball, tended to make the laser-quick cuts upfield and back that his body used to. He was up and Lair-bound before I could finish my protest groan. Sandy patted my arm across the table sympathetically. Dad, you could feel, was reverting into cold storage.

"He has pictures in there?" Ma said. She hadn't ventured into that realm for years. "Really? Pictures of us?"

The answer was headed our way, and even whistling as he did. The tune was unidentifiable but suggested malicious intent all the same.

"This is my file," Lloyd said.

I still had my head buried. Slowly I raised it to see Sandy's open and happy holiday face fade into shade as Lloyd opened The File to begin the tour. *The* File.

"Jesus, Lloyd," I said.

Nobody else said a word to protest. Dad, well, this wouldn't have been his moment. But Ma? This would have seemed to be precisely the time for one of her intervention swoops to save a situation.

But. Ah. Right. Conflicted.

And if Sandy came to understand some of the life lessons of sport?

Let us give thanks indeed.

"Oh, now there's a picture of me," Lloyd said to her happily. You could almost buy into his enthusiasm. "And that one there, that's our little Arlo. Isn't he precious?"

Sandy looked at me, her complexion with a worrisome gray-meat kind of effect.

Not unlike the damaged brain slices laid out before her.

"Boy, am I suddenly sleepy," Lloyd said, rising, stretching.

"That turkey chemical thing, it'll get you every time. I'll just leave that with you then, Saundra, huh?"

He walked around to my side of the table, which was not the route to his room. He leaned himself heavy on my back, draped himself over me, and got right up in my ear.

"I'm so proud of you," he breathed.

I waited. Waited for the punch line, or the punch.

Then he was off me and toddling away to his bedroom.

# THERE ARE NO OFF-SEASONS

I wanted to be great. That's what I knew. I planned to pack on another twenty or thirty pounds before I started sophomore year. I let Dinos know that I would be training day and night, every day, and he could jump in or out as he wished, but I didn't have time for off days anymore. I left for school early and even though there weren't practices anymore, I came home later than ever, splitting afternoons up between lifting and running on the track.

In other words, I started spending all my time at school, at exactly the time my brother quit spending any time there at all. Kind of a universe-balancing equation in there someplace.

One fine, strange morning, Lloyd summoned me into his lair after I had finished my push-ups, sit-ups, pull-ups, biceps curls, which I did for an hour every day. *Strange* would be inaccurate, actually, as there was no longer any strange with him because every day the realm of that possibility got bigger.

As I walked in he sparked up, pulling his product out of his Pop Warner Defensive Player of the Year cup. He took a hit of his breakfast, offered it to me.

"Of course not, man," I said. "I have no interest at all. And don't you worry about Ma and Dad smelling that stuff?"

He took another hit, shrugged, exhaled a response in my direction. "God knows I've tried, but they seem to be turning a blind nostril. They probably like me sedate. Weed's harmless, though. Certainly are worse things you can do to your brain. Like that shit you do. What's it called again? Right, football." He offered me the smoke again as if we had not already settled that.

I shoved it away. "Never. And even if it wasn't never, we have to get to school."

He exhaled, then waved the smoke—and school—away from his face. "No time for that shit, man. I have to get on with life, and high school ain't life. Not for me anyway."

"What are you going to do?"

"Gonna make money, like a man's supposed to do. That's why this is so fortuitous that you just happened to drop by."

"I didn't just happen to—"

"Steroids. Human growth hormone. That's your ticket. And it just so happens I can supply these things to you at a family discount."

"Hell, Lloyd. Jeez. Hell no, not a chance, not ever."

"Huh," he said, his voice constricted as he held in some smoke, "you don't want greatness. Stop wasting my time. Go to *schooool*," he drawled as he let the smoke roll my way. He said the word *school* as if he expected me to pull my cape over my head and slither down through the nearest sewer grate with the shame of it.

**\* \* \***

February: eight pounds. March: ten. I started spending a lot of time around the spring track-and-field guys, working on intensity sprints, and I found that I enjoyed this dynamic, this feeling of being my own athletic bubble, my own pod working right in the midst of this team I did not belong to. There but isolated.

The track-and-field varsity coach came up to me while I stretched alongside the track.

"You ever try any of the events?" he asked.

I looked up from my spot on the ground, my right leg extended and my head almost touching my thigh. "What events?"

"Shot put, discus, javelin, hammer throw. I've seen you and I would bet with a little coaching you could throw a hammer a country mile."

Thing was, I was so into a zone, right then and whenever I was training, that this kind of unscheduled interaction sounded to me as foreign as somebody talking to me underwater. I received his words, reconstituted them in my head, but I was afraid I did not engage like a fully functional human.

"Why would I do that?" I said, looking all around the infield of the track oval where throwers and jumpers were throwing and jumping to no purpose I could figure.

He laughed. "Competition? Fun? The purity of noble athletic endeavor?"

Well, yeah, all right. But I couldn't feel it. That was the thing, the hard reality thing. All those things were just things to me. Just stuff. Like disjointed pieces of some larger game that wasn't fully assembled yet.

Where was the contact? How boring it would be to train for a sport that had no contact. Those weren't even actual sports but just training exercises for sports.

Sports with contact.

"Thanks for asking, Coach," I said, the return of my interpersonal skills indicating I had been pulled out of my training zone for too long. "But I'm just too busy."

He nodded, shrugged, and walked away without saying anything more. Which I really appreciated.

Sandy was already looking at me kind of sideways over the workout thing. She liked me in shape, but once Memorial Day came she seemed to think a clock had been punched somewhere, a bell had rung for recess or something.

"Ah, I think it's safe to say you're *there* now, muscles," she said when we got down to the beach on the first really warm day. I took my shirt off, as guys do.

"Where is there?" I said, laughing. I grabbed her in a quarterback sack and tumbled her into the sand.

"There," she said, poking her sharp nails into my chest, then my deltoids, then my abs, "and there, and there, and there."

"Ha," I said, squirming and twisting away. Little thing that she was, she had a mastery of debilitating me that I was helpless over.

I was helpless all over, over her, to tell the truth. She was the only person in the world who made helpless feel good.

"Now that it's summer, you'll back off the hard-core training for a while, right? You can't get better conditioned than you are right now, and off-season should be for winding down and resting up, shouldn't it?"

I had to judge the balance on this one. Sneaky notes of disapproval were starting to waft into Sandy's football opinions. I knew what I had to do to succeed, but the only two things in the world I really *needed* were this girl and that game. I couldn't have them going at each other.

I had to choose my words carefully.

So there is no excuse for what came out of my mouth. "Off-seasons are for losers."

There would be no more muscle-poking, sand-rolling Sandy this day.

"What?" I said, scrambling to my feet and spraying sand behind me as I ran like a cartoon character after her.

"Seriously, Arlo," she said, shaking my hand out of hers twice before she finally let me hold on. My heart rate came back down then. "At a certain point hypertraining becomes a kind of sickness."

"Are you saying I'm sick, Sandy?" I said, giving myself away by being too happy about it.

"I swear, boy, if you're doing that thing of using the word *sick* to mean awesome . . . I'll show you real sick by barfing right on you, right now."

Which of course made me laugh out loud but also made me surrender. I yanked on her hand for her to slow down and stop trying to pull away from me. "Okay, okay, I get your point. I don't

**87**

entirely agree with it . . . but that should make it all the more meaningful that I'm going to take your advice and ease up. A little."

She faced me. "What's a little?"

"Ah . . . okay, how 'bout one gym session a day instead of two? But you'll give me till the Fourth of July. To taper off."

She pulled her hand away yet again, then offered it back to me in the form of a handshake. "You do hear yourself using the language of the addict, however."

I took that hand, and gave it a good shaking. "I'm addicted to *you*," I said.

"Yeah, well don't be that, either. Just try to be normal."

"I'll write that on my Hit List."

"God, if I ever find that you have a real, physical hit list . . . ," she said, turning away and laughing as if she were picturing it.

I made a mental note to stop talking about my Hit List.

* * *

Dinos was off to stay with relatives in Greece for the summer and I was all two-a-days solo by the end of June. The school facilities were open for community stuff, and the only people I saw were parents taking their little kids for swim lessons and the summer school dopes who didn't take any better care of their bodies than they did their grades but needed a credit or two to graduate. Sounded like Lloyd, except for the giving a hoot about graduating part.

After Lloyd did not graduate and made it clear he was not going to summer school, there was a sort of Lloyd Conference at a nice Indian restaurant where his short- to medium-term future was brought up. Dad and Ma were good, well prepared, as positive as possible, and spoke with one voice. That voice sounded like it had two different and recognizable tones within it—one signaling concern for his future happiness and the other that Lloyd had to realize that stay-at-home deadbeating was not a route to that happiness. They managed to blend the voices well enough.

Lloyd remained silent for a while, pounded himself with enough of the four-alarm lamb *bhuna* to make the sweat start running down his forehead, until Ma insisted he stop that.

He did, and then he responded.

"I just want the summer," he said with watery curry eyes and a surprisingly earnest tone to his voice. He even made a point of glancing from Ma, to Dad, back to Ma again, and then for emphasis back to Dad, looking him respectfully right in the eyes for a change. "I have some ideas but they aren't worked out enough for me to talk about them yet. If you guys just give me space, let me do my thing, I promise I'll have a plan once the summer's over."

I don't think anybody was expecting something like that. Something more combative would have been truer to form. My parents were wrong-footed enough that they didn't say anything at all until they finally said okay.

So Lloyd went back to the tandoori.

As far as I could tell, for the first month those plans involved getting high and at last working on his motorcycle in the garage. You could hear him clanging away in there, and you could smell him, at all hours. Well, all except the morning hours when regular people were up and about.

* * *

Every week I was bigger. My clothes told me that. Which made me want bigger still.

A one-hour gym workout in the morning, hard and fast and sweaty, followed by a protein shake. Home for lunch. Nap. Running. Back to the gym for an hour in the afternoon. Hard, fast, sweaty. Protein shake.

* * *

By July I was *hard*. I was a hard individual, which I never was before.

Sandy took off for a month with her family on Nantucket, starting the second week in July.

I was reduced to one daily workout and zero Sandies.

Five days in I was so bored and achingly lonely, I started thinking that swimming to Nantucket was not only possible and sane but a pretty darned good workout within the bounds of our agreement.

I did not, ultimately, attempt the swim.

My one-a-day workouts got a little longer, though. Then a little longer. Goals.

Nobody had ever yearned for sophomore year to arrive like I did, I was certain of that.

# LIGHTER AIR

Sandy was due to get back two weeks before the start of school, followed by Dinos the week after that. That was when I was expecting to emerge from my training bubble, and my life would settle back into something like a more normal routine.

A little before that, however, it settled into something very different.

I got up one morning and just like every morning, my feet landed on the carpet and I started my stretching. I reached for my toes to wake up the hamstrings. Then I pressed my hands to the wall in front of me and my heels to the floor behind me to work out the calf tightness. I latched on to the chin-up bar mounted in the doorframe to my room and pulled a quick twenty, then hit the floor for an eye-opening thirty push-ups. And by the time I got to my feet again, I was double-espresso awake without needing to subject my body to any caffeine at all.

Then I reached for my thirty-five-pound medicine ball with the handles, to do my torque exercise that leaves me feeling like my core muscles could repel bullets. *That* is the way to leave the house in the morning.

The medicine ball was MIA.

"Where is my medicine ball?" I said. The shock of its absence had me speaking out loud to the spot on the floor in the two-foot space between my dresser and my closet where my medicine ball was *supposed to be*. It was always there. Unless one of my parents decided they just had to take my medicine ball with them to work, I could not think of any conceivable explanation. Because Lloyd sure wouldn't have any use for it.

"Lloyd," I said, banging on his door aggressively enough to prepare him for how seriously I would take it if he had in fact screwed around with my medicine ball.

When he, unsurprisingly, didn't answer, I barged in.

No Lloyd. I knew he was there last night, because I heard his music. But the idea of him getting up before me this summer made even less sense than the medicine ball disappearing. I headed outside and as I moved down the driveway, I could faintly hear the clanging from the garage but did not smell the smell.

"What are you doing, Lloyd?" I said, walking through the side entrance, the *only* entrance since the main garage door corroded shut years ago.

He dropped the dumbbells to the concrete floor.

"Who would understand better than you what I'm doing?" he said. "I'm working out."

He certainly was, and he had the sweat-drenched T-shirt to prove it. His hair was matted to his head. The motorcycle was in the far corner, dismantled into so many pieces that the original factory would have trouble getting it all back together. In the center of the garage, Lloyd had unrolled a tattered old Oriental rug that was in our living room when I was in kindergarten. Arranged around the rug were the components of a pretty sad version of a home gym. There were the rusted iron weights that I forgot we ever had, the weight bench that was in the basement, which Ma used to hang shirts and blouses on for drying. And my medicine ball.

"Is that my medicine ball?" I asked.

"Sorry," he answered, picking it up by one of its handles and walking it over to me. "You were asleep, so I thought borrowing it quietly would be better than waking you up."

I took the ball from him and watched him walk back all businesslike to the dumbbells and resume his curls.

"Why are you out here?" I asked as he curled. "You know I'm doing this stuff every day at the gym. Didn't it occur to you to just tell me and maybe we could go together?"

"You didn't want me," he said, pumping harder and looking at the floor. "Anyway, this is fine. Works out great for me."

I held the medicine ball by both handles, in front of me like I was about to begin my torque routine. As I walked up to where he was, my abdominal muscles started twitching. "What are you shaping up for all of a sudden, Lloyd?"

He let his arms drop and his head rise, and he looked grateful for the excuse to stop. The sweat was beading up on him, he breathed audibly, and his eyes were clearer and more focused than I had seen them in a long time.

"I'm joining the army," he said, flashing a wide smile that had likewise been a stranger to me lately.

If he told me he was forming his *own* army, I'd have been less surprised.

"The army?"

"Yup."

"The United States Army?"

"Yup." He sounded completely sincere.

"Wow," I said. "This is kind of amazing. I never considered you'd do anything like this. I mean, you'll make a great weapon, that's for sure."

"Kinda what I was thinking. I figure, I was trained all those years to be the most devastating free safety imaginable, and then they took that away from me. So I was thinking about how I could build on what I was already building on with football."

"The military, of course."

"Exactly. Take everything I learned from the game—field position and possession, following orders, defending my zone, being lethal—and add a gun to that?"

"It's a wonder the army didn't think of it first and send a car for you."

"This is no joke, Arlo," he said in his familiar not-joking tone.

I lowered the medicine ball to the floor by my feet and offered him my right hand to shake.

"I know it isn't, brother, I can see it all over you and I'm impressed. You didn't opt for any easy path."

He shook my hand proudly, with a tight grip that was not

show-offy but just strong. The idea alone seemed to have done something for him already. I was relieved that he was getting himself together—and yes that he was getting himself out of *here*. But my admiration for the guts this took was genuine, too.

"No," he said. "I wanted it to be tough."

"Ma's not going to like your chosen path," I said, releasing our handshake and wagging a finger at him.

He leaned forward and poked me in the chest, "She'll like it better than *your* path," he said, then looked at his finger as if he'd hurt it on my pecs.

"Still . . . ," I said.

"Ah, she'll like it fine eventually. When she sees what it does for me. Anyway, Dad's gonna like it enough for everybody."

"Ha." We both laughed and pointed at each other. He was right about that one.

"So you know what all's involved in the enlistment process, yeah?" I said.

"Oh, yeah."

"They are going to test you, right? Like, a written exam, and fitness tests . . ." I couldn't step around this. "And a medical? Including drug and alcohol testing?"

The last thing I expected here was a smile, but smiling seemed to be a hobby of his all of a sudden. "Two and a half weeks, my man," he crowed. "Not a drink, not a toke, not a nothing."

I looked at him sideways to see if he was pulling my leg, and could instantly tell that was not the case. The pride was radiating off him like he had swallowed a bar of uranium with his breakfast.

It had been months since I saw him cleaned up for even a couple of days in a row, and a lot longer since he displayed anything like pride—or had any reason to, frankly.

For almost a year, since Lloyd left the team, we'd been in such a weird place. I felt more like I was the big brother and he was the junior member of the firm. But when he saw this project through, when he was a real soldier and all that, then it would go back the right way. Or at least, he'd be gone. That was something to look forward to, even if I was a jerk to think like that.

I didn't like this feeling at all, so after a moment I said, "Seriously, man, let's do this stuff together."

He considered, nodded.

After that the Brothers Brodie were hardly ever apart. Upper body weight machine group, lower body group, free weights, middle distance track running. Lunch, protein shakes, nap. Back up, running—easy pace—to the afternoon sessions at the school.

"Don't you think it's getting time to tell them?" I said a week into training as he jolted me with one after another heavy hook to the bag.

It was my idea to hold off a little bit on letting our parents know his army plan. I thought it would be good if they could see how he was changing already, working, getting his body fit and his head on straight.

It also couldn't hurt for them to notice the two of us spending all this time together after so long.

"Probably is," he said. Bang. Bang-bang. "She'll be all excited one day when she gets to go to the White House to meet the president when I get my Medal of Honor."

"Yeah," I said. "It'll be sweet but not such a big deal, since they'll already know each other from when I won the Super Bowl."

"Ha! We'll see who gets there first."

"My turn," I said, and we switched.

Bang-bang. Bang-bang-bang-bang-bang.

Boy, did I love tattooing the heavy bag. I had almost forgotten what a rush it gave me, especially now that I got the extra juice from seeing my big brother getting rocked as he tried to hang in against the weight of my big punches. That never happened when we used to do this.

"Kind of like old times," he said as I slammed him one way and then back the other.

"Yeah," I said, "except that you're not kicking my ass three times an hour."

"Do you miss it?" he said. "'Cause I have a lot to do, but I could schedule a session just for you if you like."

It was that moment I really loaded up, the bomb, the heavy straight right hand that was going to loosen his molars, and as I reared back, I spied him there on the other side. He knew, too. He was bracing, clutching hard and leaning into the coming shot.

And grinning madly.

Yeah. Yeah, this was a lot of fun.

"Hey, why are we walking, anyway? We should run," Lloyd said when we finished the workout. We were tired and sweaty—it was about a hundred degrees out—but it was an invitation that could not be refused.

So I started running.

He started running.

I got a good jump, then he shocked me by pulling even. I brought it up a gear, and when his breathing and footsteps did not fade into the distance behind me, I realized I had a race on my hands.

The sun was already blistering. I was mopping my face every ten strides, and I knew I was running too fast a pace, but with my brother challenging me there was no way I could let up even if I wanted to. I pushed harder still when I heard him actually draw closer, and there was no way, no way I could let this happen even though there was obviously no way, no way he could let this happen.

After around seven minutes of running flat-out, I reached the front of the school. I was so intent on my goal—and huffing like a steam train—that I had no idea at what point I lost contact with the sound of my brother. But I was seriously happy when I reached the broad granite front steps and I could sit down and pretend to be cool and unfussed when he eventually arrived. I draped my head in my towel, already soaked with my sweat. I was looking forward to being able to greet him hobbling down Baker Street, checking my watch and shaking my head sadly.

I stayed like that, dodging the crazy hot August sun and catching my breath for a few minutes. He was still not approaching.

I got up and walked Baker Street, to Centre, turned left toward home, past the shops, and Tony's Pizza, into the small green park ringed with benches.

He was facedown in the grass, mostly underneath a bench. I walked over, climbed onto the bench, and peered over the backrest down to where I could see his left cheek, and his left eye sort of rolled to see me.

"Seems to be some vomit there," I said coolly.

"Where?" he said. Nothing moved, not even his lips.

"Right there," I said, pointing to be helpful. "Just about that spot where your mouth ends and the park lawn begins."

His eye rolled away from me and toward where I was pointing. Then it came back.

"I don't think that was me," he said. "Pretty sure that was already here when I pulled in."

I was laughing as I hopped over the back of the bench, and him. I helped him sit up, then mopped some of the barf off his chin with my towel.

"I can do that," he said, testy, snatching the towel from me.

I wasn't entirely sure that he could. He still looked wobbly as he sat there, dabbing at his face as if he was just guessing where stuff might be. But in a few minutes he looked like he was pulling it together. I gave him my hand, and pulled him to his feet.

"All right?" I said.

"Yeah."

We walked between two benches, back to the Centre Street

pavement, where we took a left, toward home again. "We can try this again tomorrow," I said. "Or possibly even later today if you're feeling better."

"Yeah, right," he said.

I took pity on him. "We shouldn't have been sprinting that distance, in that sun."

"Hey, you're the one who set the pace. You throw down, boy, I'm throwing in."

"And up," I said, making a quick dash out of his reach. "Pace yourself now, Lloyd. You're not a kid anymore."

He walked right up like he was going to push me. He grabbed two tight fistfuls of my sweaty T-shirt. I was a couple of inches taller than him, and much bigger, harder now, and he looked small, a little desperate, a little worried as he said, "I gotta do this, and do it right. Y'know?"

I knew. I nodded. We turned around and headed back to the gym.

It was remarkable to think that Lloyd and I were plotting together like this, but that was exactly what we were doing. And it was worth the scheming because it was plain to me what good this was doing Lloyd, would do for him, would do for our family.

But it was just as plain that this would be another blow for Ma, every possible danger of military life suddenly flooding her already overloaded head with misery for however long. We could lessen that blow. We could at least try.

"Remember, don't make a big deal of the physical side of it, right?" I said as I lay on the weight bench lining up one last set of presses. He was spotting for me, looking down from straight above. We had really turned up the intensity, and I was feeling it, ready to be finishing with the weights. "Talk about the trade and training opportunities that could lead to a nice career down the line, the structure and discipline and worldly experience . . ."

"I'm not a dope, Arlo. I know what she doesn't want to hear."

"Okay," I said, and lifted the weight off the rack. I held it for three seconds, breathing, breathing, then lowered the weight to my chest. "Grrr," I said, bouncing the bar off my chest and then blowing out, blowing the weight back up. A one-second pause, breathing in as the weight came down, then blowing, bellowing the weight back up again.

I could see my arms shaking with the strain as I pressed that bar up again, then again, up to six reps, seven, then I was tiring quickly, slowing.

Just made the ninth rep, when Lloyd yelled, "All right, boy! Done it!" clearly expecting me to do the smart thing and hang the bar on the rack.

But I had ten reps as a goal in my head.

"Whoa!" he said as I brought the bar down again, and then, "Come on, come on, push it, push it, lift!" as I very, very slowly pressed the weight upward, blowing, shaking, stalling. The bar simply stopped going anywhere as I put every ounce of everything into moving it upward and it put exactly the same amount into pushing downward.

My brother barked and roared me on to do it, until the instant when the weight began descending on me, when he reached out and grabbed the middle of the bar with both hands, and together we guided the heavy beast back into its cradle.

I stayed motionless and relieved, on that bench.

"Time to punch out," I said.

"Since you mention it," he said, "can you just hold the bag for me once more? Then we can quit."

"Grrr," I said, and hauled myself up for a bit more.

He looked a little edgy, a little twitchy. Only when he was in the middle of punching or lifting did he look at all settled. It was Saturday, the afternoon of the night of our return to the Indian restaurant for Lloyd Conference II, so maybe he was getting a kind of stage fright as it approached.

He started hitting the bag with more intensity than I thought I had in me at this stage. But as I hung on, absorbed his impressively stiff shots, he looked all right. Then, about two and a half minutes in, he tired visibly, as any fighter would at that time, at that pace. He slowed, punched lighter, then lighter, then spoke through his panting.

"I'm thinking I might go out for a while," he said in an odd, tentative voice.

"What?" I said.

"Just for an hour maybe. Go hang out with some friends, relax. Worked hard all week, right? Just for a chill. Be back in time for the big dinner. Or meet you guys there. That would probably be even—"

"What?" I said again, this time straightening up to make it plain that I wasn't holding anymore.

"Don't get so worked up. I think I could have one beer at this point. Don't you think that would be all right? I earned that, I think. Don't you think?"

"Hold the bag," I barked, seizing that big brother role I wanted no part of.

As he clung to the other side of the bag, I hammered it, peppering punches with new energy.

"And maybe a quick smoke, too, Lloyd?" Bang. Bang-bang.

"What could it hurt?" he said.

This was a good question to answer nonverbally.

Bang-*bang!* Left-right. Bang-*bang!* Left-right.

"It's been a long time," he said after a pause. "I've been really good. Clean all this time, sober, and good. I should be able to, just to relax a little."

"After all this?" I said. Bang. "After doing everything right?" Bang. "And after working so hard *for* something worthwhile for a change?"

Bang-bang-*bang!*

My right wrist hurt with the jolt of that last big punch, but I continued anyway, popping away at the bag with both hands while waiting for my holder on the other side to say something back to me.

It took about a dozen more punches for me to conclude that he was not talking anymore, so as I threw one more sweeping left, I peeked around at him from the right.

He was clinging to the bag just to stay up. I lunged forward and grabbed hold of him, bumping the bag aside to catch him under the arms. I balanced him there and looked closely at him. "Are you okay? Man, I'm sorry. I didn't mean to do anything like . . . Look at me, will you?"

He was standing, holding himself up maybe three-quarters of the way by himself with me making up the difference. Then he looked up and I saw his eyes unfocused and kind of twitchy, darting side to side.

"Hey," I said, locking onto his eyes. "What's wrong? You all right? You with me, Lloyd? Talk, man," I sounded dumb, useless and childish.

He blinked, and blinked, and blinked, and his eyes pulled into focus within several more seconds. "It's nothing, man," he said, putting his hands up on my shoulders. He held them there briefly, shook his head a little, then nodded at me. "Thanks, kid," he said, slapping my shoulders. "That was my own fault. I shouldn't have been leaning in so hard with the side of my head up against that part of the bag. I know better. Just got my bell rung a little bit, is all. I'm good."

I stood there, looking at his eyes, listening to his voice, holding firmly under his arms.

"I said, I'm good, Arlo. Let go now."

"You sure you're all right?" I said, though I did let him go.

"Come on," he said, "we're outta here."

I walked slightly behind as we headed up Baker Street, so I could check out his movements. His balance did not look outstanding, but as the cobwebs cleared he'd get it back fine, I figured. I caught up to him just after the Centre Street turn.

"You were right, though," he said without seeming to notice

how close up beside him I was walking, almost touching. "I don't need any of that. That was just stupid talk. I *shouldn't* need it, is the main thing. Not after all this."

"Not after all this," I said, hanging right there on his shoulder.

* * *

After I finished showering and started getting dressed for dinner, I began to come down out of the lighter air that I always felt I was breathing during intense exercise. That air made it possible for me to get outside of anything else that was going on in my life and just be pure physical drive.

I found myself wedged between tonight's complicated family navigation and tomorrow's more straightforward delights, when Sandy was coming back. Even though she was certain to growl and scowl at me for being a fanatic, I couldn't wait. I'd have to explain that I hadn't been able to taper off because I'd been helping Lloyd, and the truth was I was aching to show off for her. To get her to feel this muscle and now feel this one, and go ahead, punch me here as hard as you can. As silly as it all sounded, I was dying to pick her up and hold her in the air until she shouted at me to put her down. Which I would do immediately.

That was what all the work was for, at the end of the day. Knocking guys down, and picking Sandy up.

I looked at Lloyd as we pulled into the restaurant parking lot. He looked back at me, his eyes clear, his demeanor just serious enough. I slapped his knee as Dad put the car in park, and the two of us rolled out our respective doors like a couple of commandos.

Twenty minutes later, after we had each spoken more words to the waitress than we had to each other, our orders were in and Dad thought it was time.

"Well?" he said, folding his hands and resting them on the edge of the table. Ma leaned a little bit forward and a little bit sideways to bump up against Dad. They both looked like they were bracing for their first skydive.

"I'm joining the army," Lloyd said.

So, then. The big *it* was right there fat in the middle of the table between us.

A beat, then Dad reached across the table and shook my brother's hand.

Lloyd took it eagerly, and I could just about feel the looks of all the other diners as he let out a *psssht* of a release of steam pressure.

"I think that is a sound and brave decision, son," Dad said. "I think it shows maturity, and serious thought. And for what it's worth, I believe you are going to make a fine soldier."

"Thanks," Lloyd said in a breathy whisper that spoke for the table generally. So far, the program was going even better than we could have hoped. "That means a lot, Dad."

Dad withdrew, leaving a clear line of vision between his wife and their number one son.

It was obvious this exchange would not be nearly so untroubled.

She looked like she had been mugged. Her body sagged forward and her eyes doubled in size and soupiness as she looked pleadingly, and angrily, at Lloyd.

"Traumatic brain injury is worse, *worse* in the military," she said. Her face had that fractured, confused expression people always seem to have at one of those senseless tragedies when they show them on the news. "Have all my words meant that little . . . ?"

The waitress came then and politely cut the discussion right off. All the lovely foods and drinks and condiments were distributed while my mother held her stare on my brother. Then it was just us again.

"It's all in The File," she said, sounding exhausted and defeated enough already that this could have been the end of the debate rather than the beginning.

Lloyd had somewhere found the ability to help himself with silence for once. He nodded, understanding, but held his tongue. He began scooping and sharing the various rices and curries and papadams and chutneys in a gentle family way.

"Look at him, Emma," Dad said, gesturing at the undeniably fit and unclouded version of the boy. He didn't have to elaborate, because he knew she knew she'd already given in. Lloyd didn't just have a physique—he had a goal, he had an idea. And he didn't have those the last time we sat here. "Look at where he's gotten himself, where he's seeing himself. There has to be good in that."

We all looked at her, and finally she gave a slow, reasonable nod.

I wondered if all four of us were thinking the same thing at that exact moment: what other options are there?

I bet we were.

"What would you say to an amaretto sour?" Dad asked, his lips brushing her forehead.

"I'd say take me, amaretto sour, I'm yours."

Dad gestured for the waiter, ordered Ma's drink and a solidarity manhattan, and the two of them turned Lloyd's way. They were kind of linked and twined like a couple of old folks facing a big storm together.

"So," Dad said, "fill us in on the details. What happens from here?"

Lloyd jumped in eagerly. "Okay, first I have a date to report to—"

"Bup, bup, bup," said Ma, her fingers doing that shushing thing. "Please don't answer until the drinks come."

The drinks appeared, the parents sipped, and Lloyd proceeded.

"I have a date a couple weeks from now, at the MEPS," he said brightly, clearly expecting to be asked.

I volunteered. "Okay, what's MEPS, Lloyd?"

"Military, ah, Enlistment . . . dammit," he said, making both Dad and me laugh as he reached into his shirt pocket for his crib sheet. "Military Entrance Processing Station," he read irritably. "I worked on this, too. Memorized this stuff, so you could see I knew what I was talking about."

"Just relax," Ma said. I sorely wished we could get Lloyd at least a small amaretto sour, just this once, just for this.

"So I report to MEPS in the morning. Then all the evaluation stuff starts. First stage is the ASVAB. . . ."

Oh boy. We all waited as if nothing weird was going on in the empty seconds as Lloyd turned red with the effort and embarrassment of trying to recall this one, too.

"The military is so swamped with acronyms, Lloyd, nobody would expect you to be committing them all to memory this soon."

I thought that was decent and well played on Dad's part.

Lloyd glared at him, then growled before reading off his sheet again. "Armed Services Vocational Aptitude Battery. Then is the APFT, which stands for Army Physical Fitness Test," he went on without even bothering to look up from his sheet, which he then crumpled right up and spiked on the floor at his feet. "Now I'm really pissed off because I know I would have remembered *that* one without reading it."

It would have been ideal to record this moment so that some-day we could replay it and share a big laugh over the whole thing. What would not be ideal would be to take any note right now of how not funny it was.

"So the vocational thing," I said, "what's the deal there?"

That direct question lit him up like a Christmas tree. "It's multiple choice, takes like three hours—which is kind of scary right off the bat. Two hundred questions. I don't know when the last time I took one of those things was. But I'll be fine. They say that no one fails. Then the medical exam and the fitness test, sit-ups and push-ups and a distance run, which thanks to my trainer here I will be able to pass in my sleep. Then they evaluate the whole thing and decide what they're gonna do with me."

"Sounds like a lot to fit into one day," Ma said cautiously.

"Could go into a second day. I'm supposed to pack a bag in case they have to put me up."

She did the slow, reasonable nodding again. "Sounds so . . . real," she said.

"'Cause it is, Ma. It's really real." His odd, funny, really real smile would be enough all by itself to pretty much carry the day with her.

So the dinner finished quietly, warmly. When we left, Dad patted Lloyd's shoulder from behind and Ma slipped an arm around his waist. My father got sort of caught up in the moment and put an awkward arm across not quite my shoulders, holding it really across my shoulder blades. I think we both realized in that instant how much bigger I was than him, because he was shooting a look up at his hand planted on my back just as I looked down at him.

So I swung my arm around and draped it heavily over his shoulders. It was a nice feeling all around. But not as nice as the feeling that was rapidly sweeping it away: sixteen hours.

Sixteen to Sandrine.

# HOW HIGH SANDY

*Plinnngg.*

That was definitely it. That was the text message alert. I raised my head from the pillow, adjusting to sudden consciousness. I had given myself the morning to sleep in, and the sleep I was sleeping was deep and happy, with fuzzy unspecific dreams of sweetness coming my way.

In a little while I was going to specify them.

Gym bag. That's where I left the phone. I stretched as far as I could reach without falling off the bed, and just snagged the canvas handle of the bag with my middle finger. I dragged it across the floor, unzipped it, and rooted around inside. The ghosts of many sweaty summer days rose, and I realized I needed to put the bag and all its contents into the washing machine without delay.

I shoved the toxic bag a safe distance away, fell back onto my bed, and flipped open the phone. A little stomach jump at the sight of Sandy's name.

*Did you get my text?*

No. Jeez, no. Arrrgh. I swept that message aside and got to the one hiding behind it, the one that came two hours earlier.

*Miserable rain so got early ferry. Dying to see you big ape. Nice if you wanna meet me at mine. Be home at . . .*

I looked at my watch.

"Woooohoooo," I howled, jumping up out of bed and dashing around my room to get myself together and out and Sandy-bound.

"What, you got bedbugs or something?" Lloyd said, leaning casually in my doorway. "I was letting you lie in, but I'm starting to get itchy. So, ready to rock and roll, yes?"

I stopped bopping around the place and paid closer attention to him. He was in regular grunt gear like we were going to have another workout day.

"It's Sunday, man," I said. "You've earned your day of rest."

"I don't want one."

"The school doesn't even unlock the facilities on Sundays. Relax, Lloyd."

A look of real discomfort took over his face, and he stopped the casual leaning. He grabbed the chin-up bar above his head and lifted himself up and down, up and down.

"I don't want to relax, Arlo. We don't need the school. We'll pull something together, and it'll do us fine for today. We'll do urban adventuring kinds of things. Like we're kids again."

I gestured toward the window. "It's Sunday, *and* it's raining."

"That's no reason to give up your discipline," he said, letting go of the bar and standing rigidly with his hands on his hips.

I grabbed my phone off the bed, and gestured with it as if this would get him to see reason. "Sandy's home, man. She sent me a message. She's back early. She told me to meet her there, and so . . ." I started digging through a couple of drawers for the charcoal T-shirt I knew was going to be just right for this. Got it.

"So what?" he said. "So you can go over there after. She can wait."

"No," I said, going on about my business.

I pulled on my nicer sneakers, retrieved my black almost-waterproof windbreaker from my closet, and spun for the door.

His face looked pained as it hung there right in front of mine. Looked like he was trying to pull out his old snarly, intimidating self, but something a lot less sure was failing to get out of the way.

"I *need* to do our workout," he insisted. "We need to do our workout."

He was practically pleading. It was a moment to savor, except that it was kind of sad, and I didn't have time anyway. "Excuse me, Lloyd, I have to run. I think you should chill out for today, but if not, have a good session yourself, and I'll catch up with you later."

He gave way slowly and stiffly, like a rusted gate, as I passed him by.

"So," he snapped at my back, "Sandy says jump, and you say *how high*?"

"Phwaa," I called, continuing happily toward the front door. "That's supposed to bother me? Yes, I say how high, Sandy. I say how high, and how far, and what would you like me to wear."

And as I slammed the door behind me, I broke into such long

strong strides I looked like I could have, in fact, been training for the triple jump.

By the time I got there, her family had all already been working together to be getting all their Nantucket gear out of the car and into the house. To transfer operations out of the fun summer and into the serious business of fall. They were like carpenter ants, carrying their lives nugget by nugget from one place to another through the light misty rain without ever breaking the rhythm.

So I just stepped into the rhythm.

"Hello, Arlo," her Dad said, handing me a box that was labeled *Condiments*.

"Hello, sir," I said, pivoting with the box toward the house.

"That's for the kitchen," he called after me. Good thing, too, because I was about to head for Sandy's bedroom with the condiments.

"Ahhhh, you!" Sandy shouted as I walked into the kitchen with the surprisingly heavy condiment box in my hands. I had to raise and defend the condiments as Sandy slammed into my rib cage and squeezed me fantastically, her claws sinking into both of my kidneys. Actually, I just wanted to drop the box.

"I'll take that," said Sandy's mom as she relieved me of the box and freed my hands for more pressing matters.

It was a really nice, vacuum-packed hug as the two of us melded together just the way you should after four hot summer weeks apart.

Then she pushed me away but held on, too. She held me at arm's length while maintaining a death grip on my biceps. She looked me all over while squeezing the merchandise at the same time. "What have you been up to, boy? You look—and feel—like you've been built out of molded plastic."

I tried to wriggle politely out of her grip. "I've been working to make the varsity squad, Sandy, you know that. That's what this is all about, and in two weeks time we'll see if I met my goal. Then it'll all be worth it."

Sandy's older sister, Catrine, the one with her own kids, came in with another box. Sandy grabbed it out of her hands.

"Catrine, here," Sandy said, "feel this," and she placed Catrine's hands here and here and there on my physique, just for scientific purposes. "Now, do you think this stud I left at home all summer has done enough to make the varsity?"

Catrine held a firm, polite grip on me for a few seconds, then smiled delightfully right in my face. "You've made the varsity, sweetheart," she said.

Her mom was just making her way toward us when Sandy seized my arm with more strength than I thought she had, and announced to the world, "We're gonna be in my room." She yanked me to the stairs and then we were tumbling up, and as I said "We are?" she said "Yes, we certainly are."

"I thought this wasn't allowed," I said as she shut the door behind her and wrapped me in another Greco-Roman hug.

"It wasn't," she said. "But I got bored near the end of the trip and decided to give them a good talking-to. Now it is."

"Good decision," I said.

"I also decided I like you very, very much. More than I thought I did before I went away."

She had the right side of her head planted flat on my chest, so pretending that my heart rate didn't just triple would have been pointless.

But also, I thought I sensed something kind of complicated buried somewhere inside that wonderful statement.

"You're not saying anything," she noted.

"I'm not? Oh, sorry. I'm a jock, so, you know how we are—men of few words and all that."

"Nonsense."

"Yeah, that was nonsense. I like you, probably twelve or thirteen times as much as you like me."

"Hmmm," she said, pondering. "Twelve or thirteen? If we factor body weight into the equation, I guess that sounds about right."

She grabbed her laptop off the dressing table, ran, and launched herself into a flying sit, up by the pillows of the bed. She opened the laptop and patted the spot next to her for me to sit, too.

"Umm, Sandy, I would think that after all this time apart, you'd be a little more interested in interacting with the actual physical me rather than—"

"Here he is," she said to somebody, right over my protest. Then she quickly turned the computer screen toward me. There, a girl with a lava mountain of black hair was waving. I waved back. Then the computer and the girl were gone again.

"Didn't I tell you?" Sandy said.

"Who is that?" I asked.

"That is Sasha, my island friend and one of my training partners."

"Ah," I said, "I noticed right away you are more buff." She still seemed to be ignoring me. I might as well just have been a screen grab. She waved at the computer again. "Wait, *one* of your training partners? Who else—?"

She turned the screen my way again, and I returned a wave, again.

"So *now* do you believe me?" she laughed to her friend, a guy. Who looked like an Olympic rower. Silver medalist. And I only withheld the gold out of spite.

"Right," I said, "I'm going home."

Sandy slapped the laptop shut and fell over sideways with laughter, restraining me.

"Wow, that was easier than I thought it would be," she said, hanging on tight to my arm while I pouted in a manly way.

"Right, fine. I'm a fool," I said, turning and seeing her laughing face, which changed my mood by quite a bit. "Now, who was he?"

"That's just Gordon," she said. "He was kind of a personal trainer to Sasha and me while we were on the island."

Personal trainer. I stood up.

"Oh, stop that, will you?" she said, yanking me back down and holding me securely in place.

"Tell Gordon he did a great job. You're really strong. Your arms are like bridge suspension cables."

"Why don't I feel complimented by that?"

"Because maybe I don't feel like talking anymore about how you got so ripped on Nantucket with Gordon."

"Fair enough," she said. "Instead, let's talk about how *you* got so ripped on only one normal-person workout a day."

Genius, Arlo. Just throw *yourself* under the bus, why don't you.

"What's the most impressive about your program," I said, gripping her biceps and admiring them closely, "is that you got serious muscle density without putting on too much mass." I kissed that muscle, and she kindly allowed it. And then went right back to what she was saying. "Talk. Now."

I gave in. It's not like she would believe me anyway if I told her I'd been working out with some tramp. "Lloyd. It was Lloyd, the tramp I was spending every minute with. He's getting in shape . . . to join the army."

"Oh," she said after a fat pause. "Wow."

"Yeah, that's the standard response. I'm hopeful it's going to be good for him. It has been so far, because he's clean and sober as well as working himself into pretty stellar shape."

"Well, okay, that's promising. Fingers crossed, I guess, huh?"

"Yup. The only problem we seem to have so far is I think now he sees you as a rival."

"What? Jesus, no, Arlo."

She was leaning way into me now, and I had my arm around her. Made me want to scare her more often.

"He didn't want me to come here today. Resents you competing for my time and attention."

"Great, that's great," she said. "The last thing I need is to become part of the world's freakiest love triangle. If he starts following us around and stuff, I will go crazy. When does he leave?"

"Two weeks. And I'll keep a close eye on him till then."

"Yeah, you do that. And get him a hamster or something to keep him company. You also have my blessing to spend all the time you like with him, working out. Because I'm certainly going to increase my weight training and boxercise during that time."

I knew this was going to be a great day, but it was exceeding all expectations.

We nestled down lower into the comfy safety of the bed, protecting each other from all those dangers out there, like Lloyd.

# DINOS DESCENDS

So the Brothers Brodie went back into the gym. I'd see Sandy in the evenings, although Lloyd continued to be territorial about it.

We just trained our brains out, and the universe was pleased.

"So you're feeling good about where you're at?" I said as we geared down on our run and started walking down Baker Street to the school. It was the last Monday of the summer. Five days before preseason football workouts and tryouts began, seven days before classes began, eight days before my brother's MEPS date.

He nodded, but I could see I had made him tense just by asking the question.

"You have nothing to worry about, Lloyd," I said, shoving him sideways because when a guy shoves you sideways everything's probably fine. He stumbled, maybe a little more than an aspiring soldier should. Still, probably fine. "You're smart, and your fitness level at this point would probably get you into the space program."

He smiled a little bit at that, but it was work. "I don't test well," he muttered just before we reached the school steps.

"Hey, fatass!" I said, genuinely excited to see Dinos standing there, deep Greek tan coating his face, arms, and legs, and Greek cooking adding inches to his middle.

"I am aware of my obesity," he said, stepping down and bear-hugging me. "It's not my fault that every Greek person I met treated feeding me like it was an Olympic sport. . . . Hey, Lloyd, how are you?" he said, reaching over me and giving my brother a nice warm greeting like I hadn't seen anybody else do in quite some time.

"Hi . . . Dinos, welcome back," Lloyd said, completely failing to make it sound sincere. Jeez, no, Lloyd. I was touched, honestly, at how much he was valuing our summer together, but this was already embarrassing.

Dinos ignored the awkwardness and started in on the curious change in his European bowel movements compared to his North American ones as we walked into the gym. Normal was back.

We started working out every day. The gym was getting busy as people began returning from whatever summer trips they went on. The buzz and energy of the place was great, and I was glad to be working out with Dinos again, even if it made Lloyd silent and suspicious and hostile. The Brodie bonding was gone now, and I had a few moments of regret. But that was that and it was done, and now that life was getting back to normal and noisy it was easier and easier to simply ignore him.

I was happy to have him joining in, fitting in. But the territorial intensity was not something I could handle.

On Friday, when I got ready and headed out to the gym, Lloyd was elsewhere.

My brother would have to be his own keeper.

* * *

The weekend was taken up with the first organized football of the season, and I was crazy anxious and crazy prepared for the two-a-days in the sun.

It was almost easy. Lots of guys were in shape, but nobody had outworked me, I could tell, and nobody ever would in the future. I almost took a sadistic kind of satisfaction watching them drop like potato sacks when hamstring cramps seized them right in the middle of a stride. Others were running hobbled and holding their sides with abdominal cramps. There were enough guys on their hands and knees puking along the sidelines, you could have thought it was just one more scheduled team activity.

It was *great* to be back.

# SOPHOMORE YEAR

# VARSITY

"So everything's going your way, is what I'm hearing," Sandy said. I had gone early to her house so we could walk to school together the first day, and I guess I'd been boasting.

"I didn't think I was putting it that . . . overconfidently."

"Ah, don't worry about that. You've earned the right to crow. This is your time, and it isn't overconfidence if it all comes true. Which of course it will."

"Was I really crowing?"

Sandy took my hand and squeezed it with a little pulsating action while we walked. "I'm glad you still worry about stuff like that anyway. It means you might be savable after you finish being a big-head jock football star."

"Thanks. That was kind of you. Not that there's going to be any finish. Not for a very long time, anyway."

I could feel alterations to the pulse as she pondered that. I waited for the results.

"You mean this year, and junior and senior years," she said.

"Hey, I won't even know if I've made the varsity until tomorrow afternoon. Let's not get ahead of this already."

There was no real chance that was going to slow her forward progress on this.

"So you're talking college, then? You're planning to play college football?"

Might as well just go for it. "Yes. And only big-time Division One programs will be considered. If I intend to play pro ball, nothing else will do me any good."

"If you . . . Well, I have to admit, Arlo, you aren't bashful about it at this point."

"Oh, but I am. I'm loaded with bash," I said, trying to inject some humor into what was rapidly becoming a dangerous situation. She looked straight ahead, focused and serious like she was working out a math problem at the blackboard. "You should have seen the last two days of workouts. More bash than the next two guys put together."

"Yeah, that's very cute," she said as we passed along the old familiar low wall and turned to mount the school steps. "Your ambition is a little scary. But at least it's out in the open where I can see it."

We walked straight through the doors, where she turned left down the corridor to her homeroom.

"Oh, you'll see it all right. You'll see it up close and every step of the way, Miss Sandrine, 'cause you'll be there for the whole ride."

"Maybe," she said, waving me away toward my own homeroom with two hands.

*Maybe?*

"Hey, man . . . hey . . . hey . . . hey, Brodie." I heard it all the way down the hall, *already* more than I heard any such greetings my entire freshman year.

Yes indeed, a whole new ball game now.

* * *

By the time the rosters for freshman, junior varsity, and varsity were posted beside the locker room entrance, there was no real suspense.

Still, when I crowded in with scores of other sweaty, desperate football hopefuls to check if my name was where I needed it to be, I was shaking with nerves.

But there it was: *Arlo Brodie/Sophomore/Linebacker/Varsity.*

Even after I had all that I needed to know, I lingered there in the crowd of jostling bodies, guys pressing in, guys pushing to get out. Right in front of me, I saw the back of a head drop forward at the precise moment a guy I recognized from practice got the bad news. I had no doubt he was feeling the opposite of what I was feeling. From what I had seen of him on the field, he was a decent enough character, and it wasn't his fault that he sucked. But I would have hated to be on the same team with him.

"Aaahhhh," Dinos spazzed in my ear as he piled on my back. He was celebrating, I could only guess, making the varsity after a very slow and worrying start.

Dinos used his size and strength to clear a path that led us both out of the area and then out of the school altogether.

"Feels pretty great, huh?" I said as we walked up to the corner of Centre, where he would turn right while I cut left.

"It does," he said, "but it would feel better if Coach didn't warn me that I'd better deblub myself in a hurry if I expect to see any playing time."

"Ha. He didn't say exactly that, though."

"Deblub. That is an exact quote, my friend."

"Harsh."

"We'd better get used to it. Much harshness lies ahead for us in Varsityworld."

"What *us*? I'm not fat. My life's going to be golden."

We were stopped at our corner parting spot. "You know, I think that's exactly what your life is going to be, Arlo. It looks bright ahead for you. Asshole." He gave me a fist bump and said he had to run. "I promised Jenna if I made the cut I'd go over to her place and let her swoon and coo and whimper and tremble in the presence of my awesomeness."

"And you're expecting her to do that, with the noises and all, yeah?"

"No," he said, crossing the street and waving over his head, "she's gonna make ape noises at me like usual. But at least now I'm a varsity ape."

As soon as I was walking again, I found myself alone with my thoughts. The very first one was: with that one stroke, my name on that sheet, I had already surpassed everything Lloyd had ever achieved.

I didn't care to be alone with thoughts like that.

He better get into the army.

I pulled out my phone and called Sandy.

"Let me guess," she said without a hello in front of it. "Because you are so incredible, they jumped you from the Junior Varsity, right over the Varsity, to the Extreme Varsity. And because you are so special and on a different plane from everybody else, you are the only one and have to spend the year running around an empty field looking for somebody to bash into."

"I just shouldn't have told you exactly when the cuts would be announced," I said. "Then you wouldn't have had the whole afternoon to spend making that up."

"You thought that took the whole afternoon? Now, that is not a compliment. It didn't take more than an hour, I swear. Congratulations, Arlo," she said in a tone that was altogether changed in an instant. It was warm and sincere and happy for me without even a hint of wise guy.

"Thanks, Sandy. I know I was talking big and all, but I have to admit I was nervous when I went to find out."

"Ah, well, that makes it feel even more satisfying, right?"

"Right enough," I said.

"So then why do you sound so flat?"

I sighed. I was glad she asked, and in truth I probably called for this more than to tell her about the football. "Lloyd," I said.

"Right. It's today."

"He was gone first thing this morning, and Ma started being a wreck over him a whole twenty-four hours before that."

"Okay, so now you get to go home and tell your folks your

news. Your father will love it. And your mother at least will be distracted by it."

"Hnn," I said. "I never even thought of that, but you could be right."

I was within a block of the house, and wanted a minute to clear my head before seeing them.

"Thanks, Sandy, I'm going to go now."

"Okay. Get in there and be a big distraction. The team's counting on you."

* * *

You would think that being a clean-cut, fit, and healthy, no drink, no smoke, no drugs, no-nonsense fifteen-year-old guy with a strong work ethic, good manners, good grades, and natural athletic aptitude would satisfy any parent. That in most households I would be pretty much the model for what would be considered successful son building.

You would think.

My father was predictably proud, but I thought my mother was going to cry. I thought she was going to cry this morning and last night, too, so it wasn't all about my announcement, but the announcement didn't help, either.

They were getting ready to go out to a movie because it was two-for-one night at the community theater, and on two-for-one nights they eat dinner early, then do the his and hers washing and drying tag team before sprucing up a little for their date.

I caught them midspruce. I upended their spruce.

"Ma, come on now," I said as I watched her stare into her three-mirrored vanity. All four views made my heart sink a little as her shoulders sagged, her mascara brush suspended in the air before her eye, and she squinted, like with a little stab or two of pain.

"Emma," Dad said, going to her and squeezing her shoulders. "Now, we knew this day was coming for Arlo. And we hope something is coming for Lloyd. They are making their way in the world."

He was trying to sound upbeat, but being my dad, he ended up sounding like a preacher needing to say something positive about a guy drowning. He's swimming with God now. Or, he died doing what he loved, enjoying the ocean.

"I'm fine," Ma said, shrugging him off and going at her lashes again with a shaky hand. "Put on a little bit of cologne, Louis, will you? We have to get going."

He kissed her head and stepped lightly toward the bathroom.

"A *little* bit," she called.

I approached her from behind, and all her eyes stared at me hard from the mirror. "Get away from me, you," she said, "before you spoil my movie altogether."

I ran straight through that blocker and wrapped my arms around her shoulders. She leaned right back into me, reaching a hand up to lightly touch my face. We looked at us there in the vanity.

"How susceptible might you be to a little emotional blackmail over this," she said, allowing herself a small linear smile.

"Probably a whole lot," I said. "But not enough."

"I won't ask you not to play, for me, then."

"Thank you for that. I'll be fine, Ma," I said. I kissed the top of her head and let go. "And so will Lloyd."

See, right there. I did it. Overplayed my hand because we seemed to be doing well.

Her eyes, all of them in all those mirrors, seemed to swell three times their size with welling tears. Then she made a shape with her hands, lacing her fingers together like she was holding a large orange. "Your little heads," she said. "They were this big, and soft, and the smell . . . Lord, I think you both stayed bald an extra six months because I kept inhaling any hair that tried to grow."

This was really hard. I felt indestructible lately, but I wasn't tough enough for this, I knew I wasn't tough enough for this.

"He's going to be fine, Ma. I'm sure of it." Saying it would make it true.

"I want him to go, Arlo. I realize everything involved in this, and your father is completely right this time, it is a positive step in many ways. . . ."

Good. Good, good, good. She's helping her own self up out of this because she realizes I'm going to be useless.

"But now I feel awful, for wanting him to go."

"Ah, Ma," I said as she covered her mouth with her hand. "I feel so guilty," she said in a manner that sounded as much like an accusation as a confession. I want him to go, too, but I won't let myself feel guilty about it.

She stood and faced me. Grabbed my arms.

"You may look like a man, Arlo, but you are still my boy. You're still *a boy* for a while yet."

"I am still your boy, I know that," I said.

"Good." She kissed my cheek and pushed off me like launching a boat from a dock. She collected Dad and they headed out for their date.

But I'm not *a boy* anymore was the thought I did not share.

Fifteen minutes later, with my feet on the coffee table, a reality cop chase on the TV, one egg and tomato sandwich in my hand and another waiting on the plate, my phone went off.

"Hey," I said.

Silence.

"Obviously, I know it's you, Lloyd. Your name comes up on the screen."

Near silence. Breath.

"Did you call to stare at me, Lloyd?"

"I'll be staying over tonight," he said. "Staying for a second day."

"Oh," I said. "Okay, fine. Long day, huh? How's it going?"

This silence was one too many. Not right at all.

"Lloyd?"

"I think I forgot how much I hate multiple choice exams, Arlo."

Oh. Oh no.

"You struggled, I guess."

"Nobody fails this test, man. I mean, nobody. It's famous that way . . . like a joke. I can't be that stupid, can I?"

"You are not stupid."

"I scored below what I was supposed to. By a lot. It was like, I would stare at a question forever. Then the four choices with the little oval you were supposed to fill in for the answer, they'd start getting blurry, swimmy, moving back and forth a little. I had to close my eyes, then I'd open them and a whole ten minutes had gone someplace."

"You're out of practice, is the only problem."

"Yeah, maybe. Maybe. You think?" His voice went quickly up toward hope, then down even quicker. "Well, anyway, they're giving me a retest tomorrow."

"Good, great," I said, despairing over his prospects. "Right back in the saddle. Best thing. You had just a bad day. Tomorrow you'll be sharp as can be."

"I hope so," he said sullenly.

"How'd the rest of the evaluations go? All clear?"

"Well, no," he said. "Something in my medical they weren't too crazy about. There was a thing with my balance, which is just stupid. And response time. And the way my eyes reacted to stuff wasn't as quick as they like to see. I mean, come on, slow eyes? Who has slow eyes? Right there I knew, it was fixed, and the truth was they just didn't like me."

"Come on, Lloyd, everybody likes you."

He just let a fat blob of a silence hover over that.

"Okay," I said. "If you still *maintained* any of your old friendships, you'd be a very popular guy. But still . . ."

"The plan," he said, "is to add a few more advanced tests tomorrow. Then, I guess, we'll see." He was saying the words of a trouper, but he sounded more worried than that. "I slaughtered

134

their fitness drills, though, which is all they should need, goddammit. Don't you think?"

"Well, I think it's great that you're so fit."

"They have me rooming with a total shit heel here, too," he growled loudly, "just to make it worse."

"Lloyd? Can the guy hear you?"

"Yeah, but so what? He's a shit heel. Oh, and the funniest thing of all? Besides fitness, the only other tests all day I know for certain I passed were those drug and alcohol screenings you were worried about. How funny is that?"

That was very, ironically, funny.

"Funny," I said, barking it. "More than funny, though, it's great, and who'd have bet on *that* result not too long ago?"

Find pride someplace, man, for everybody's sake.

"Oh yeah, I'm proud as shit. So proud, I'm gonna celebrate. Reward myself for all my goody-goody self-fucking-control. And I'll tell you what, the bastards fucking better not try screening my blood tomorrow."

"No, Lloyd, no!" I shouted at him, even though I knew he was already gone. Well, I wasn't going to tell him about making varsity just yet anyway.

It went without saying that it was the only phone call he'd be making, and it was left to me to provide our folks with a carefully worded update on Lloyd's progress.

Police chases were way too tense now, so I flipped over to Animal Planet, where schools of fish shifting through coral reefs made a much better backdrop while I finished my food and prepared to sift through some facts.

"Hey, how was the movie?" I said as my parents came through the door. I knew that I was already failing to set the right tone by being too keenly interested.

"It was silly," Ma said. "Have you heard from your brother?"

No warm-ups, then. Straight into the game.

"I did," I said. "He called, sounded kind of exhausted."

"Well, fair enough," Dad said as the two of them came over and hovered above me where I sat. "I imagine that whole process is tough going."

"It is, Dad," I said, happy for the assist. "That's exactly how it sounded. And it's going to spill over into a second day, obviously, which is why he isn't here."

"What does that mean?" Ma asked intently. "Does that mean anything? Being kept for a second day—is that a good thing, or a bad thing? Are many people held over for a second day?"

"Sounds pretty routine to me, Ma. I know there were other guys with him. He has a roommate, and everything."

"Oh," she said, and her shoulders slid down slowly from where they had ratcheted up near her ears. "Well, I like the sound of that, anyway. Better than thinking of him being alone through a night like this."

It was hard now, and definitely going to get harder if I didn't cut and run. I hated to be deceptive with them, though the way my dad was looking at me hinted that I might not have been completely successful there. No way could I give it to them unvarnished, and leaving it like this at least left the distant hope that Lloyd could pull it all together by tomorrow.

"Anyway," I said, standing up and stretching, "there is no third day no matter what. So by this time tomorrow we can all be here getting it from the horse's mouth. Good night."

And a good night to the horse. Bring home a winner. Get it together, brother, please.

* * *

It was hard getting to sleep as I thought about the possibilities, the odds, the fallout of what tomorrow could bring us.

It wasn't hard waking up. Because tomorrow brought it. Early and heavy. In the form of Lloyd himself.

"This cannot be true!" I heard Dad bellow just before the wall of my room nearly caved in on top of me.

The two of them roared and rumbled as I yanked open the door to find Lloyd and my father slugging it out right there in the hallway. Ma came flying out at the same time and screamed, "Arlo, do something! Make them stop!"

The scene was as horrible as anything I had ever seen. They were in a kind of death clutch, choking and sticking short sharp jabs in each other's face as Ma pulled tight fistfuls of hair on both sides of her head. I felt as small and big as it was possible to feel, like a little boy who wanted to run and hide and the big boy who needed to do something.

I heard my involuntary bull bellow as I drove myself blindly into the two of them, smashed them into the far wall, and dumped

137

them right on the floor. I stood over them, steaming as Ma sobbed in front of their bedroom door six feet away.

"You see what you're doing here?" I said when they looked up at me. I pointed to Ma. "I don't care who you are, but if either one of you gets up and does not go to his own corner, I swear I will throw you out a window."

Dad got straight to his feet and, more out of embarrassment than out of any fear of me, took a brisk walk into the bedroom. Ma followed him and the door shut crisply behind her. Muffled but urgent discussion seeped out.

As I stood there looking down at him, Lloyd fixed a cold stare on me. It was then that I realized the conk I had given my own head when we all hit the wall. It throbbed.

"What did you do?" I asked him.

He stuck out a hand for me to help him up. I did.

Once on his feet he leaned forward, too close to me. He reeked of booze.

"Nobody's watching now, big man," he said. "You gonna throw me out the fuckin' window?"

Even I couldn't tell how much of my tone then was disgust and how much was pity. "Ah, Lloyd, man . . . ," I said.

He nodded, grinned, breathed extra poisonously right in my face, then stumbled toward his room.

"Didn't think so, big man," he said, and slammed the door hard.

There wasn't much chance of my going back to sleep after that, so I returned to my room and did some light working out, just to steady myself as much as possible.

He had completely blown it now. If he just showed up, just went through whatever tests they wanted to run him through, no matter what they concluded, it would have to be a better result than this. Now what have we got? Now where could he go?

I realized when I heard my parents start bumping around in the kitchen that my light workout with the push-ups and medicine ball routine had gone beyond light. I was breathing too hard and breaking a sweat. I wiped my face, threw on a robe, and went out to them.

The two of them were sitting down over coffee and bagels. Dad had a couple of welts on his face and Ma's eyes looked hay-feverish, but otherwise they looked like people who could walk into their offices without dragging an ugly home story in with them.

I got myself orange juice from the fridge and a glass from the cabinet.

"You going to throw him out?" I said as my father scowled down into his cup.

"He has nowhere to go," Ma said, staring at him. "He was very upset."

"He was very drunk," Dad said.

"If you hadn't confronted him. If you just could have let it go, just until later when we could have—"

"What, Emma? Could have what, later?"

"He needs to find something. That's all. He was counting on the army, and so this was devastating for him. He needs time. He needs to find *something*."

Dad got up abruptly, left his half-finished breakfast on the table, which never happened.

"Then he'd better find it soon," he said, then collected his jacket from the back of his chair and marched out.

"He'll be fine," Ma said, reaching across and patting my arm before taking her plate to the sink.

"I know he will," I said. We both knew we did not mean Lloyd.

Nobody had the answer to Lloyd. The question alone, however, could tear all of us down if we let it.

I, for one, would not let it. The only thing I knew how to do for sure was to take care of Arlo.

Put your head down, dip that shoulder, and run hard, Arlo.

# YOU HAVE TO EARN IT

## HIT LIST
Pay your rookie dues. Suck it up, shut your mouth, move on.
Never take it again.

* * *

There is a reason why there is a barrier between the varsity and junior varsity teams. If it was just about moving from freshman to sophomore to junior to senior teams, then Lloyd would have eventually made the top team and maybe even gone to college—and who knows where he would be now. No, it's more. It's about development and skill and dedication and ultimately producing the maximum football that results in the awesomeness you see weekly in NFL games. And when you make varsity, you realize it's a lot more.

Almost as soon as I hit the field, more was what I got.

*Bam-shazam!* I got slammed from down low, the guy coming up under my armpit and shoving me up, over sideways, and with a huge *crunch*, driving me right into the turf.

"Yo, Rook," said the guy standing over me, hands on his hips while I stayed flat on my back where he'd put me, a giant of a left guard and offensive cocaptain named Arsenault. He was also a senior, and while the varsity was theoretically all one team, the seniors were very keen for you to know they were seniors. "That *nose for the ball* stuff you did last year is all well and good, but it's only gonna get you so far. In fact, it's not gonna get you very far at all if you just have your eyes on the runner and not his blockers. Vision is gonna matter more than your nose. See what I'm sayin'?"

"I see," I said.

"Excellent. And your nose is bleeding."

As Arsenault walked away I reached up to my nose, saw the blood all over my fingers, and started laughing.

"What, do ya like it down there or somethin', Rook?" said Stopes, the big receiver and big senior. He looked like he was going to do the sportsmanship thing and offer me a hand up. But he stepped right over me. "Get your ass up, for God's sake, Rook. You're embarrassing yourself."

Rook was my name. There were a few other new players, but I seemed to absorb a lot more of the focused rookie treatment than anyone. I was clued in some by a junior named Galvin, who told me on the first day, "Your rep says you're somebody to watch."

"Yeah?" I said, overly pleased to have an unfamiliar upperclassman taking me aside, and even more thrilled to have a rep of any kind.

"Yeah. So prepare to be *watched*."

That last part didn't sound entirely like friendly mentoring.

And since Galvin played inside linebacker like me and I was his backup and potential rival for the job, it probably wasn't.

It was also not inaccurate. I was *watched* mercilessly, daily. Staying on my feet and in one piece the first week was a constant struggle. My nose probably did not stop bleeding for more than twenty minutes at a time, and for certain my head never stopped hurting. I couldn't even take the time to see how Dinos was doing. The second week was when they upped the challenges, having tenderized my meat. I took my beatings at linebacker, but my field vision was getting better. I got my legs knocked from under me with a wicked chop block, but then I didn't. I made one interception that caught me totally by surprise when the quarterback threw a perfect ball, right to me, as if I were the intended receiver. And since there was no actual receiver anywhere near, maybe I was. Although I was brought down as quickly and brutally as a wildebeest by a pack of high school lions that was so big it must have also included several who were supposed to be on my side. Senior lions, naturally.

And then there was that one memorable play, in case I was getting too cocky. Trying some snaps at the lineman, I was just going for it, all out, driving ahead and being physical as the only reliable alternative to absolutely anything. But before I could reach my man, he reached me, I got a slap across the side of my head that was so hard it sounded like a great big church bell, and felt like he had used a pipe. I went down sideways, landed on all fours, and stayed there for several seconds watching that bright nose blood forming a red motivational pool on the ground below me.

I was pretty sure the head slap had been illegal for a long time.

I wasn't going to complain about anything, but when I got to my feet I took a look over to the sideline to see if this was registering at all. Standing there with his arms folded, Coach Fisk was staring right at me, motionless, silent, just watching.

Okay, then.

Bit by bit, smash by smash, I found I could take it. Then, take it just fine. Then, the best part, came the rush. There was a thrill, hidden behind the first several layers of combat, like a video game quest, until you got to what had to be called the true violence, and once I got there I *loved* the true violence.

And I learned.

By the end of the second week, I played as if I invented the linebacker position. My nose for the ball was enhanced greatly by my improved field vision, and even more by my *preparedness* for a whole new level of tough.

The following week I played almost half the plays. I made more than four tackles, then I stopped counting. I got several head slaps, and they weren't the nosebleed kind. Galvin stopped talking to me entirely.

My name was still Rook. But it sounded different now.

# STARLO

"Everyone's calling him *Starlo* now," Dinos said as he and Jenna and Sandy and I left the crap movie halfway through.

"No, everyone is not calling me that."

"Okay, true. Galvin's in a couple of my classes and he mostly calls you Starhole."

"Does he?" I said as the girls laughed out loud.

"Oh yeah. But don't worry, to everyone else, you're Starlo. Or at least you will be by the time I get finished spreading it."

"Don't spread it, Dinos."

It looked as if the girls were one couple and the guys were another. They were "thick as thieves," as my mother would say, strolling arm in arm ahead of us and appearing to find everything wildly comical.

"Do spread it, Dinos," Jenna called back to us. "It's great."

"Yeah," Sandy called, "spread it, and we'll help."

I turned to my good pal and teammate. "Happy now?" I said.

"I'm a little happy. But I'll be a lot happy when we eventually trademark it and surf a pile of money together off your own private island."

I shook my head. "Man, you do think big, don'tcha?"

"So do you, boy, so don't think you're fooling anybody."

"Pit stop?" Jenna called, hauling Sandy diagonally across wide Washington Street as she did.

We followed them to the baseball field, sitting all dusky and deserted the way a baseball field should at this time of day at this time of year.

"Why are we doing this?" I asked as we walked past the back-stop to the bench on the first base side. The lights from the street reached just enough to make us visible to one another.

"I told you," Jenna answered, "for a pit stop." Her face briefly became more illuminated than the rest of her as she click-flicked a Bic and lit up. She took a big inhale, then passed the joint to Sandy.

I watched in not quite amazement as Sandy inhaled and passed on to Dinos. I continued staring at her until it became too much for her and she spluttered out a little storm of smoke and laughter straight my way.

"I didn't know you smoked," I said.

"I don't, mostly," she answered. "Just for the odd laugh. Nantucket could get really boring sometimes."

"*Nantucket?*" I snapped, making the girls burst out all over the place.

Dinos laughed, too, but in a slightly more sympathetic way. He exhaled, and put a big paw on my shoulder.

"I do not want that, thank you," I said.

He handed the joint back to Jenna. "I wasn't offering it to you, Grandma, relax. Anyway, I wouldn't let you have it even if you did want it. Your body is a temple."

"You're on the team, too. What's your body, then?"

"Mine's a frat house. I hardly even play. C'mon, man, you've seen it. A guy like me, an upperclassman with no remaining untapped potential is just another big body filling out the roster. I'd have to work ten times harder than you just to be mediocre, and that ain't what senior year's about in my book. You, however, are an investment. Everybody here, and the children of everybody here, is going to be counting on you financially for many years to come. So, no fun for you. I'll see to that."

"Thanks, pal." I wasn't kidding.

Jenna shook her head and said sympathetically to Sandy, "My no-neck boyfriend might not be a star, but at least he knows how to loosen up."

Sandy sighed and shrugged. "What can I do? Maybe we *should* get him to smoke."

"Hey, my neck is hungry," Dinos said. "Where should we go?"

"Home, to bed," I said, and started walking back to the street.

A few seconds later Sandy caught up and took my hand.

"Hey, that was a joke, you know," she said, "I do wish you wouldn't be so serious."

"Maybe I should smoke."

She yanked on my arm like she was trying to ring a church bell really hard. "Grrr," she said.

"Okay," I said, "less serious. I'm working on it."

We walked along in silence for a bit.

"Are you bothered that I smoked there?"

"There, no." I said. "Ask me if I'm bothered that you smoked on Nantucket."

She sighed. "Are you bothered that I smoked on Nantucket?"

"Pffft," I said as casually as I could fake. "Of course not. Why would you even ask that?"

"Um, because you just—"

"Who was there, when you smoked? How much did you smoke? How often? What were you wearing? Who was there?"

"Ahhhh," she said, wrapping her arms around my arm now instead of tugging on it. "That's more like it. I was wondering where you were for a minute there."

She pressed into me and I pressed back, and we walked home that way and mostly quiet, secure in my sappiness.

We sat for a while on Sandy's stoop, huddling happy against the chilly breeze coming up.

It was becoming one of my favorite spots anywhere, that stoop. The only things that mattered to me at that point were becoming a better football player and being with Sandy, and neither of those things was helped by spending more time at my house.

At home I was like a watchdog. Even when I was closed off in my room, I couldn't help tuning in to all the sounds and silences of the place, trying to get a read on what was coming next. The silences were mostly Dad's. The sounds were mostly Ma's as she tried to help Lloyd somehow, and Lloyd's as he tried not to be helped. And I needed to do all this while remaining in the shadows. Since he found out I made varsity, it seemed like he felt the need to take me on, challenge me every time he saw me.

"The only upside," I told Sandy, "is that Ma's so wrapped up in keeping my brother from falling completely through the cracks, she's stopped fretting about me getting hurt."

"That's nice," she said. "Less stress between the two of you at least. For now."

"Ha," I laughed. "Yeah, there's plenty stress enough to go around. For now. She'll be back, though. Making up for lost time, with The File."

"Hnn," Sandy said in a funny way.

"What?" I said.

"Dinos is right, right? How this is becoming a big deal. How *you* are becoming a big deal."

"I sure hope so," I said, pulling her closer under my one-arm bear hug.

I felt her stiffen. Not quite resist me, but not quite fall all in, either.

"Don't get carried away with it, though, huh?"

"No," I said, feeling myself doing my own version of the stiffen-resist. "No, not carried away, no."

We sat through a minute or two of silence, the cold feeling cold now, before she removed my arm and escaped from under my hold.

"It's time, Arlo," she said, hopping to her feet.

"Yeah, I guess so," I said, standing up on the step, facing her, both of us being awkward.

"The Starlo thing," she said, "is pretty funny."

149

"Yeah, I guess so."

"I won't be calling you that, though, even if it does get to be a thing. Might not be mentally healthy, y'know?"

"No." I laughed in what I thought was a convincing way. "I don't know. But you, miss, can call me whatever you want and I'll still come running."

"Hmmm, we'll see about that," she said, and slipped away inside.

# CHEERS

"Do we really think this is a good idea?" Sandy said when I came over to her in the stands, pumped so full of adrenaline I could hardly see straight. Honestly, I had to look at her and Jenna at an oblique angle to get them in focus.

"Of course it's a good idea," Jenna said to her.

It was halftime of the first varsity start for both Dinos and me, and I had come to the railing to talk to them while Dinos crawled to the locker room, winded and speechless. Or rather, I came to listen in as they consulted about me as if I wasn't there.

"Just because they say he's fit to go back in doesn't mean he's fit to go back in," Sandy said, looking at Jenna while gesturing at me.

Jenna cackled like she thought Sandy was really joking. "That is exactly what it means. If they tell him he can play, he's okay to play. Don't be such a girl, Sandy. You sound like you're his mother."

She did, worryingly so.

Truth was, I had had my bell rung on one fast-moving pass play during which somebody blocked me at the knees when I was at full speed. Landed on my face mask. Then on the next play I had collided full tilt with a tight end as big as me. I was pulled off the field after that for precautionary measures, that was all.

"You got rocked, Arlo," Sandy said.

"Maybe so," said Jenna, reaching and slapping me a high five that I caught just in time. "But that tight end's not coming back into the game. You, however. Look at you. You're fine as wine."

"That's what they tell me," I said, laughing, with Jenna laughing. Sandy, though, failed to see the humor.

Second half, Dinos was happily resting on the bench, but I was brand-new. Shook off the earlier dings, and felt like I could do anything out there. The bounce back after getting banged up could produce a surge of energy and clarity. Like the body was so pleased about feeling fine after feeling not-so-fine that there was a slingshot action that shoots it up into better performance. Almost better than never getting smacked in the first place.

I was in on practically every tackle, part of the pack if not the man himself. We were jumping up and howling after pretty much every play, and it felt fantastic. We weren't even trying to rub it in. This was pure football, fun football, a real war, dominated by both defenses.

Then late in the fourth, their quarterback suddenly figured out he was allowed to throw the ball, and he started slinging it all over the place.

Our rhythm on defense was all messed up from having our own way all day. I was out of position on two twenty-yard pass plays, and I was furious at myself.

They had a third down inside our thirty with under a minute to play. Only needed three yards for the first down, but I was certain they were going to keep at it and go for the big gain in the air. We were at 7–3 and in trouble.

Coach Fisk was thinking the same thing, because he called for an all-out assault pass rush. Our corners were playing man-to-man on their two deep-threat receivers, our safeties bumping up to play more like linebackers watching their slot guys across the middle. Linebackers got the green light to go after the passer.

There must have been spittle gathering at the corners of my mouth, I was so hungry for this.

The quarterback started barking out signals, then "hut-hut," the snap, and we were off.

The play seemed like it was already a replay, rolling out in high-def slo-mo before me, and that was great because I already wanted this to last as long as possible. I tracked the passer like a number 9–seeking missile as the trench warfare of the line-play churned in front of me. He stayed in the pocket an impressive amount of time as his blockers did stellar work fighting for his space and time. But as everybody seemed to be fighting to a standstill, the quarterback did a spin move, rolling to his right as he left the pocket and legged it far to his weak side sideline looking for his deep threat in the end zone.

It was totally unexpected and I never lost him.

I turned on the burners, beelined it right for him. A big, slow left tackle rolled out, braced for me, and blasted up toward my chin.

My legs and upper body were like two complementary machines doing very different jobs. My lower half continued like

I was just doing another of the endless sprints I had run to pre-pare for exactly this, and my upper half went into no-prisoners attack.

I slammed into that guard with both forearms up, then I jammed him with my right, tipping him the other way. Before he could right himself, I took my left and just smacked him with everything I had, smashing him toward the right sideline, where he crashed at the feet of my coach and screaming teammates.

The quarterback was my reward. He had pumped and was looking to unload his Hail Mary when I leaped, towered over him, cast a death shadow that just erased him before he tucked and I crash-landed on him so hard I was sure there would be nothing but a stain there when I got up.

I was still on the ground when the place erupted. Teammates came over to mob me as time ran out and the game was ours. They pulled me up off the quarterback, who writhed on the ground howling and pawing at his throwing shoulder.

When they had hauled me, jumping and laughing to our side-line, the big tackle I had dumped was screaming at my coach and pointing at me. "Head slap! Head slap!" he yelled over and over as Coach Fisk merely shook his head no at the guy before banging me hard on the shoulder pads and leading the team to the locker room while the home fans roared us off.

After showering and dressing I looked around for Dinos, but he had been quicker than me for once. I hurried to where we were supposed to meet Sandy and Jenna in the parking lot, but when I approached the spot, Sandy was alone, arms folded, on the hood of the wheelless old Ford that had sat in that same parking spot forever. She did not look thrilled.

"What's the story?" I asked.

Then the story revealed itself.

"You really do get it," Lloyd said, popping out of the Ford's driver's seat and startling me like a corpse emerging from a grave. He wore a black polyester track suit I had never seen before but already looked like it needed washing.

He was a funny old mix of things there, excited and sad, crystal clear and distant. His mouth was smiling but his eyes were definitely not.

"Thanks," I said. "What are you doing there?"

"I'm taking it for a test drive, thinking of buying the thing. What do you think I'm doing? I came to watch you play."

"You . . . were at the game?"

"Yes," Sandy said irritably as Lloyd slammed the car door and sat on the Ford's front fender, close to her. "Apparently he was."

"You can *play*, dammit," Lloyd said, pointing at me in case I didn't know who he meant. "You reminded me of *me*. Even more than last time I watched. Progress, or what!"

That would not have sounded like a compliment to anybody else, and all things considered it didn't to me, either.

"Thanks. Well . . . you were right, I have to say. About hitting. As long as you hit 'em correctly you can hit them as hard as you like and you'll never feel a thing. Except great. I feel *great*."

This left Sandy well underimpressed and me wishing I hadn't said it. She slid down off the hood of the Ford, and looked anxious to get going. "You're a stud, Starlo," she said, using her unfavorite nickname like a pointy stick. She walked right up to me, with her back to my brother.

"Starlo," Lloyd said with a grin, pointing at me again. Then he hopped off the fender, turned and abruptly walked away.

"Hey!" I called after him. "What are you doing? Where are you going? We were going to grab a pizza or something, why don't you come along?"

Both of Sandy's feet were suddenly stepping on mine. I shrugged at her, like what else could I do, even though I had no clear idea why I did it. Because I was feeling all-powerful while he was now all-pitiful? I hoped that wasn't it, and now I hoped he wouldn't accept.

"Can't," he called as he kept walking.

"Why not?"

She grabbed firmly on to my sides. "He looks, and smells, like he should be eating in a Dumpster, not a restaurant," she whispered forcefully. Then her nails started digging in around my kidneys.

"I just told you. 'Cause I can't."

"Tea for two then, huh?" I said to Sandy as I watched him skulk off into the not-quite sunset.

"Excellent idea," she said, keeping her firm grip and walking me backward in the opposite direction.

"What happened to D and J?"

"Well, they were waiting, then J met your brother, and suddenly they were too wrecked to go out."

I sighed. "He sure can tire people out."

"Oh yeah," she said. "Wait till you're playing in the Rose Bowl or something, and he shows up rank and half wasted to tell you for the fiftieth time how much you remind him of him. Imagine how tiring that'll be."

I inhaled deeply, sighed loudly. "I can imagine it, since it's got me pretty exhausted right now."

* * *

We sat across from one another in the same old booth in the same old place that I had been going to for as long as I could remember. And it looked just this old, with yellowed mirrors and cracked vinyl upholstery, for as long as I could remember. Every little school or church something, like honor roll or First Communion, would bring all or part of my family here to celebrate. Little League all-star game when I still saw the point of baseball, then peewee and Pop Warner late-season victories would be cause for modestly marking the occasion. These guys did a series of burgers named after New England states and I always got the Vermont. And their thin-crust pizza was the equal of anybody's, partly because they stuck with it and kept it consistent even when half the city seemed to be switching to stone-baked, flatbread stuff that tasted like pizza toppings smeared across a paper plate. My mother still loved football, in this old place. Lloyd and I laughed at every stupid thing, in this old place.

Sandy and I sat on opposite sides of a shared sausage and black olive pizza, with two vanilla Cokes from the fountain.

"So," I said as I reached for a slice, "do you love me more now?"

157

I was, admittedly, still running on an overdose of adrenaline that made me as stupid as a football player.

She reached for a slice. Then she put it back.

"I can't possibly come to all your games, Arlo."

I had folded the pizza slice in half and bitten off pretty much everything up to the crust. So I had to let that float in the air while I chewed. Sandy took a sip and waited for me.

"How can you say that now, when it's all just getting so good?"

"It's torture to watch. My stomach still feels like it's full of bees. And they're *stinging*."

"You should eat something then—that'll smother 'em." I gestured in the direction of the pizza for good measure.

"It's not hunger, thanks. It's . . . gruesome stuff going on down there on that field."

"But you've always loved football. You told me that yourself."

Now she took up a slice. She bit it in such a tentative way the thing looked like it had healed over again when she put it back on the plate.

"I did say that," she said. "But that was before."

"Oh," I said, "you mean, before my mother started filling you up with the propaganda."

"No," she said. Shaking her head emphatically, she added, "Yes. But more than that. I loved the game before anyone I cared about was playing it. That says something, don't you think? That has to say something."

I stopped eating. I started nodding, without even meaning to.

"Yes indeed," I said. "It means you care about me. Ha." I was this close to jumping up and doing a foolish quarterback sack dance and jeopardizing everything.

Sandy sighed. "Yes, Arlo. That. Of course, that. But beyond that—"

"There's nothing beyond that. Have some pizza."

"There is a whole world beyond that. If I can love a sport, but then only love it if I don't love anybody inside it . . . There is something wrong with that. Can't you see what I'm saying?"

The involuntary nodding returned, and brought a doofus smile with it. "Love. *Love* is what you're saying, right? What a day I'm having. What an amazing day."

She stood up, leaving all the pizza but taking her drink.

"I'm going to go now," she said.

When I moved to get up, she reached over and pushed me back down into my seat with her palm flat on the top of my head. The spot was surprisingly tender, like I had a bruise up there.

"I don't think I can talk about this with you right now. You're still buzzing from your big game, and that's only right. But I'm not going to be able to feel the same way, so we'll talk another time."

When it was clear she had subdued me, she came around to my side, kissed me on the cheek.

"Someday, Sandy, I'm going to replace all those awful stories in that file with good ones, great ones, about my achievements. Magazines, newspapers, the works, all positive stuff. Change The File, change the story, change everything—that's what I'm going to do."

"It's good to have goals," she said softly, kissed me again, and left.

I watched her go, looked at her empty seat, looked at the un-eaten celebration food. Eating the whole pizza by myself was not a problem. Getting blown off by both my friendless brother and my girl on a day like this was.

Fine. Starlo would eat alone, celebrating in the same old victory place. It was still a celebration.

* * *

Sandy dodged me for over a week after the game. At first it was a case of me chasing after her—calling, texting, angling to inter-cept her in the hallways at school. She was too invisible for it to be anything but deliberate, and it was too effective for me to pretend it wasn't getting to me. I tried arriving at her house early enough to walk with her, but it was never early enough because she was always gone.

Finally I got myself out of the house stupid early, woke up the birds, walked through the dark to the coffee shop, and then staked out the school entrance. I was even blowing off my morning workout over this, and she had better be impressed when I pointed it out to her.

I was waiting on the low wall in front of the school when Sandy walked up. She was the third person to arrive, after the custodian and me. Next to me was one large café mocha and one large empty café mocha cup.

"Remember?" I said to her, pointing kind of sideways at the coffee like it had just coincidentally followed me there.

"I do," she said, taking it right up and peeling the cover off. She didn't sit down next to me, but when I patted the spot with both hands she relented. She took a sip.

"Iced coffee, Arlo? At this time of year?"

"It was steaming when I got here. Stakeouts are harder than they look in the movies."

"I guess you mean business." She drank the coffee anyway. "This isn't bad, actually."

"I'll bring you one every morning if you'll quit punishing me for whatever it is I've done. It's been awful, you avoiding me like you've been doing."

"I know. I'm sorry. I haven't handled this very well."

"Well, what is *this* anyway? I don't even really understand the *this* that you're handling so very unwell."

"This football thing," she said, breathing in the coffee before sipping on it.

"Well, that's easy. Leave that to me. I'll handle the football thing."

"Thanks, Arlo, but I still have to handle my own thoughts about it. When I see you out there . . ."

"You should have seen me last week, Sandy. Oh, man, I wish you could have seen me. It was the best—"

"I did."

"Huh?"

"I did see you. I went. Thought I should. To give it another try. To see if maybe I'd feel differently."

"Good," I said, truly hopeful about this development.

She was shaking her head sadly, looking down.

"Don't say no, Sandy, say yes. I played really well. I know I did. Everybody told me so. Coach told me so. Said if I keep progressing at the rate I am, who knows where I can go. Who knows, is just what he said. . . . Please, stop shaking your head."

"When I see you out there trying to hurt people . . . and people trying to hurt you—"

"That is not the objective. When you play the game right, and you play it hard . . . there's a lot of complication to it. It's a very sophisticated game, a psychological game as much as anything."

She took a long drink of coffee, then continued.

"When I see you out there trying to hurt people, it has an effect. I don't like it."

"So then what? Are you telling me to quit football?"

"Never. Never would I. You need to play, for you. You're great at it and, yeah, who knows. You might even be the perfect football player."

You could probably hear the unspoken *but* at the end of that from ten blocks away.

"Are we splitting up here, Sandy? Over this?"

Thank goodness she now employed the head shake no in service of something good this time.

"Let's just take a break. For the remainder of the season. Makes sense, huh? You can just focus on your football, and I can just not focus on football at all."

My heart felt like there was a zipper on it, and it was being yanked hard up and down.

"Makes sense, I guess. I mean, the way you say it, not the way I

feel. Jeez, it's only just October. That'll be, including any playoffs . . .
about two months. Arr, Sandy . . . Can't I do something else, like
collect litter or volunteer at an old folks' home or something?"

"Phwaa . . ." She covered her mouth at least while she laughed
at me. "It's not community service, Arlo. Get it through that thick
helmet head of yours. It's not punishment, and it's not even breaking up. It's kind of the opposite even. We're trying to avoid a certain period of time when there's a good chance we'll have big fights
about big things."

I laughed. "I'd never fight with you about *anything*."

"That's sweet, Arlo. But I'm pretty sure even if that were true,
if one person wants an argument bad enough, she can make it
happen."

She looked sufficiently serious that I figured I'd ditch the wisecracking and the mush that wouldn't get me anywhere anyway.
"Did you just threaten me, Sandrine?"

"I didn't intend to, but I see how it could have sounded that
way. It was a threat of good intentions, at least."

"Hnn," I said. Growled, actually. "Two months sounds like a
long time. Doesn't it sound like a long time to you?"

"It does," she said, leaning close to me and making it that much
worse. My heart felt like it was infested with fishing worms. "But
we're tough enough."

"Ahh, taking a shot at my toughness now," I said.

"It's a pretty big target," she said, and held out her hand.

"I'm not shaking that thing unless you kiss me first. If you can't
even do that, like you mean it, then this is all just a—"

"Shut up," she said, and met my demands. Really, really nicely.

Then, yup, we shook on it. That's how mature we were about this, and civilized, and respectful of each other's position on the subject. Even though her position was absurd.

We didn't need this. But I'd do anything for her. Except give up football.

# A FUNNY THING

I couldn't stand the "take a break" idea.

But I had to admit she was onto something. The only thing seriously competing with football for my attention had been Sandy. Add in feeling angry and helpless about the weird situation she put us in, and I reached another level entirely.

I had more focus. I had more fire.

I had more meanness. A lot more meanness.

"Jeez Louise, calm down, will ya?" Dinos said after I dragged him out one morning to practice a few one-on-one maneuvers I had thought up. We were dressed in regular sweats, and he was wearing the fat oversized coach's training pads, pretending to be an offensive lineman.

I stopped bashing him. "What?" I barked.

"What did I do to you?"

"Nothing. What did I do to Sandy? Huh? She said this wasn't any kind of punishment. But that's exactly what it feels like, a punishment."

"Sandy?" he said, smiling slyly. "Oh, a picture emerges. . . ."

"Pads up!" I bellowed, and he got them up just in time to avoid serious harm as I tore into him as ferociously as I had any opposing player all year. "Punishment!" I roared as I drove big Dinos back and back over the whole length of the field, and he was helpless to even slow me down. "Punishment! Punishment! Punishment!"

It only stopped when I had driven him back through the end zone, under the goal posts, and off the edge of the field to the running track.

"All right!" he yelled when I kept bashing. "Time out, time out."

"Sorry," I said as I stopped, then walked a small circle with my hands on my hips and my heavy breathing clouding the air.

"I think I need to revise your long-term prospects a little," he said, joining me in my little circuit like we were a couple of circus ponies. "Instead of the NFL, I think maybe prison could be an option if you don't get a grip on yourself."

"I'm already in prison. That's what this feels like."

"Well, I meant a prisoner of the state, but prisoner of love must be pretty harsh, too. Come on, pal, this is enough for today." He tugged me by my shirt and we walked the half lap back to the locker room.

"I think I'll run a mile or two," I said as he veered off the track. "Want to join me?"

"Nope. I don't want to get in too good a shape or they might play me more, and that'll make me too hurt or tired to enjoy my Sensational Saturday Nights. But by all means you should. Game time isn't for another two days and you are giving off a whole lot of menace, my friend."

"I hate not seeing her, Dinos," I said. "I mean, I really *hate* it. It's worse than I even thought it was gonna be."

When, at that moment, my best guy friend started laughing, loudly and for real, I went cross-eyed angry. "Are you trying to provoke me right into prison, Mr. Dinos?" I asked in a voice like a bear's.

"Nah, nah, nah," he said, holding up the pads as if he could defend himself. "I was just thinking how on Saturday some poor unsuspecting sap of a running back is going to pay the price for your lonely heart. Ironically, Sandy is turning you into a better and even more ferocious football player than ever before. Coach says he might hold you out of the next couple of practices, just to make sure we have enough offensive players to take the field on Saturday."

I found myself smiling. "Coach said that?"

"Something like, yeah. Anyway, do some laps there, Starlo, channel that ferocity. Meanwhile, since *I* am still allowed to talk to Sandy, I think I'll go tell her how she's making you an All-World linebacker."

"Yeah," I said, starting out on my lap. Then I threw it in reverse. "No! Don't do that. I'm not crazy or ferocious or brutal or any of that. I'm normal. I'm a normal athlete playing a normal game. Nothing else, got it?"

"Got it, Chief," he said, saluting before walking away.

"Oh, except, hi. Dinos, tell her hi, please, for me."

"Hi-ho!" he called, and was gone.

I lit out on the track at an impractical pace that there was nothing I could do about.

\* \* \*

I had more stamina, on the field, and in the weight room. First in, last out, every day. It was as if some kind of restriction had been lifted, a supervision order had been removed, and I was free to test the absolute outer limits of what might be possible for me both physically and mentally. So I went mental. I think maybe I even knew there was another level of brutal I could reach, but I had held back because I didn't want Sandy to see.

"What has gotten into you, young man?" Coach Fisk asked when he found me in the weight room late on the day before Thanksgiving. "I am well aware that you've taken your training right off the charts, and that's jim-dandy. Nobody appreciates ambition and effort more than I do. But it's the Thanksgiving holiday now, lad. It's not possible to pump yourself any greater between tonight and tomorrow."

"Ah, but conference playoffs . . ."

". . . can wait. So go spend some time with your family."

Right, the family. This would be the Thanksgiving I wished the whole day could be spent on the field. Lloyd will be wasted, Ma will be fretting, Dad will be quietly tensed up, and Sandy will be elsewhere. The team was my family this year.

"Maybe it is possible," I said with a laugh.

"Go on home now," he said in a voice that made it clear he did not disapprove of my line of thinking just the same.

* * *

Twenty-four hours later I was sitting in the front passenger seat of Dad's car, with the game ball in my lap. He could not stop smiling. We had won and I had been everywhere, in every play. He let every other car pass him or enter into traffic ahead of him. He was my only guest at this year's Big Game, which made me a little blue. Lloyd was threatening to come, but he couldn't get out of bed. Not that I cared much about that, but at least he would have been a distraction from the absence of Sandy.

After a while, breaking his happy silence, Dad said, "It's almost a shame we have to go home, son, because I feel like taking you out for a great big steak and a beer."

Steak and a beer sounded just great to me, since Sandy wouldn't be with us this year and who knew what Lloyd would be up to by the time we got home.

"Let me take a rain check and cash it sometime in the future, Dad."

"That's a deal," he said. I noticed him sneaking peeks at the game ball, like it was going to do something at any moment and he didn't want to miss it. "It is Thanksgiving, right?"

"Oh . . . I almost forgot, but I think you're right."

"It's a shame Sandy can't come. She really brightened things up last year."

"Yeah," I said, looking out the window. "Yeah, she did, didn't she?"

"Why, by the way, can't she be here? If you don't mind my asking."

"I don't mind. Sandy and I are great. It's Sandy and football that aren't on speaking terms."

"What about football?"

"She doesn't like the aggression of it, I guess. And she doesn't like the way I play it in particular. And she doesn't like the way I train for it, as in too much, too hard, too everything."

I was still looking out the window, but I sensed a change inside the car and looked over toward Dad. His happy smile fell away somewhere on the road behind us.

"Everything okay, Dad? You all right?"

He took a deep breath, then let it all out, all full of words.

"You have done nothing wrong, son. Sandy is a lovely girl—and so is your mother, for that matter. But it almost sounds like you have done something wrong, and that's just not true. From what I can see, you are doing it all right. Righter than anyone else on the evidence of it." He reached over and tapped the game ball for emphasis. "You are a remarkable young man, Arlo, and I could not be prouder of you. So you go right ahead and continue to be remarkable, and go wherever that takes you."

I stared at him, this man of few words and even fewer these days, as he exhaled hugely again. And now he looked better. Maybe handing out unqualified praise was good for him and he should try it more often. But I could hear in there, that "righter than anyone else" and "could not be prouder" came with built-in comparisons to his other son that couldn't help but make me look better than I otherwise would.

Too bad for both of them, I thought, that they didn't have this.

But he was also right. I wasn't doing anything wrong.

I was doing everything the best I could.

"Thanks for coming, Dad."

He smiled that smile again. "Thanks for having me."

I slid the football over onto his lap. "Happy Thanksgiving, Dad," I said.

# RIGHT AND WRONG

Sandy was right the whole time.

The season played out, and I never felt better about the game of football or my place in it. The game came naturally now because I did everything humanly possible to prepare for the games, and when you do that you cannot miss. I was wearing blinders from Monday through Friday because I was dedicated to nothing but training, and because it had become so hard for me to even see Sandy just in passing.

We had one last game after the pointless two-week layoff between the season's end and conference playoffs. It felt to me like any other game. I did my job in a highly efficient, professional way and did not miss a single tackle all day.

I played with menace but without passion.

When the whistle blew and we had lost, I was largely unconcerned. I didn't even know for sure what the final score was, but it wasn't close enough to sweat about letting this one slip through our fingers.

Then I ran to the locker room and through the door, knowing

also that it was the official end of the season, and I ran to my locker and threw down my helmet and dug out my phone and pressed the right button and walked out into the parking lot while it rang just the one time.

"Hi," she said, laughing.

"Hi," I said, smiling hard enough that I knew she could hear it.

* * *

The break seemed to have worked flawlessly. From the moment we reconnected that first week of December, we were hardly ever apart, and neither one of us wanted to be apart. I was always going to be at a disadvantage in this thing because there was no way she would ever be as gone on me as I was on her, but as long as she was half as gone that would be plenty. The halls had the usual pre-holiday lightness, and I felt the added bounce of being known by everybody and treated special just for walking around. It was like the football gift that kept on giving, without the complication of football season itself getting in the way and mucking things up.

We were like royalty. And our ball was the Christmas Dance held the Friday night when school had just let out for the holidays.

"There's dancing?" I said as we walked into the gym and I saw a mass of bodies milling at a midtempo pace in the middle of the floor.

"Of course, it's a *dance*," Sandy said, covering her face with both of her hands as she giggled helplessly.

I was deeply embarrassed. What was I thinking? It was right there in the title the whole time, one of only two words and so, really hard to miss. Christmas *Dance*. Dancing would probably come into it at some point.

"But I've never danced before," I said.

"Never?" Jenna squealed, coming up and taking my hand gently between her two as if her next words were going to be "So sorry for your loss."

The lighting in the gym was low, and they had some strobe thing going on, which also contributed helpfully to the camouflage, but still I could feel people looking at me. I felt even bigger and more public than I already was, and I could see in this situation why fame might not be all that desirable a thing.

"We cannot have this," Sandy announced. "Starlo can't dance? Unacceptable."

A low-level terror swept over me as she started tugging me toward the dance floor. I was surprised at how helpless this scene made me feel, and I put up no more resistance than a kite to her pulling.

It only got worse when we reached the fringes of the dancing population and I stood like an oaf in front of a swaying and shimmering Sandy, who was looking electric in satiny blue, the low light doing nothing at all to dim her.

I was mortified. Whether people were all looking at me or not, it sure felt like they were. Give me the football field any day.

"I'm sorry," I said, gesturing top to toe at the rusted tin man of me. "I'm spoiling everything. You should go dance with whoever you like, honestly, I don't mind."

"Hmmm," she said, "anybody I like . . ." She put her hands on her hips like the peppery type of actresses seemed to always do in old Hollywood movies. Then she spun to survey the dance floor, her swishy skirt fanning out to catch every last flicker of light to advertise her.

I hated having my bluff called. Whoever the lucky guy was, I'd kill him first and then myself.

And she knew it, too, milking the moment viciously.

The song changed to something slow, and while this would still be no help to me, it made me bold and stupid.

"Will you dance with me?" I said.

Sandy swung around effortlessly, weightlessly. "You mean me?" she said, touching herself lightly on both collarbones with her fingertips.

"Yes, Sandrine," I said.

She sidled up to me. "Is your oil can around here someplace?" she said much too loudly.

I was definitely not imagining now that a good portion of the immediate crowd was watching, and enjoying, the spectacle.

"Please?" I begged quietly in her ear.

Pity, when you need it, is a fantastic thing.

She firmly took my right hand and placed it on her hip, seized my big left paw in her right hand, and exerted a series of push-and-pull pressure moves that had me suddenly, for the first time, dancing.

"How does this work?" I said, genuinely surprised at how she was able to make the big bulk of me do what she wanted it to do with just gentle manipulation.

"There are wires that come down from the ceiling," she said. "Now shush."

I did what she said, and happily shushed. And my body did what her body told it, and followed. I couldn't even tell her what I was feeling as we glided—she glided, I shuffled—through this song and then the next two, which were different in rhythm and tempo but still the same to my dancing. I couldn't believe how much more *intense* this was, this whole experience was. Sitting with Sandy, touching Sandy's hair and her face, dropping my arm over her and keeping her tight and mine were already exciting to me in a way that nothing else ever was. I felt my face flush now, as I thought about what I couldn't even tell her because I would sound like some mountain creature that just crawled out of the forest for the first time, but it was true, too. This, dancing, *mixing,* with Sandy like this was simply a whole other category of being with her. I wanted to throw my head back and roar and let the horrible gymnasium acoustics repeat after me for the whole night.

But at least I understood that that was crazy. It was just dancing.

"Are you having a good time now?" she asked when the third song morphed into a fourth and then a fifth, and we were the only ones who were slow dancing anymore.

"Pretty good," I said in my unconvincing croaky calm voice. At least I managed not to roar. "How 'bout you?"

She didn't say anything but laid her head flat against my chest, and pulled me tighter to her. I pulled harder then. She pulled harder.

* * *

Apart from Sandy, the holidays themselves were not a lot of laughs around the Brodie household, but there wasn't any mayhem, either, so settling for a draw was fine by me.

Every year the four of us would get up and open our gifts, then get dressed nice, go to church together—yes, the four of us. After that we would drive two hours north to spend the remainder of Christmas Day with various relatives on my father's side, or two hours south to spend it with my mother's people. This was a due-north year.

As always my parents paid close attention to selecting things that matched up thoughtfully with the person who was on the receiving end. Once again they came through, and I opened up some classy high-end shaving gear and cologne as well as several items of underarmor underwear designed for athletes that cost more than almost any overarmor attire I'd be covering them with. Equally thoughtful, perhaps more surprising, though, was when Lloyd opened his gift from them to find a seriously serious leather motorcycle jacket like professional racers wore.

He had put in the hours to get the bike in good working order, and was working as a courier. The jacket he usually wore was so threadbare that mosquitoes could penetrate it at high speed. Lloyd stared at the jacket, squeezed it, and pulled it, nodding at the quality of the thing. "Thanks, guys," he said, kind of whispery.

Their choice of gift was a statement, an investment in whatever modest undertaking he was willing to pursue. I hoped it would be worth it.

For my part, I dipped into my modest lawn-hedge-leaf maintenance money—which came from my parents in the first place—to give them a pass to the community cinema that would cover their two-for-one date nights for the year, including popcorn and a medium drink they were going to have to share.

Lloyd's and my tradition with each other had long been cheap and comical gifts for the occasion, so when he opened up his can of meadow-fresh bathroom deodorizer spray and I opened up my economy-size tube of Ben-Gay muscle ointment, we were both gracious and grateful for the thoughtfulness.

But it was Lloyd who stopped the presses and the clocks and probably Dad's heartbeat for a few seconds by not only remembering the holiday gift-giving tradition but also presenting the folks with a Fruit-of-the-Month Club subscription that was so high quality we all briefly gathered around the illustrated brochure like a 1930s family around a big wooden radio. As each page revealed another exotic fruit that was hand-grown, hand-wrapped and, no doubt, was going to be hand-delivered, it just reinforced my suspicion that Lloyd's job as a courier wasn't quite what he made it out to be.

We all ignored our thoughts about how Lloyd had paid for his gift, though, and a good quiet settled in then, the quiet that floated on Ma's cinnamon candle scent, and on her Boston Symphony Orchestra's *Messiah* recording that played low while everyone disappeared into their bedrooms to get dressed and move on to the next stage of the day. It was, in a modest and mildly surprising Brodie way, as fine a morning as we'd had all year.

Which could have explained the dejected look on Ma's face when Lloyd came out of his room not in his holiday glad rags but in his usual grunge plus one deadly sharp leather jacket.

"What?" he said, seeing Ma's expression. "Aw, you didn't think I was gonna go to church. C'mon, Ma, I hung in there a long time, but this year I have officially lost my faith."

"So?" Dad said. "What's that got to do with anything? It's Christmas."

"Sorry, no," he said. "But tell Uncle Rodney and Aunt Babs ho-ho for me. And grab some of those whoopie pies to bring home if you can."

I didn't think this was such a terrible turn, myself, now that I thought about it. I had heard a lot of people tell stories of relatives acting up something horrible at Christmas, and this was certainly preferable to that. Dad surely agreed, because he headed out the door without a word. "I'll be warming up the car."

But Ma was going to take some time to adjust to this new state of things.

"Son?" she said, making him wince with the very word. "Are you sure about this?"

He pretended to get all casual and busy as he put on his helmet and failed to look at her as he followed Dad outside. "Gotta work, Ma," he said, shrugging.

"Who has to work on Christmas?" she asked, pursuing him to his bike. "Who needs courier service on Christmas?"

"Santa Claus," he said, and then proceeded immediately with the kicking to life of the bike's engine.

"Ho-ho-ho-house," I said to the empty place as I shut the door behind me.

# A NEW YEAR

"You want to come running, with me?" I said into the phone as I pulled on my socks.

"Yes, I do," Sandy said.

"Listen, I'm okay with that, Sandy, but I'm gonna tell you now that I have to keep up my pace. If you can keep up, then great, but you can't expect me to slow down. Holidays are over. This is training for real now, not for fun."

"Okay, sir. Yes, sir. I'll try not to be a drag on your training, sir."

"Good," I said, ignoring her mockery because the "sir" thing sounded pretty nice. "I'll come by your place in a little bit. While you're waiting, you should do some stretching. Hamstrings, Achilles tendons, calves . . . Do you know these stretches, or will you need me to show you when I get there?"

"Ohhh," she drawled " I will *neeeed* you to show silly little me."

"Hey, wise guy, I just don't want to see you get hurt. And it is cold, but don't overdress. Layers are key. If you come outside in some old bulky sweats—well, you might as well just go right back inside again."

"Arlo?"

"Yes."

"Are you trying to make me regret this idea? Because if you'd just rather not have company on your run, then I'd rather you just came out and said it. Because I'd hate to think you would think you needed to go to all this trouble just to discourage me. Or worse, that you are seriously this much of a *snore* on the subject."

I paused long enough to let her think about her behavior.

"I am not a snore, on any subject. And I would love your company."

"Good. Shut up now and get over here." She hung up then, which was probably for the best.

By the time I had reached Sandy's house, she was out front and running through her stretches of all the important areas.

"Well done," I said.

"Thanks, Coach. How long do you usually like to run?"

"Sometimes three miles, sometimes five."

"How 'bout we do three today?" she said, bouncing up and down and toggling her neck muscles all around.

"Of course," I said, giving her a minibow. "Remember, though, don't tear out at too quick a pace or you'll never make it."

"Right," she said. "Okay, I'll watch it. So from right here if we go straight up Belgrade, to the private tennis courts on Cypress, go around the tennis courts, and come straight back, that's a solid three miles right there."

"Really?" I said as she stretched her calves once more, pushing up against a maple tree in the corner of the yard.

"Really," she said when she was done. "Ready, and we're off."

And so she was.

"Pace yourself," I reminded her, hoping at the same time she wasn't planning on a lot of chatter during the run.

As it turned out, there wasn't another word of chatter until the run was done.

"Okay, okay, okay," I said, striding up to the front of her house at least two minutes behind her. She was sitting on the porch with her legs stretched out down the steps in front of her, leaning toward her toes to stretch those hamstrings. "What's the story, jackrabbit?"

I was way more winded than her.

"The story is, you should have paced yourself, young man."

"Yes," I said, "I should have. But you didn't need to. Why?"

"Because I am an experienced runner, Arlo. What did you think I did with myself while you were building Starlo, Master of the Universe? Sitting around eating caramel popcorn and watching soap operas? I told you before, stud, I'm not going to let myself get fat if you're not. Stretch those hammies before they freeze up."

I bent into the task as quickly as if Coach Fisk had screamed it at me. Then when I was down there, I started groaning.

"You're really good, Sandy. A natural runner."

"That's what Gordon said," she said. "That's why I started running more seriously, on the island."

Gordon.

"I am *going* to Nantucket this summer," I insisted.

"We'll see," she said, sitting up there on the porch like it was a throne, and lording it over me good. Just as she should have.

**183**

We ran together sometimes after that, more often apart since we had different agendas. Dinos and I had a loose schedule we kept up through the winter and into the spring, which was looser for him than it was for me but I understood. He was going into senior year, and football was very much part-time for him, very much just a piece of the *delicious senior-year pie* he said he planned to savor bite by bite.

In the spring I was more the sideline fan anyway, as Sandy made the track team, competing at three thousand and five thousand meters. This made it a little less weird and a little more fun when I once again worked out with the track team without joining the track team.

I got to stay in shape, and hover around my girl all the time, too. Could it get any more win-win than that?

# ISLAND ARLO

"So where you goin', big man?"

Damn. I hated that. When he called me big man it meant his shoulder boulder had grown so massive it was crushing him and he needed somebody to knock it off for him.

"I'm going to Nantucket, Lloyd," I said and continued to jam a week's worth of stuff into a bag that had *The Weekender* printed on an inside label.

"Oooh, Nantucket. Nanfucktucket and kissitgoodnight. How'd you ever get a pass onto that snobby little island?"

"Sandy and her family rent a place there every summer for a month."

"A month? You're going there for a month? Goin' for it now, boy, ain't ya? Seriously think you're leaving the riffraffers behind."

"I'm only going for a week," I said.

"Oh, good," he said, draping himself over me and almost toppling us both onto the bag and the bed. "There was no way I could get more than a week off of work."

Oh, dear god.

"You're not coming, Lloyd."

"What? Why not? We used to do everything together. Remember? I never left *you* behind."

"Yeah?" I said, stuffing random socks and shorts into the bag and zipping it up before I could get drawn into this any further. "Well, we called ahead, and Nantucket said, unfortunately, you're banned." I grabbed up the bag and pulled a spin move that left him toppled on my bed.

"Dammit," he said, lying there comfy and motionless, "I'm running out of islands."

"Yeah," I said, leaving him there to go get some stuff from the bathroom, "maybe next time."

He had no response, which was good. I came back to my room a few minutes later to find him gone, which was also good. Finding my bag also gone was something else entirely.

"What do you think you're doing?" I said as I found him jamming his own stuff into my bag. Half of my things were dumped onto his bed and the floor.

"I just figure we should consolidate, share one bag. No sense overpacking."

"Lloyd . . . ," I said, my teeth hurting already from gritting them so hard.

"Like, for instance," he said, holding up the box of condoms he had found in the bag. "I *know* you ain't gonna need these, Humpty Dumpty." He leered at me, with such utter, demented sleaze, he managed to look like some mangy scuzzball with half his teeth missing. But for the moment, he still had them all.

If I lost my cool now, it would only inspire him.

"I need my bag," I said, walking calmly right up to him and taking the box of condoms out of his hand. His expression didn't change, and it was hard to be up so close to its creepiness.

"Of course you do," he said after several more uncomfortable seconds ticked away. He started removing his things from the bag while I collected mine and dumped them back in. "Relax, will ya?" he said as I took the bag and walked back to my room. "You're no fun anymore. You really do need this vacation."

I didn't answer, just went silently and quickly back to my room, finished packing, and spun for the door.

Where I found him, the leer on his face and a backpack over his shoulder.

"You are not coming."

"I could have pissed in your bag, you know."

"You're not coming."

"Could have pissed in your bag, but I didn't. Could have done a lot of things, but I didn't."

"What, am I supposed to thank you?"

"'Course not. Think I don't know by now you're a fuckin' ingrate?"

"I have to go, Lloyd. And you have to stay. And that's that."

I walked toward the door, and he stayed, blocking it. "Maybe that's not that, big man. Maybe this is that. And maybe you should stop hurting my feelings."

I practically spit laughter in his face. "Your *feel—*"

"Laugh away, big man. Though, if you really want to get out of here, maybe you should stop acting like you can tell me where I am going and where I'm not going."

I knew he could go on with this kind of thing forever, since time only appeared to matter to one of us.

"I would appreciate it if you stayed home, Lloyd. This time." I said, feeling my face flush with restrained rage.

He stepped aside, nodding happily. "And I'll keep an eye on your room for ya," he said as I stormed out the door. "In case anything happens to it."

* * *

"Is that what he said?" Sandy said as we hung together over the rail of the ferry. I had given her a highly edited version of events, ending at the part about all the islands he'd been banned from.

"Oh yeah," I said. "He's a barrel of laughs to spend time with. As long as the time is limited to like a minute and a half. After that it's downhill, and he can be kind of unpleasant and dangerous. Or sometimes before that."

"Does he need help, Arlo?"

"Help? What, like professional help or something? No, no, he just needs direction, something. I still think if he had just held it together for that one more day . . . he might have gotten into the army, and then we wouldn't even be here talking about him now."

"You're the one who brought up the subject."

"Hmmm," I said, "I don't know why I even did that."

"Well, as long as you did, what do you think is wrong with him, aside from being just plain nuts? I mean, you know him better than anybody, right? You knew him when he was partway normal, yes? Sounds to me like it goes beyond Lloyd just needing something to do. What are you thinking?"

I was thinking this was making me way uneasy, trying to hang words on what I thought might be wrong with my brother. Who was I to do that? And when I did sometimes let myself go there, I got right back out again because I didn't like even the notion of diagnosing the guy, never mind the possible ramifications.

I was thinking that ferries steaming toward Nantucket on perfect late-July days with perfect girls like Sandy were supposed to be a vacation from thinking.

"I was hoping we could leave Lloyd behind for now. Could we do that?" I asked her as the wind whipped us and the sun toasted us.

"Of course we can, for now," she said, leaning into me as we leaned into the sea breeze.

I hated that *for now*.

* * *

I had never been on an island before, but I quickly understood what people meant about the whole pace of life being different, the relaxed feeling that was everywhere.

"I could get used to this," I said on the third straight hot and sunny day. Sandy and I were in the water, far from the shore, watching the island posing pretty for us.

"Yeah," she said, kind of dreamy, "every year when we return I think I'm not ever going to want to leave here again."

"Yeah, now that I see the place for myself, I'm going to always worry when you leave that I'll never see you again."

"Ah, don't be silly. By the third week I usually get tired of it. But if I don't, I'll send for you."

"Good. My bags will be packed."

Those first days were unreal to me in the best way. Sandy's sister and her family wouldn't be down until the next week—taking over *my* room—and her folks were totally relaxed about doing their own thing and leaving Sandy to do hers. So we had a kind of freedom and space . . . and *calm* that I had never quite experienced before.

It agreed with me.

"I haven't gone this long without breaking into a run in a long time," I said as we took another long, easy walk through dunes and beach grass and out to the squat lighthouse.

"Yeah," she said, "I didn't want to mention that in case you panicked and started running laps of the island and lifting cars up over your head and stuff. But seriously, three days now and nothing but walking and cycling for exercise. I'm impressed with Island Arlo."

Of course, as she put it into words, Mainland Arlo suddenly started rustling around inside, agitating.

"Well, I guess my muscles—our muscles—earned a short rest after this year."

"Yes, they did."

"I think I am almost all rested up now, ready to get back to work."

She sighed and laughed at the same time. "Well, see you around, Island Arlo. It was nice knowing you."

Oh, jeez. Down, Mainland Arlo, relax just a little longer.

I took her hand and started tugging her away from the water and toward the fried clam shack that had already become Island Arlo's favorite place to eat.

"Hey," I said, "third straight day of fried food. I think we can agree that Island Arlo hasn't left us just yet."

"Good," she said cheerily. "A little bit of summer fat never hurt anybody, right?"

"Right," I said.

"And tartar sauce, right? It shouldn't be anywhere near that good, should it? But the clams just scream for it."

"And the clams are absolutely right," I said, nearly breaking into my first run of the week just to get to the counter that much quicker.

\* \* \*

The fourth day I woke up knowing right away things were different. Nothing drastic, but as I lay in bed right by the window, listening to the surf pounding just a couple of hundred yards away, I couldn't quite *feel* it like the other mornings.

Island Arlo was giving way to Mainland Arlo.

The partly cloudy morning may have had something to do with it. The fact that August was only twenty-four hours away surely had something to do with it. It meant football was coming over the horizon like the sunrise coming up on the whole year.

And, maybe, the fact that I was finally going to meet Sandy's Nantucket friends could have been influencing my feelings.

\* \* \*

"He has a *boat*?"

"Yes, Arlo, the answer to that is the same as it was last time, and all the other times. Gordon has a boat."

Since we were walking along the wooden pier of the marina, between rows of boats—because we were invited out on Gordon's boat—I did pretty much believe that he had a boat. But I still couldn't believe that he had a boat. I never knew anyone who had a boat.

"I'll have a boat, when I make it," I said, sounding so stupid even to myself that I was going to have to raise my game a lot just to achieve *jock moron* level.

Sandy skidded her flip-flops to a halt and grabbed both of my arms.

"If you could stop acting like this, that would be really good, Arlo."

"I'm sorry, Sandy. I'm just a little nervous, meeting your friends."

"Well, that is sweet but unnecessary. As much as I like seeing you be underconfident for a change, I've seen it now, so . . ."

"Right, I won't be a dope."

"Great," she said, and led me by the hand toward the sleek, handsome boat with the two sleek, handsome people on deck waving at us.

"Is it actually *his* boat, though? Not his father's, or a family boat or a rental or something?"

Her fingernails started digging into my hand until I yelped.

Happily, the boat was one of the smallest in the marina, and

Gordon and Sasha couldn't have been more friendly, so I was starting to settle down nicely as Gordon began *putt-putting* us out of the marina.

"Boat Basin," the skipper called back over his shoulder to the three of us sitting on benches behind the wheel.

"What?" both Sandy and Sasha called.

"Boat Basin," he called a little louder. "Somebody back there keeps calling this the marina, but actually, it's known as the Boat Basin."

I stared at a spot right between our host's shoulder blades, wishing there was a number twelve there.

"Thanks, Gordon!" I yelled. "The someone was me. I'm still getting up to speed around here."

"Ah, we'll get you straight," he said with a no-look wave.

"And we *will*," Sasha said, patting my knee warmly. Sandy stared just a bit wide-eyed at the hand-knee contact.

I decided my quick judgment was a little rash, and that Gordon was maybe a little less down-to-earth than I figured. But Sasha seemed even more friendly than I'd guessed, so that seemed to even it out.

The girls launched into such a high-speed debriefing of each other's lives, it seemed in stretches to be an entirely different language. I smiled with what I hoped was a mysterious, intelligent smile and looked at the predominantly white sky, then around at the other watercraft, then back at the girls. The motion of the boat was nice, and I could have settled into this state happily.

"Arlo," Gordon called just as I had closed my eyes, "come on up here, man."

193

"Aye, aye, Captain."

"What do you think of my boat?" he asked in a voice that was so openly proud and not bragging that I couldn't even get irritated over it. Not much at least.

"Nicest boat I've ever been on," I said. I turned back, hoping Sandy could see what a good guest I could be.

"Thanks, man," he said. "Here, want to take the wheel for a bit?"

"What?" I said quickly. "Really? Thanks, but I never even—"

"Don't worry," he said, stepping aside and pulling me into the pilot's position. "It's open water now, so you can't get into too much trouble. Just steer gently, and early, away from anything out ahead. And this lever down here is the throttle—up for faster, back for slower. Don't touch it."

"Aye, aye," I said, taking the wheel and already stupid with excitement.

"Good," Gordon said as I steered away from the smallest floating objects. "But usually, the seabirds will get out of your way, so you might want to focus on boats and buoys and that kind of thing."

"Right," I said. "Cool." But I was glad when he moved away.

As I focused on the mildly choppy waters ahead, I heard the *schtick* of a match and turned to see him inhaling on a joint about the size of my middle finger. He held his breath and extended the offer to me.

"Sorry, man, but I take my responsibilities here very seriously. Never on duty." I left out the part that I am *always* on duty.

"Cool," he said, exhaling forcefully enough that the smoke

overcame the wind and entered my airspace. I coughed a little as he headed back to the girls.

I didn't miss him. It was thrilling, soloing already. I enjoyed the ease with which the thing maneuvered in my grip. Another small boat was coming our way and I turned the wheel easily, but then too easily, and I made the turn just a little too quickly. I heard my passengers tumble around a bit and yelp in protest, but I called right back, "I got it, relax, you people," and gave it a calmer, more measured turn. As the other boat passed about twenty yards off to our right, I looked over to the guy at the wheel, half suspecting him to yell at me, too, for some breach of water traffic code that I knew nothing about.

Instead, he gave me a quick salute.

"Oh, I like this," I said, feeling like a brand-new member of the Society of Boat Captains.

"You like what?" Sandy said, appearing beside me.

"Oh," I said, "open water. Steering. That kind of thing."

"See?" She put an arm around my waist. "I knew you could fit in here."

She sounded kind of dreamy-dopey already, so I just hummed a sort of agreement.

"Okay, okay, your time's up," Sasha said, bumping me and Sandy aside with one sharp hip-check.

I reluctantly gave way, and we went back to sit with Gordon.

The two of them then went off on their own session of catching up, aided or otherwise by the joint still—or a new one?—live and circulating.

"No, thanks," I said when Sandy offered it to me, maybe thinking that Island Arlo might feel differently.

"There's beers there in the cooler," Gordon said.

"Thanks," I said, but returned to my earlier routine of looking around while the wind whipped and the boat bounced on choppier waters. It wasn't as good this time, partly with the rockier conditions making it less relaxing, and partly because Sandy and Gordon began to talk about plans for high-intensity summer workouts.

I found it hard to speak. In my head I was obsessing over being at the helm again, in charge of the boat instead of back where I was. I started feeling a little nauseous. And panicky. Like I never, ever felt at home.

To make things worse, Gordon jumped up and whipped off his shirt to reveal his Olympic swimmer physique.

"Stop here, Sasha!" he yelled, and Sasha cut the engine. As soon as she did, he was overboard, diving fearlessly into the water.

"Come on," Sandy said to me, stunningly stripping down to her bathing suit and dropping her clothes right there into a pile with his.

The boat now rocked and rolled in a dramatic way.

"What, swim? Right there, in the ocean?" I pointed at the thing for emphasis.

She giggled machine gun–like. "Yeah. It's the same ocean we've been in all week."

"No," I insisted. "That was the *beach*. This is the *ocean*."

"Suit yourself," she said, shrugging. Before I could say another word, she had dived right in and was splashing around with Gordon.

The ocean, as if it heard me and was insulted, increased its churning.

"You can take the wheel now," Sasha called as I sat on the bench and stared at the shiny white painted deck.

"No, thank you," I called.

"Come on. I want to go in. You just need to steer in a circle so the boat doesn't float away while we're swimming."

"No, thank you," I called again. A lifetime of good manners was being wiped out in short order, but I could not manage to care enough now.

Sasha started yelling something angrily at me when I gave in to the inevitable and hurled myself to the side, then hurled my insides into the water.

I saw before me every clam I had eaten this week and probably ever, returning to the sea.

I was utterly convinced now that the ocean knew just what it was doing. It had such absolute power.

And I had less than none.

I continued with my head over the side because my being sick just would not stop. Sandy came out of the water and sat rubbing my back like some dream mermaid-nurse until I begged her to please stop touching me. Sasha yelled some more and Sandy relieved her, while I dangled over the other side, puking helplessly until saliva just trailed out of my mouth and into the salt water and I didn't even bother wiping my mouth on the back of my hand anymore. If my chumming up the waters managed to attract Jaws and I saw him rushing straight up at me, my head was going to be all his and he was welcome to it.

Somehow time stopped and restarted, and I felt the engine rumbling underneath me again and the rolling of the boat lessening as we chugged back toward the island.

"I'm sorry," I said to Sandy.

"It's not your fault," she said in a voice that was about equal parts sympathetic and *yes, it is your fault.*

"You should just drop me and go back out," I said.

"No," she said. "Of course not."

It was kind of weak.

"You're thinking about it," I said. "I wish you would. . . . It'll help me be just a little bit less humiliated."

"Good point," she said. "Win-win."

"Stretching the idea of win-win a bit," I said, my face still only a few feet off the surface of the water, "but basically, yeah."

She patted my back gently. I asked her not to, gently.

Eventually I was aware of the boat powering down and I sat up to see us very near the shore. It was not the spot we had launched from.

"Not taking him back to the marina?" Sasha asked.

"Boat Basin," I said, congratulating myself inside my head for finally showing my fun side.

"No," he said. "We'll take him into the cove. He can wade in, and we won't have to deal with all that boat traffic so we'll be right back out to sea."

"Okay?" Sandy said, and as I spotted the bottom underneath the clean blue-green of the water, I was overjoyed enough to say okay before basically allowing my carcass to slide over the side like a navy burial at sea.

I went under and then right back up, feeling chilled and thrilled and grateful all at once. I stood and started wading in to the beach.

"We won't be too long," Sandy called as Gordon immediately peeled out or whatever it is that boats do in that situation. "Hang out here or head back to the house, whatever."

"Whatever," I said, waving with what I hoped was nonchalance.

I wobbled onto the perfect white sand of the empty cove beach, just like a scene from a shipwreck movie. As I got my feet into the dry, warm sand, I had a sudden urge to hit something, get up a good head of steam and just crush the first thing to cross my path. But my legs were still shaking and my stomach still flipping, so the only thing I managed to hit was the earth itself.

I dropped to my knees, then fell forward onto my hands, then my chest. I closed my eyes and fell quickly asleep. I dreamed, vividly, about playing football. Running, howling, throwing off blockers and destroying ballcarriers.

I woke up out of breath.

And hungry. For normal food. So I headed toward the Boat Basin, past anyplace that looked like it sold seafood of any kind, until I got to Joanne's Burgers and Fries. There was a girl my age slumped and bored on her little counter behind the window.

Several minutes later I was walking toward the docks once more with a 7-Up in one hand and a basket of fries in the other. The burger, which was a little dry but otherwise glorious, didn't last the time it took me to dump the wrapper in the closest trash barrel. I was no longer feeling sick, but I was not back to my full strength, either.

Uneasy, was how I felt. Wrong. Weak. I was nobody here. No one cared how much I could lift, how well I could read an offensive formation, or what my time was in the forty.

Tomorrow was August. August was football.

I was certain I was not where I belonged.

* * *

"This is really stupid, Arlo," Sandy said as she walked me to the ferry the following morning.

I was upbeat and took no offense. "Yeah," I said.

"Lots of people get seasick. It's no reason to go running home. This is an insane overreaction."

"It's not the seasick, I keep telling you. Don't get me wrong. I had a great first few days, but I realized that's my limit. You have a fine island here, but as far as I'm concerned they should change the name from Nantucket to Krypton."

Somewhere in there she stopped walking, because I found myself unaccompanied. I stopped and turned back toward her.

"You are not Superman, Arlo Brodie."

I marched back and took her by the hand.

"I know that," I reassured her. "Not here, I'm not."

She tried then to yank her hand out of mine, but I pulled her toward the ferry and home and my strength was surging back to me.

"All right, you," she said, laughing but also growling. "By the time I get back, after training with *Gordon* every day, you'll never be able to hold me like this again."

It was a brilliant play on her part, because it caused me to release the grip instantly and stop in my tracks.

Her killer smile said she knew just how well played it was.

"All right yourself," I said. "It's *on*."

Not sure if it was a make-up call on my part for being weird, or on her part for Gordoning me, or more likely both, but the kiss we had at the dock just before I got on the ferry was the sweetest thing that ever happened to my big stupid face.

As I watched her waving to me from the pier for much longer than I deserved, and I hung over the rail waving back, I was thinking how great it was that she fit wherever she was. And I was thinking I never wanted to feel that powerless again.

We needed to be home, to be *us*.

* * *

"Hey, Goldilocks, what are you doing in my bed?" I said when I finally returned to my home and my room and my brother.

He slowly rotated like a big bony rotisserie chicken. He raised himself up on his elbow, blinked seventy-five times at me, then scanned the surroundings.

"Christ," he said, "this is your room."

He rattled his bones up and walked blindly across the room in his underwear and out. I walked all around, sniffing every corner for foul smells before finally relaxing.

Welcome home.

# JUNIOR YEAR

# SEPTEMBER

I had arrived home feeling fat and slow and furious with myself for letting this happen. Your conditioning is one thing that is always within your control, and when something is within your control, you *control* it. No excuses.

Which was why I was happy enough that Dinos wasn't home from his Greek holiday for another couple of weeks, because I was ready to pay the price for slacking and he would never have agreed the price was worth it. I ran and lifted and ran and lifted and ate and slept and ran and lifted every day leading up to football camp, to the point where I was almost satisfied with how my body felt and how my mind felt about how my body felt. Almost.

Then finally, camp. Two-a-days. Sweaty, backbreaking, soul sapping, officially sanctioned varsity tests of strength, stamina, intelligence, commitment, and manhood. Morning and afternoon sessions.

I wished they were four-a-days.

I have always loved September, ever since I was a little kid and started school and recognized differences in the calendar that didn't involve Christmas or my birthday. A lot of my friends would start complaining about being told what to do for another nine months, but that part of it never bothered me.

I loved the change in the weather, the knowledge of the more serious changes coming right behind it. I loved the structure of school, and the work.

But now all that stuff was just background music to the opening of football season. I was delirious. I was established at this point, a junior, with a year of varsity behind me and big expectations ahead. I was no scrub kid anymore. Now I would be a leader, and a force, and I thumped my way around that preseason camp like I wanted everyone to recognize that fact, and if they didn't like it to just do something about it.

Nobody did anything about it. Not a single senior.

"Easy there, Brodie, easy!" Coach Fisk yelled as we neared the end of our first practice during the week before our first game.

"No problem, Coach!" I bellowed as I pulled Anderson, the right offensive guard, up off the ground. We had been beating on each other all afternoon because so many of the offensive plays were being run through him and right at me, and it was a war.

"Save it for the game, gentlemen!" Coach roared.

Anderson allowed me to help him up, but his hate was written in his bulging eyes and the explosiveness of every block he laid on me. I hated him, too. It was glorious.

It was pretty commonly assumed that Anderson was on the 'roids, which explained the inhuman bulk of him, the back acne, and the fistful of Division 1 recruitment letters that started pouring in for him on September 1.

I didn't care what Anderson did to himself, only what he did to me. Scare me, dare me, hurt me, improve me.

"Comin' atcha, Brodie!" he barked from down in his stance.

I was in a half crouch but straightened right up to give him a bright smile and welcoming wide arms.

The quarterback took the snap and turned for the handoff as the lines engaged. Their job was to open that hole between the center and right guard to spring that halfback through and onto open spaces. Ours was to see that that hole never opened or was plugged again just as quick if it did. But the defensive tackle, Ottaker, who'd been lining up opposite Anderson all day, had clearly had all he could take. He might as well have started every play already down on his back with his hands covering his face.

So the big boy was mine. All day.

*Down* went Ottaker, with Anderson trampling right over his chest. Open was the hole, Anderson leading the ballcarrier at a gallop right up through the seam toward my left. I shifted, planted, and took Anderson on at full strength.

*Crrrasshhh.*

I thought I was going forward when I connected with Anderson's shoulder, but somehow I was keeling backward, looking into his face mask and the sky beyond it, and then the blur of a running back leaping over me to greener pastures.

Anderson had me good and down, then good and forearmed for good measure, then I had a hand jammed up under his chin strap bouncing his head back, then he had a big hand inside my face mask and away we went, snarling and snorting.

We were pulling and pounding at each other's helmets as I rolled him over and then he rolled me—and as stupid as it is to be punching a helmet, we were both wildly doing just that when it seemed like fifty football players and coaches and heavy machinery and Tasers and fire hoses got in there and pried us apart.

It was amazing.

\* \* \*

"I admire your spirit, gentlemen," Coach said, his arms folded and his red baseball cap tipped way back on his head. The field was completely cleared of people, and we were sitting on the bench. I knew it was going to go like this. Publicly he had to pretend to be angrier than he was, but privately this is exactly what coaches want to see.

"Thanks, Coach," I said.

Coach Fisk had his face at about the midpoint between my left ear and Anderson's right, but was staring straight ahead like he was talking to somebody way beyond us.

"Your decision making, on the other hand, makes me want to horsewhip you in front of a full stadium."

I might have been inaccurate about his feelings.

He just hovered there, letting the words fizz, while the three of us held our positions. Until a screech broke the calm.

*Phweeeeeeeet!*

He blew so hard into his coach's whistle, police whistle really, it would have knocked me over if I were in front of it. It just about punctured my eardrum. Anderson and I both groaned and rubbed hard at our ears.

"That, gentlemen," Coach Fisk said as he fell back into normal Coach speechmaking position, "is the sound of the whistle that signals the stoppage of play. I expect all players, but especially top-of-the-food-chain players, to learn that sound and to learn how to respond to that sound. Regardless of whether it is in real game-time action or in practice, my players heed that sound, or my players do not play. Is there anything ambiguous in that statement?"

"No, Coach," we both said enthusiastically.

Anderson slyly turned his gigantic head in my direction and opened the sound-making hole. "*Ambiguous* means not understand—"

"Really?" I cut in, "I thought amBIGuous was what happened when you took too many ster—"

"Great, men," Coach cut in. "Great. Camaraderie, good-natured horseplay, team building, *that's* what I like to see among my leaders. Now, shake hands and make up for the first and last intrasquad altercation of the season."

Anderson looked like this was killing him, which was a bonus. For my part, I was happy to shake his hand. Not out of love but out of thanks. He was doing more for me as an athlete than probably anybody, even Coach.

I stuck out my hand. He took it.

Lord, he was strong. We shook long, and we both squeezed, but jeez, I was starting to feel the cartilage in my hand crackle and hoped I was the only one who could hear it.

*Phweeeeeeet,* Coach screeched with his whistle, hurting my ears again but making my hand eternally grateful.

I would not forget that sound again.

# SUBS AND SCRUBS

"Maybe you'd do better lifting the weight with your belly, man," I said at just the right make-or- break moment between Dinos and the last rep on the bench press. "Seriously, aren't you embarrassed about the way you look?"

"Rrrrrrrraaaaaaawwwww!" he shouted loud enough to rattle the wire-reinforced windows right out of their frames. He got that weight up one more time without any physical help from me. I was expecting some gratitude.

Instead, he popped right up off the bench and got strangely close to my face.

"Okay, so you're a stud. You're Starlo the Stud. Do you *really* need to be a jackass now just so everybody gets it?"

I was stunned stupid. Dinos was always the last guy to take that kind of ribbing seriously.

"Calm down, man," I said. "What happened in Greece to make you come back all sensitive about yourself all of a sudden?"

"I'm not all sensitive about myself," he said, going so far as to poke me in the chest as he said it. "I'm sensitive about *you*. I mean, it's great to have a whiff of confidence, but Arlo, you smell like shit so far this year."

For the first time since football started up again, I was back on my heels. Dinos, my best friend whose name wasn't Sandy, was putting it to me in a way I shouldn't have had to tolerate from *anybody*.

"I'm not that bad," I said.

"You are exactly that bad."

I was starting to get mad. "Well, maybe I was doing it for your own good, Dinos, ever think of that? Maybe I have to push you a little harder because I see what's happening to you, and I don't want to see you stuck with the subs and scrubs for your senior year."

"I *am* a sub! I'm perfectly happy being a scrub. If Coach gave me more snaps, I'd ask if I could give them to somebody else. I'm going to the University of Wisconsin–Madison next year because I'm putting in the work to make that happen and I can't wait. Football will have no part in my life. Football is for numbskulls. You know why I'm playing football this year? Two reasons. First is that it's a laugh and a nice part of my portfolio of senior year experiences. And second, because my best friend is a numbskull."

"Okay, fatboy, now *you* listen to a couple of things—"

"No. No couple of things. I have committed to this unreasonable workout schedule with you even though I don't need it anymore because it's our thing, and I am supporting you while I can. So you can puff out your chest for the rest of the world and act superior to everybody else if you want to, but you cannot do it to me. And the next time you say something to throw me off instead of hollering brainless encouragement like you're supposed to when I'm trying to complete my last rep, I will take that steel bar and whatever plates are on it and as my *final,* final rep I will shove the whole show right up your ass."

Holy hell.

"Holy hell, Dinos. Jackass, and shit smell, and numbskull?"

He nodded, right up closer to my face than I would ever again let a guy get.

"You're gonna miss me," he said.

And only at that exact second did it occur to me that I would, possibly, in the future. Right now it was only out of respect for our history that I held back from pile driving his fat head right into the concrete floor.

* * *

"Not as much as *I'm* gonna miss him," Sandy said as we sat on her porch and I related the whole thing to her. "Who else is going to force anything like that kind of humility on you?"

That was not at all what I was aiming for in sharing this story with her.

"One, nobody's forcing anything on me. And two, what's humility ever done for anyone?"

She rushed her words then, like that airspace had to be filled right away. "Please tell me that was a joke, Arlo. No, really, please."

I pulled her close to me because I thought that was the smart thing to do.

"Absolutely," I said. "Sandy, I'll tell you anything you need me to."

I thought, wholeheartedly, that I had said a really good thing there.

But when she yanked out from under my grip—and true to her word, she had gotten even stronger over the summer—and disappeared into her house with nothing more than a sharp "Night," I had to consider otherwise.

The nightly walk between Sandy's house and mine was suddenly a lonely and uncertain thing. I had managed to piss off both of my most reliable supporters, just when I was hitting my stride everywhere else. Maybe this was going to be something to get used to, with every year, with every new level and bigger stage. People would get used to it. We'd all adjust. If I was just patient, people would catch up and everything would be fine.

"Again?" I said, finding Lloyd in my bed when all I wanted was to fall into it. "What is going on? Get out of there. I need to crash, Lloyd, right now, and I have no time for any more of this nonsense from anybody today. I mean it, get the hell out. Now." I shoved the side of his head, and he still didn't stir.

"Can't you just leave him alone?" Ma said from behind me.

I spun toward her. "Are you joking?" I said. "Ma, the freak has come into *my* room and stolen *my* bed, and you are telling me to leave him alone?"

She looked at me as if I were blowing snakes out of my nose rather than being the only rational person in the room.

"You have everything, Arlo," she said. "You are on your way

to getting everything you have ever wanted. Everything you *both* ever wanted. Can you show just a little kindness and leave him be for now? Would it be such a big sacrifice to just trade rooms for tonight?"

"No, Ma," I said to her tired and sad face because you'd have to be an even bigger jackass, stink breath, numbskull than Starlo to say all the things I was thinking to that face.

"Good boy," she said, then patted my cheek and headed off to her own room.

"Good boy, big man," I heard at my back.

I entered the hallway and ran right into Dad, who was standing there with a scowl and an opinion. "Maybe he's the way he is because of crap like this, Emma," he said.

"Don't start, Louis," she said, brushing past him on the way to their room.

We stood looking at each other. "You don't have to do this, son," he said. "I'll go in there and haul him out myself, rather than see him get away with what he's doing to—"

I reached out and squeezed his arm, to reassure him, thank him, and quiet him. He was right but Ma was frazzled, and it was going to be a serious no-win for everybody if we blew this up. Instead, we were going to have to live with a win-for-Lloyd, whatever it was he was playing. "Just for tonight, Dad, we'll let it go. But thanks. And good night."

"Good night," he sighed, and turned away.

"Good night," Lloyd chirped.

I was fortunately tired enough that I was able to walk away, and to make my way through whatever state his room was in, fall down onto the bed, and reach unconsciousness before I had to think too much about it.

I thought I was dreaming unpleasantly, but then I realized my dreams at their worst never came with that smell.

"You have everything, big man," he was saying, and my eyes opened to the sight of boxer shorts that should have been changed five days ago hovering six inches in front of me. "Do you have to have my bed, too? Can you leave me nothing at all, big man?"

I had no idea how much I had slept, other than to know it wasn't nearly enough. But like a radio-controlled zombie, I heeded his wishes, because of Ma's wishes, and got out of his bed and his room and his wicked way.

"Good boy, big man," said my personal sandman, again.

Big man would not be good boy much longer if this kept up. Ma or no Ma.

# HITS AND LISTS

Two days before our opening game of the season, Coach made me defensive cocaptain.

On our team it was an almost completely ceremonial title, since Coach Fisk made every important decision himself from the sidelines. But still, it meant something. It meant he had faith in me. It meant the other guys were going to look to me as a leader. It meant I was excelling not just among this group here but also in the bigger picture, because he announced that I was the first junior ever to receive the honor.

That meant the most to me. That meant Coach considered me special.

And making captain was on my Hit List.

"What is this stupid thing?" Lloyd said, laughing in a not so nice way as I walked into the house all pumped up with the news.

He was walking again out of *my* bedroom, holding a small notebook. The Hit List.

He was coming straight in my direction, with his head down so he could keep reading and cackling.

He used to know better than to keep his head down like that.

I burst forward just as he started to look up, and I cracked the top of my skull right into his forehead, sending him sprawling backward across the floor.

He was lying on his back, his head and shoulders across the goal line and into my room, when I stood over him. He was wincing with pain, still grinning like a jack-o'-lantern, and incredibly, still reading.

"Does that say MVP?" he croaked, turning the notebook toward me so I could help him out.

I snatched it out of his hand.

"You should reverse a couple of things, though. You shouldn't marry Sandy before you go number one in the NFL draft."

"Lloyd, cut it out. Stop digging around in my stuff."

"It was right there out in the open, in the third drawer down underneath all your underarmor big man shirts."

I crouched down low to him. "Why are you doing this stuff? Why are you all of a sudden obsessed with being all into my shit?"

He stopped grinning, increased wincing.

"I was the big man, you know, big man? I was *your* big man. I'm the one who showed you how to hit."

He waited.

As far as I was concerned he could keep waiting. I liked him right down there where he was.

"You probably ain't even doing it right," he said. "Not since I haven't been there to show you. They'll figure you out, then they'll bring your chicken ass down. I remember, don't forget. I remember how scared you were. Don't forget. You should add to the very end of that list: *Everybody figures me out and I crawl home to Lloyd.*"

Every molecule of me was voting for the same thing, and that was to give Lloyd such a pummeling that he would remember nothing else his whole life.

But fortunately something smarter, something better, overruled the impulse and I stood up. I stepped over him into my room, and slowly pushed the door closed, plowing his head and shoulders right out into the hallway as it shut. "Stay out of here or else, Lloyd."

He laughed as he slowly bumbled to his feet. "That act might be working on the rest of the world, big man. But you *know* you're powerless with me. I own you."

His laughter was fading as I punched my door hard. Then it got twice as loud.

At least I could now stop pretending that the head-butt didn't also punish me. I cupped both hands over my skull and flopped down onto the bed.

* * *

Friday, the last practice before opening day, Coach shut me down.

"What?" I hollered at him as I came off the field while man-on-man blocking drills raged on behind me. I adored man-on-man blocking drills.

"Calm down, Mr. Brodie, calm down," he said in a not-so-calm voice of his own that reminded me cocaptain was still not superior to Coach.

"Sorry, Coach," I said. "I just don't understand—"

"You're ready."

"I sure am," I said. "Ready for anything and everything, which is why I want to be back out there banging."

"Which is why you're gonna stand right here next to me for the rest of practice and observe. You don't need to be using up any more of your bang on our own guys."

"Don't worry about that, Coach, I feel like I've got enough bang for everybody."

"Tomorrow," he said, turning his attention back to the guys on the field.

"Yeah, but Coach . . . ," I started, but he continued watching the guys and made a pointing gesture with two fingers, indicating I should be doing the same.

"You see big Anderson there?" he said as the monster lined up across from Dinos.

"Kind of hard not to."

"Watch after the snap. Watch his feet."

The center snapped the ball, the quarterback took it and started into his usual very deep drop back. His linemen pulled back into the mobile force field of beef that gave him time to read the field, find an open receiver, plant and unload a throw strong and accurate enough to connect. Dinos was as usual no more than a minor threat, and I watched Anderson's feet the whole time he dominated my pal.

Anderson had great feet for such a hulk. Light and fast, seeming like they were always moving but always somehow rooted as well.

"He has good feet," I said, trying to be accurate without being generous. "But to be fair, Dinos has ridiculously small feet, so the balance matchup there is way one-sided."

Pass completed, and the players lined up again.

"That it?" Coach said, unamused. "If that's your idea of analysis, Captain, you might not go all that far in this business after all."

The center snapped the ball. The quarterback dropped back.

"Every third step," Coach snapped. "Pay attention."

The offensive linemen again did a pretty job of protection, dropping into a perfect sickle shape as they backpedaled in sync with each other and the QB. It would look impressive enough just as an agility exercise, but with each guy also manhandling his opposing lineman at the same time, this was real art.

And Anderson the fat jerk was the artist of them all. Dinos was dogged as well as tricky with his hands and strong. And he was a great big tumbleweed sailing by as the quarterback stepped up past the rush, into the snuggle of that sickle, and threw a long bomb that connected and made all the offense boys hop and howl and party like the championship was theirs already.

"He crosses over," I said to Coach as I continued monitoring Anderson's feet even though they were just taking him to the cooler for a drink. "Every third step, in pass protection, he crosses over."

"Whenever he's working his man outside and past the play. It gives him almost an extra half step of momentum, makes him all the faster in his reverse. Adds a little hitch, too, that confuses the hell out of defensive linemen."

221

I was still watching Anderson's feet as he walked back out to the field and formation.

"And it leaves him open," I said with breathless wonder and joy, as if I just caught Santa waving to me before going back up the chimney.

"It does, for an instant."

"His left foot is off the ground and crossed behind his right ankle, he's starting to lean heavy left, he's vulnerable right there to a hard left forearm—*Bam!*—ribs, under his left arm . . ."

In my head, of course, I was doing just that, and Anderson's center of gravity shifted, tilted, and he toppled hard onto the ground to the outside of the play where Dinos was supposed to go.

Coach was looking at me now, with my knees just slightly bent, my left forearm in follow-through. "Did it work?" he said with a grin.

"Did it ever," I said, grinning back.

I straightened up and watched intently as they ran one more before switching to a few run-defense scenarios to finish the day.

"Does he know he does that?" I asked Coach as the punch-and-grunt of play resumed.

"I made sure he does," Coach said. "But he said to me, 'Yeah, but Coach Fisk, it does a lot more good for my game than any possible bad. And we both know there ain't anybody in this league who'll be causing me any worries anyway.' And thing is, he's probably right."

Just for that one second, I wished I could transfer to another school within the league.

"I'd cause him worries," I said, sounding less like a human speaking than a dog guarding his house.

"Teammates don't talk like that, Captain."

"Sorry, Coach, didn't mean it that way." Though I absolutely did. "I just meant, if I had that kind of challenge presented to me, I'd like to think—"

"I know what you meant," he said. "It's good for exceptional players, the few who are going on to bigger things eventually, to learn these things so they can test each other all year in practice. Makes everybody better and more prepared for the next level."

"Yes, sir," I said.

"Pay closer attention. Arlo. To the fine details. Stay alert. Learn, and then use what you learn."

"I will, Coach."

Coach nodded, blew his whistle loudly to stop everybody where they were, and started walking out to point out the rights and wrongs of the details.

"Oh, and by the way," he said, stopping like he had just forgotten something important, "he knows you know. And he knows you know he knows. Thought it was only fair to tell him first, see if he could make any adjustments before you got at him."

He was smiling and pointed now at whatever giveaway expression I was making.

"Ah, see, I can tell already. You're already a better player. And so is he. It's great when everybody wins, isn't it?"

He spun and jogged toward the team, barking at the guys who got flattened first.

It's great when *I* win. Everybody doesn't have to win. In fact, everybody can't, or else there would be no such thing as a winner.

* * *

I woke up before five the morning of the first game. There was no chance I would get back to sleep, either. I knew that already from the adrenaline surging as the kickoff played itself out in my head.

I stood up, did some cartoonishly fast stretching.

"Pace yourself, Captain," I said, stopping mid-toe-touch. I found myself staring up close at the little kid notebook that now was so obviously, embarrassingly, a little kid's dream book.

I picked it up and tore it, shredded it over my wastebasket until it was no kind of book at all. I watched it feather down, like at the end of the Super Bowl when all that confetti hails the winners and tortures the losers right there in front of the whole world.

"Oh, I'm doing it right, pal," I said as I dressed and gathered my gear. "I know how to hit, and everybody is going to know it."

I was glad it was so early as I crept through and out of the house. This was my time.

I'd be there to greet the custodian when he opened up the locker room. I'd help load the equipment. I'd be first man on the bus. I'd drive the thing if they let me.

Hit List, I thought as I strode down the silent street. Who needs a Hit List? I *am* the Hit List.

* * *

We beat them 28–0, and I felt like I existed the whole time in some zone I never reached before. I just knew. I knew on the way to the bus, I knew in the bus on the way to the other side of town. I knew in the locker room before the game and during the kickoff.

I especially knew when I stood upright, in the center of the field, in the center of our defensive unit—my defensive unit—and I stared straight through everything right into their quarterback's eyes. I stared so deep into him that I not only knew I was breaking him before even the first snap, I felt like I had just downloaded their entire game plan directly into my brain.

I was paying attention, like Coach told me to, to every little detail. I looked over to him just before that first snap, and he gave me just what I was looking for. I had the green light to blitz, on the first play of the game.

It was like I was launching out of a sprinter's starting blocks. I scorched on an absolutely straight line, past our guys, through their stunned defensive line, untouched until I smashed right into the quarterback as he tried to set up for a throw. He never saw me, but he felt me. I drove him hard, forward and down into the turf while the ball didn't even make the trip with him.

By the time I got up, there was a big scrum for the ball right where the quarterback had been standing. When the smoke cleared, we had possession of the ball and the game, right there. I looked back at the QB as he climbed slowly to his feet. Again, he looked at me, too. Good-bye phony confidence, hello very long day.

He was mine already. I was in his head.

It went like that for all four quarters.

I focused on punishment. I was hitting every other one of their guys hard enough to either force them to play harder, or put them on the Physically Unable to Perform list. Technically, the PUP list was strictly a pro thing, and high schools wouldn't have them. But I liked the sound of it.

Late in the third quarter the QB figured he'd catch us napping and dumped a quick pass over the middle to their tight end. He was taller than me, fast, athletic, skinny, and should have stuck with basketball.

*Bam!*

The collision was violent enough to make a sound that reverberated around the half-empty stands and pop the other guy's helmet right off. There was all kinds of noise, mostly from our players woofing and their guys screeching.

I stood over the guy as he lay there flat on his back, looking dazed but holding on to the damn ball.

I reached down and offered him a hand up.

As I started pulling, the crown of my head started screaming pain like somebody was trying to open my lid with a screwdriver. I had never felt anything like this, and the sensation of tearing the top of my own skull away from my brain caused me to reflexively place my free hand on top of my helmet to hold everything together. The guy got up, but I remained hunched for several more seconds while the blood pulsed and pulsed hard enough to blast through the bone, the helmet, and the hand. Then it eased off, just enough. I lowered my hand, then looked straight ahead at players returning to huddles and a referee coming my way. It got tolerable when I straightened up again, and I could look the ref in the eye.

I got whacked with a fifteen-yard illegal hit penalty even though the helmet-to-helmet thing was accidental. Anyway, the fifteen yards meant nothing at all to the game. But the hit did. They didn't attempt a single pass play for the rest of the day.

By the closing two minutes, the game had become kind of hypnotic with its grinding regularity. You could see their team now just wishing the clock to wind down.

Except for one guy, a stocky, slow running back everybody called The Plow, who never really quit, bless his Clydesdale heart. It was kind of sadly heroic, the way he just kept taking the ball, moving a couple of yards forward, and then absorbing one gang tackle after another. Last play from scrimmage with under a minute to go and those guys inside our thirty-yard line, Plow broke through the line with the one short burst of speed he must have been saving all day.

From the other side of the field, I saw that he had a legitimate chance to score, and that our guys seemed almost to be letting him have it.

No. That is not how the game is played.

Let him have it?

Despite tiring legs, I turned on the jets and bolted for the far sideline, where he was chugging for that corner flag. I pumped and pumped, hauled, growled, and caught him at the two-yard line.

*Bam!*

I let him have it, the way you're supposed to let them have it.

The Plow had been huffing so hard for the goal line he didn't even look my way before I caught him full-on, banging hard into his shoulder and sending him sprawling and crashing sideways, cartwheeling out of bounds, and landing a good ten yards away.

That was it, really. The whistle blew and the other team finally got to slouch away.

"Did somebody kill your dog or somethin' man?" Jerome yelled as he bounded up the stairs of the bus and came my way. The bus was already rocking with rowdy celebration when I raised my hands for Jerome to slap and he ran right through them to bury me in my seat underneath 240 pounds of fullback.

"Arrrrr!" I called as he splatted me against the seat and I attempted to roll him off. "I don't have a dog! But if I did I woulda killed him myself!"

The team roared and I rolled Jerome and we crashed to the floor between the rows. We laughed and everybody else laughed as we struggled harder to get unwedged from the narrow aisle than we had struggled with anything out on the field.

Jerome had had an excellent day, scoring three brute touchdowns and dragging *four* defenders the final twelve yards on one of them. But I was on another planet the whole game. When we got back up, Jerome headed for the rear of the bus. I got to my seat, saving the one next to me for Dinos, who had just arrived. He looked at the seat for a while before deciding to take it.

"Good game," he said flatly as he finally sat and the bus started off.

"I know," I said.

228

"Make you feel like a big man, that last play, wrecking The Plow?"

"Of course it did," I said, turning away from him and looking out the window.

We didn't talk after that. We just rode. After the big man thing. We just let it go.

# A VIOLENT GAME

"Would you stop that," Sandy said, jumping up to pull my arm down. I had started doing this sort of spoof parade wave—like the Statue of Liberty with a rotating radar dish for a hand—whenever anybody yelled "MVP" or "Starlo" from the other side of the street or the other end of the corridor. When I did it in her kitchen when her parents said hello, she was finally provoked into action.

"Can't you just say, 'Nice to see you, too,' like a regular person?" she said, hanging on to the arm in case I had a relapse.

"Now, Sandrine, if I was just a regular person, I'd never have made it all the way into the kitchen of a girl like you."

Her parents laughed.

"Would you two stop that," she snapped at her folks. "You're just deliberately making him worse and you know it."

"Oh, just having some fun, honey," her dad said. He closed up his laptop, took it and his drink to another location, giving me a big wink on his way.

"And what did I tell you about the winking?" she snapped, letting go of me to take a swipe at his back as he scooted away.

"You should just relax and enjoy the ride," Sandy's mom said, gesturing for us to take the two seats opposite her. "The boy is taking it for the big laugh it is." She enjoyed referring to me as "the boy."

"No, ma'am," I said, objecting with as much politeness as I could manage. "I take the football very seriously."

"Oh," she said, nodding thoughtfully.

"See?" Sandy said, bumping me sideways and almost knocking me out of my chair.

"Well then, if you can't enjoy it so much, then just have patience. How long can this kind of thing last, right?" She extended the bag of Chips Ahoy cookies she'd been nibbling out of.

"Oh, no thank you," I said, "I have to watch what I eat. Especially at night." I checked my watch. Because it had started raining hard, we had abandoned the porch, but I needed to be getting home.

Sandy took a cookie and menaced me with it before turning back to her mother.

"A cookie, right, Mom? He has to watch his figure."

"Ah, you're a picture of strapping good health," she said, "cookie or no cookie." She giggled, started sweeping up crumbs on the table just in front of her.

"All the same," I said, getting up and stretching, "I should probably be getting to bed."

"Fun guy," Sandy's mom said, taking her cupped hand of crumbs to the trash.

"A barrel of laughs," said Sandy.

Out on the porch, I stood with my back to the weather and my forehead to Sandy's forehead.

"I think I should tell you," I said solemnly, "your mom was doing strange things to me with her feet under the table."

Sandy sighed. "You know, big head, I wouldn't be surprised if you thought everybody in the world was playing footsie with you."

"Well, they're not. Not yet anyway. But when they do, I'll tell every last foot that I am totally taken forever."

She shook her head, rolling it back and forth against mine. "Goof," she said.

"I guess I have to get going," I said.

"I guess," she said.

"Have you thought about it some more?" I said hopefully.

We had left open the possibility that she would come and see me play once this season. So I was checking on that.

The thing was, almost certainly we both wanted her to stay away now. We were good this way, and things could get complicated. She said the high-impact parts of the game were just too difficult to watch. And at this point every part of my game was high impact. So I was asking, if I was being honest, less out of excitement for the idea and more just to get as much advance warning as possible.

"We'll see," she said, making it sound a comfortable distance off. As for now, I could get quite comfortable living with our faces stuck this close.

"All right then," I said, trying to stare more deeply into her eyes, however a person actually does that.

"What's the matter with your eyes?" she said.

I wasn't aware of anything wrong with my eyes. Except maybe a little blurring. Possibly a small headache-related pressure behind them. No big thing. "Um, *love*?" I suggested.

"Your eyes are darting around, like you're expecting somebody to sneak up behind you. Does love make you shifty?" she said, her own eyes narrowing, penetrating.

"You know," I said, snagging a quick kiss and backing away down to the street, "I am sure it does. See you tomorrow, Sand." I started running home through the rain.

* * *

The second game of the season was our first home game, and the growing buzz about the team brought out a lot more spectators than we'd been expecting and they were crazy noisy.

"This is the way it should be," I said to Dinos. We were on the sidelines and pounding on each other's shoulder pads like maniacs.

"Well, you should get used to it, 'cause it's gonna get louder and louder for the rest of your life. I'm just glad I got to hear a little bit of it before it's all over for me."

The referee blew his whistle to get things going. "Don't worry, pal," I said before he rumbled out onto the field with the rest of the kickoff team. "It isn't anywhere near over for you yet, and there's plenty more of this ahead. I'll make sure of it."

This week's opponent was better than last week's. We weren't steamrolling these guys, but after the first quarter we had things in hand with a comfortable 14–3 advantage. Sideline to sideline, I followed every play, worked every angle, and delivered every hit I could. I even enjoyed the long pursuits more, because it felt like a hunt as I tracked the ballcarrier, and it felt like an explosion when I finally hit him with all that momentum.

Coach pulled me aside just before I took the field for the second quarter.

"Energy conservation, Arlo," he said. "If you run around like a madman like you've been doing so far, you're gonna be gassed when we need you the most. Trust your teammates. Let players make plays."

"Okay, Coach," I said without any intention of changing a thing.

What does adrenaline actually taste like? Something tangy and metallic was filling the back of my throat, and I could barely stand still as we waited for the snap.

I read the play immediately. I read the guy, that fullback, and knew he'd be bringing it to me.

The quarterback turned and handed off to the halfback, who took off around the left side but then handed off to the fullback, who was barreling around toward the right flank. Several of our guys went for the fake and were caught out of position, but I was zeroed in on every stride that fullback took.

It was almost an open field tackle when I motored full speed to meet him just after he crossed the line of scrimmage and we both dropped low and brought our high-caliber best into blasting each other away. It was an explosion, of muscle and bone, of padding, of helmet on helmet before we collapsed into each other and onto the turf and the ball skittered off someplace just to escape impact.

I didn't know if there had been a late surge of new fans show-ing up or what, but the sound levels just went off the charts. I was getting patted on the back, the butt, the chest, the shoulder pads by just about everybody within touching distance of me.

Coach put me on the sidelines, and on the bench.

"Well, Arlo, man, I never saw anything like that," Dinos said, getting right up to my ear. My helmet was hanging from my hand. "I think the sparks that came off you guys' helmets on that play must have set some cars on fire out in the parking lot."

"Ha," I said, nodding carefully because my head wasn't so great. I focused on the action on the field. "Our ball, yeah," I said with a single clap.

Dinos sort of curved around to look at me full-on. "Yeah, our ball. You forced the fumble. We recovered."

"Shut up," I said, pushing him sideways out of my view, then wishing I hadn't because of the jolt that went through my skull. "I know that. I was there. Jeez, Dinos."

"Jeez," he said in a funny tone. I didn't look at him.

Our offense didn't get anywhere, so we were back to work on defense. I put on my helmet and started out there, until a grab at my shirt slowed and then stopped me.

"I told you, Arlo," Coach Fisk said. "I'm resting you. There's only a few minutes left in the half, and we're in good shape."

"But, Coach, I just rested already. Just then, just there," I said, pointing to the spot where I had been idling next to Dinos.

"Good, then you know how it's done."

"Coach—"

"Sit!" he barked, and I saw the light.

I sat next to Dinos again, and got all worked up again when the brute fullback carried the ball off tackle, breaking for a fifteen-yard gain and passing right by us.

"Did he wave at me there?" I asked Dinos.

"Jeez, man, no. He did not wave at you."

"What's he doing in the game anyway? I'd think he'd need a *rest* by now."

"I don't know," Dinos said admiringly as the guy sprinted back to his huddle. "He looks pretty fresh to me."

He did, too, dammit.

This would have to be addressed in the second half.

They threw the ball a lot more in the third quarter and I realized I was going to have to work harder on my pass coverage. I didn't have the same precision when I had to backpedal, and a few times I got burned badly when I turned my back to the ball to cover my man close. Actually, every time I turned I got a little off balance and the quarterback and tight end were starting to look at me like meat.

The lack of control I was feeling was starting to get me crazy.

I absolutely needed to get it back.

Deep in the third I recognized the formation and the way the quarterback was checking, pointing, and calling audibles.

This was the time to gamble. They had momentum and they had my number and they had a chance to tie it up with a touchdown. It was my fault, and it was mine to make good.

So I threw in all my chips and ran like a radio-controlled drone right from the snap. I tuned out the mayhem all around me and I just ran to the exact coordinate the ball would be if they had called the play the way I believed they had.

I was right. Completely back-in-control right.

The ball, the tight end, and I had a brilliant star-spangled collision right at that coordinate.

I pounded him right in the numbers, jolting him forward with enough good violence that his face mask pounded into the ground at the same instant that I collected the pass that had bounced off him and waited right there in the air for me to claim it.

The noise cheering me all along down the sidelines made the sixty yards fly under my feet as if I was a hovercraft sailing right over it. I was clear for the touchdown when I became aware that someone was with me. I glanced over my shoulder to see the quarterback, who I knew was fast but didn't know was *this* fast.

He would catch me if I tried to outleg him, so I shifted hard inside, just as he was flying by. Then, rather than avoiding the passer, who was making a day out of tormenting me, I lowered my shoulder, drilled him in the ribs and off his feet, and together we crossed the goal line in the air and together we landed with a thump in the end zone. The momentum and the weight of me caused a great satisfying *oof* sound to come out of him.

By way of a small compensation, as I got up I left the ball resting on his stomach.

When I walked off the field, Coach shook my hand. "That was a lot of running," he said. "You must be gassed."

"You try and take me out of this game again," I said, laughing, "you're gonna have to come right out onto the field and get me yourself."

He held up his hands in surrender, as if I wasn't saying just what he'd want me to say.

We were on fire the rest of the game, and I was in on every play. Gassed as I was, I'll admit I was almost glad when it came to an end, feeling my head buzzing constantly now and my legs getting shaky.

"Might want to start watching it with the illegal hits, pal," the fullback said as we walked in opposite directions. Dinos was next to me.

I had just enough extra juice to engage him in a little trash.

"Sometimes helmets hit helmets. Get used to it. It's a violent game, dude. Or did they forget to tell you that?"

"Well said, sir," Dinos said, patting me on the helmet.

I could have done without that one.

# OUT OF CONTROL

"Have you changed your name? Starlo?" Ma asked, scaring me out of my socks.

"Jeez, Ma," I said, scurrying right past her and barricading myself in the bathroom. It was a bit of a Marley's ghost thing, in my groggy morning state, to find her holding up a newspaper and springing a snap quiz. About myself.

"Sorry, hon," she said as I crept into the kitchen a few minutes later. "I was a little abrupt there. I made you some French toast. Good morning."

"Good morning," I said, taking a seat opposite her. "Aren't you a little late leaving?"

She took an exaggerated swing around to the big clock above the refrigerator, then looked back to me again. "Yes, I am. One might say the same about you, as a matter of fact."

"Yeah," I said, taking a big sip from my tall glass of orange juice. "I guess I was really tired. Slept right through my alarm."

She held up the newspaper again. It was the *Citizen*, the local weekly paper. This was the first time I had any idea Ma read the sports stuff. Apparently they'd written something about me, also a first.

"Well, it's no wonder you're tired, *Starlo*."

Boy, did that sound embarrassing. And coming from my mother, somehow incriminating.

"Oh, that's just a stupid joke Dinos made up."

"Uh-huh. Eat your breakfast. A 'one-man wrecking crew' needs his nourishment as well as his rest."

"Please, it doesn't say that," I said weakly, addressing the French toast.

"Tell you what," she said, getting up and placing the paper next to my plate. "Read it yourself with your breakfast. I'll finish getting ready and I can give you a ride to school."

I found myself eating faster as I read. It was only a couple of paragraphs, but that was one paragraph longer than any of the other games got. And they had done that unhelpful thing of putting random significant names and adjectives in boldfaced type. *Starlo* jumped up at you like a neon billboard.

"Exciting, isn't it?" Ma said, jolting me for the second time.

"I think the guy who wrote it is an old buddy of the coach," I said. I remembered seeing a guy holding a notepad hang during the game. "He's exaggerating here, a lot."

"You're being rather modest for a guy with *Star* in his name," she said. "Did anybody else on your team even play?"

The guy had made it sound like our team was Arlo Brodie and the Forty Scrubs.

"I should be going," I said.

"You're right," she said. "We can talk in the car."

"I think I'll walk," I said weakly.

"I think I'll drive you," she said.

Fortunately, it was less than ten minutes by car to school. Unfortunately, she seemed keenly conscious of this as she rapidly spoke.

"My favorite was 'bone-cracking,'" she said. "What was yours?"

"Ma, please? It's nothing like as bad as he's making it sound."

"He seems to think he's making it sound good, not bad."

"He's making it sound like mayhem," I said, "and it wasn't even close." Not when I was so in control of the game.

We hit a red light because that was the kind of morning it was. She turned to face me.

"Even allowing for exaggeration, Arlo, that article makes it clear that you are putting yourself into regular and intense jeopardy."

It was a stupid thing to do, but I let out a little laugh. "Ma, if you really read it, you'll see that I'm putting the other guys into regular and intense jeopardy."

"You *know* better!" she snapped, marking the third and biggest shock of the morning. "You know your brain doesn't care whether you are the hitter or the hittee."

"Light, Ma," I said, pointing at the green.

She accelerated in a jump, zipped up the last bit of Centre, then I noticed her trying to calm both the car and herself as we rolled down Baker Street toward the front of the school.

"What does Sandy think of all this?" she said.

"She's all right with it," I said, supplying as much as she needed to know.

She pulled up to the curb alongside the wall where Sandy and I liked to sit.

"Huh," she said. "She hasn't been to the house in ages. Let's have her over."

"Oh, jeez," I said to her reasonable suggestion. I was getting out of the car at the right time, because her concern was suddenly filling me with anger. I knew it was wrong, and I knew I couldn't help it. I had to get away from her.

"Hey," she said as I started to close the door.

I stopped, sighed dramatically. She leaned across the seat and said, "My boy has better manners than that."

"Sorry," I said, bending down to kiss her. The sidewalk seemed to swim up for a second.

She stopped just short of my face. "Arlo, your eyes," she said. "They're all bloodshot and—"

I gave her a hard, aggressive kiss on the cheek before pulling right away again. "I'm fine. Worry about Lloyd instead."

I couldn't even believe myself that I had said that. She had been babying him, yes, overlooking the antisocial hours he was keeping, and overpraising his every successful venture out to make a delivery and come back unharmed, yes. So what about all that? So what if she couldn't manage to appreciate what everyone else in the world could see as my stonking great success?

I didn't need to be bothered by all that.

I slapped the door shut and scurried toward school like the rat I was.

* * *

"Oh, Arlo, you didn't," Sandy said as we sat in the cafeteria having lunch. The acoustics in the place always irritated me, making two hundred kids sound like two thousand, even stupider than they were.

"Oh, Sandy, yes I did." I was trying to tell her how my mother had taken the article all wrong, but I didn't seem to be getting my message across.

She stared at me with one raised eyebrow. "You going to get snappy with *me* now?"

"Was that snappy?" I asked, though I didn't particularly care what the answer was. "Sorry."

"Well, that was one lame sorry. You'll need to practice that before you apologize to your mother. Then you should also invite me over to dinner like she wants."

"I shouldn't even have told you that," I said. I speared a meatball off my plate and pointed to her boneless chicken and green salad with it. "You eat like a runner anyway," I said, and popped the meatball into my mouth.

"Okay. So?" she whipped back.

I wanted to follow up, but I didn't know what with. I shrugged instead and went back to work on my food.

Sandy also concentrated on eating, faster than she normally did. And she stopped talking, which she normally didn't.

"What's wrong with you anyway?" I said as she finished her last bite.

She looked at me flatly as she chewed and swallowed before responding. "I don't think I'm liking you very much today," she said.

"What?" I said. "You know, I was hoping for a little more understanding from you at least."

She stood, picked up her tray.

"I do have understanding, Arlo. For your mother. Maybe she can see that Lloyd is damaged goods. That has to be hard for her. And maybe she's trying to get through to you so she doesn't have two punch-drunk Lloyds on her hands."

With that, she took a step away from the table.

My hand shot out.

"What do you mean by that?" I said as I grabbed Sandy's arm, forcefully.

I *grabbed* Sandy's arm, forcefully.

I grabbed Sandy's arm, *forcefully.*

I grabbed *Sandy's* arm. Forcefully.

She looked at me, icy cold. She looked at my hand on her arm as I released my grip. Then she looked back at me as I opened my mouth to begin a lifetime of apologizing.

"Sandy, I—"

That's as far as I got before she opened both of her hands, releasing the tray to crash and clatter, halfway onto the table and then all the way onto the floor.

The students outside of our immediate area erupted with hoots and applause the way they were supposed to when someone dropped a tray. The ones right around us, the ones who could see, remained dead silent.

"Clean up your mess, Starlo," Sandy said, and left me there in that horribly bright light and ear-blasting racket of the cafeteria.

It felt like the evil mirror image of Saturday football as I squatted down to clean up the mess.

* * *

I didn't begin to feel right that day until I was headed to practice after school. The awful edginess was finally releasing, like when your hand or your foot regains feeling after falling asleep under you.

So I already had a bit of bounce as I walked through the dressing room door.

"Wha-heeyy!" About eight or ten guys who were in there dressing erupted at the sight of me. It wasn't any big mystery when I looked up at the far wall and saw the big banner reading STARLO TIME! In large neon-marker lettering, clearly the work of six-year-olds or football players.

I passed through the room, absorbing the love of my colleagues with my gracious Statue of Liberty wave. Then I got to my locker, started dressing for work.

"Arlo," Coach called as I was running toward the tackling sleds and the cluster of linemen around them.

I ran back to him. "Yeah, Coach?"

"It was a good laugh. Now put all that stuff out of your head, right?"

"Of course, Coach," I said, but apparently not seriously enough.

He reached out and put a hand on my forearm. "Really, I mean it. That superstar stuff is all well and good, but it's nothing but a distraction once you're back between the lines. Right? Focus harder than ever. Keep your eyes peeled and your wits about you at all times. Pay attention to what's important."

"And one game at a time. And it ain't over till it's over. Yes, sir, Coach," I said.

He shook his head dubiously as he let go of my arm, and I knew it was because I was smiling and wisecracking and he thought that meant I was taking it too lightly.

But I was smiling because I was happy. Happy to be on the field, happy to be preparing to start banging bodies with the guys, happy to be taking orders from him. I felt *good*, as I sprinted into the afternoon's practice.

I didn't feel good for long.

The very first exercise, a one-on-one blocking drill, morphed at the whistle into a three-on-one mugging as the defensive players to my right and left froze in position. As I dug in against my man—Anderson, naturally—I felt an almighty thump as another lineman banged into my right side. I was straightened out again by another one thumping into my left. I heard roars all around as I did my best, hanging in there for maybe four seconds before they started driving me back, and back, and—*Bam!*—down on my back, mashed into the earth by about seven hundred pounds of offensive oaf.

I was aching already as the guys got up, and there was laughter and camaraderie all around. Even my guys, the defensive unit I served side by side with so nobly, were all high-fiving with my muggers.

"Sad thing, I used to remember when he was great," somebody called out. That somebody sounded awfully like my good friend Dinos.

"Catch the falling Starlo," somebody else called, to wild laughter. That somebody had a lot of Jerome in his voice.

I got it then. Every drill was going to be some kind of survivor challenge designed specifically for me.

"Okay," I said, climbing to my feet, "so this is how it's gonna be."

"Yeah, yeah" was the mob response, along with heavy slaps on the back, ass, and helmet.

"Well then, bring it, boys!" I hollered.

In retrospect, that was a questionable approach to take, really.

I was battered all through blocking drills, never once winding up anywhere but in the dirt. I had to line up for sprints against every guy on the team who was faster than me. Then I lined up against the next one without a break. Then the next one. Then the next. Until *every* guy on the team was faster than me. Coach Fisk had the honor of taking me on for the last one, crossing the line only six yards or so ahead of me.

After that I was made to play cornerback for several pass-protection run-throughs. Cornerback! It looked like a game of keep-away on the elementary school playground when we'd take the lunch of the nerdiest kid in the class.

247

Wherever you are, nerdiest kid, I apologize with my whole heart.

When the rest of the squad took a break after a particularly exhausting stretch of no-huddle, shotgun-formation plays, I got no break. Although being the water boy, carrying the cooler around to each player to get him a drink, was kind of a break compared to everything else.

I was chop blocked, sandwich blocked, blindsided, and pigpiled. One time when I thought I had actually broken through the line to rush our second-string quarterback, it turned out they were all just copying a scene from an old movie. I jumped high to block the pass attempt, and he just drilled me straight in the crotch with the ball.

I took it, every bit of it, with a shut mouth. The fact that I didn't have the breath to spare on words did not diminish my grit.

When the whistle blew to end the day, something happened that I had not expected.

Every guy, everywhere on the field, broke into applause. They clapped loud, and held it for a good minute, and it even choked me up a little, making me raise one arm with great effort to acknowledge it.

As they started walking toward the locker room, big buff Anderson ambled toward me. I was suspicious, naturally, but he made a point of extending his hand well before he reached me, indicating his peaceful intentions.

"How's it feel to be a star?" he said as we shook.

"Oh, just the way I'd always imagined it," I said.

"I'm glad," he said, finishing the shake, then blasting his left flat palm into the middle of my chest.

I flew over backward, my feet in the sky as my shoulder pads dented the earth. The remaining players who saw roared laughter on their way off the field.

"What on earth are you smiling about?" Dinos said when it occurred to him to come and check if I was breathing.

"I love football," I said.

In the locker room I dressed slowly, gingerly, under the mockery of the shining Starlo banner.

"Oh, stop milking it already, will ya?" Dinos said impatiently. Everyone else was long gone, and he wanted to be likewise.

"Hey, I could have been killed out there today," I said, finally zipping up my jacket. I didn't want to tell him I really couldn't move any faster.

"Oh, you could not have. We had careful instructions on how and where to abuse you since we will have need of your services again this weekend. You're just sore because we tapped some of the muscle groups you don't ordinarily use. Like failure and humility."

"Haha," I said. I pointed up at the banner, my head doing its swimmy thing for a second. "Can you take that thing down before we leave? Some of those animals will see it there tomorrow and forget that we already taught me the big lesson."

He laughed but jumped right up to yank the thing off the wall. "And that lesson was . . . ," he prompted, as if I could possibly forget. I was forced to repeat it twenty times while four fatasses sat on my prone body—including one on the side of my helmet—before they would let me up.

I went into zombie voice. "Football is a team game. No star shines brighter than the galaxy. I do the dance of the sugarplum fairies when nobody's watching me."

Dinos laughed robustly for the twenty-first and most gleeful time yet. "I wrote that last part," he said, helping me up from the bench.

"Of course you did," I said. "Who else would have known about that?"

I had a lot of time during the short, slow walk up Baker Street to fill Dinos in on the day's other highlights and my sudden inability to get along with the women in my life.

"Hell, man, you did have a busy day."

"Yeah," I said, exhaling heavily. "I can hardly keep up with myself."

"You're gonna wear out some pants legs with all the groveling and apologizing you'll be doing."

I bristled. Of course I would apologize, but we didn't need to make this out to be bigger than it was.

"It probably sounded worse the way I told it to you."

"Uh-huh. Did you grab Sandy's arm?"

"Yeah."

"Were you angry when you did that?"

"Yeah." We were stopped on the corner, where we'd go our own ways. "Come on, Dinos. What about with Jenna, have you honestly not once—"

"Honestly," he snapped. "Not once."

It was the most serious I had ever seen him.

He started walking away.

"Hey, aren't you the guy who's supposed to help me feel better about myself when I'm feeling low?"

"Stop being low, dude, and start being yourself, then everybody will feel better," he said over his shoulder.

In a day loaded with ass whippings, *that* was an ass whipping.

Not too surprising that Sandy didn't answer calls and texts from me, which was why I was already walking toward her house as I was attempting them, even though I would be late for dinner. When I rang the doorbell several times and nobody answered despite lights being on all over, I just dug in and rang some more.

Then, my phone alerted me to a text. *Don't want to see you right now. Don't want to talk to you. Go away. Don't make it worse.*

I stepped back from the door. I stood there looking the house up and down like if I could just somehow show how serious I was, how much I meant business, then something would have to give. Like my powerful will combined with good intentions would cause doors and windows to fling themselves open and welcome me inside.

That didn't happen. I stood there for several minutes, growing angrier, squeezing and releasing, squeezing and releasing my fists.

"Sand-riiiine!" I bellowed up into the air.

My text alert sounded within seconds. *I said don't make it worse. Dad wants to call cops. Go home now or I might let him.*

As I marched down the stairs, I growled almost as loudly as I had howled her name.

I heard the familiar motor coming a couple of seconds later. The perfect ending to the perfect day. Lloyd pulled up beside me. He whipped off his helmet.

"Yes?" I said.

"What's taking you so long? Starlo's gotta make a big diva entrance or something?"

"That Starlo shit's gotta go," I said.

"Well, he's got a special dinner waiting for him right now."

"Humble pie?" I said.

"I imagine you'd choke to death on one bite of that right now, big man. So you're lucky she only made your favorite beef and black bean stew."

That was my favorite, a long time ago, back when I was a quiet, good kid with manners.

I started quick-stepping toward home.

He revved and caught right up.

"You can't walk," he said. "She's hired LB Courier Services to deliver you back personally, and you ain't costing me a payday."

"Seriously."

"Seriously."

"I don't have a helmet."

He reached down into his opposite side saddlebag and produced a helmet.

I laughed out loud. It was an old chipped and scarred football helmet I didn't even think still existed. Then, just as quickly,

I stopped laughing as I lost myself in feeling the surface of the thing. I ran my fingers lightly over it, front, back, sides, locating and remembering every ding. It was like a map, of the old us, and one by one each collision, each assault—and each lesson that came along with them—returned to me clearly.

He really was teaching me, while he was killing me.

I swung a leg over and got on the seat behind Lloyd. The sides of my head throbbed as I fitted the helmet down on my skull. "This thing is ancient," I said. "I can barely get my head inside it."

"Whose fault is that, big man?" he said, peeling out rapidly and forcing me to grab on to him for safety.

* * *

"I always deliver," Lloyd said, sweeping the door open and marching in ahead of me.

"Just barely," I said after experiencing the current state of his operating skills up close. Maybe it was the extra weight, but I felt like I was doing the balancing for him.

Dad was waiting at the table, looking up at me angrily as I stuffed the old helmet like a handoff into my brother's gut. I went into the kitchen to Ma, who had her back to me, as if the stew that should have been served an hour ago needed any more tending.

I tapped very lightly on her shoulder and I hardly gave her a chance to turn fully before I grabbed her up in my arms. I put everything I had into that hug, short of crushing her ribs. I lifted her right up off the ground, buried my sorry face in her neck, and just held her there, through resistance, into reluctance, and finally through to the point where the hold was mutual. I held her, all shut up and sniffling, unable to say what I needed to but unable to let go, either.

"All right," she said finally, softly but not weakly.

I still held her there until she made me put her down, punching lightly on my shoulders.

# STRUCTURES

I spent the next week making an effort to avoid the jerk-jock stereotype that seemed to be creeping into my profile. I concentrated on not offending anybody who didn't deserve it, on making sure the manners I had always taken pride in were kept as sharp as my reflexes. And I made sure my football intensity didn't dip at all while at the same time distancing myself as far as possible from Starlo.

On most counts my life was back on track. The team won again, with me leading a quietly efficient, vicious defensive effort that allowed only three points. And I didn't have a single disagreeable interaction with anyone who did not go by the name Sandrine.

I tried every which way to apologize for being a brute, but she stonewalled me every which way. Calls and texts ignored and unreturned. Inside and outside of school encounters suspiciously nonexistent. She was putting work into avoiding me. Even dream Sandy didn't like me.

I wished so badly that she could somehow see, like with a heart-and-soul monitor or something, how I really felt, because every time I thought about how I grabbed her, meaning thirty times a day, my disgust with myself grew.

I sent her a card. I had never sent a card before. Not ever, to anyone, for any occasion. Well, maybe one in second or third grade when we exchanged them in class just before Valentine's Day. Even then the cards were tiny, I only wrote my name inside, and I handed out thirty of them. Way different. This was *me* I had mailed away.

I didn't hear from her.

Who was I kidding, that life could be back on track without Sandy on board?

* * *

We'd entered the fourth week of football season. One of the precious truths handed down from generation to generation of football players at our school was that there was a lot of slack given to varsity starters after games. Especially if we won. I had been sleeping in, pretty late on Mondays and tapering down as the week wore on. On Tuesday I would have gotten myself to school to see the beginning of third period.

But my dad came in before I was even out of bed. I knew right away things were not how they were supposed to be. This was my dad, who was always out of the house before I woke up, even when I used to wake up early, who hated talking about *anything* unless he absolutely had to.

"Dad?" I said, bolting upright. Blinking to clear away the red haze. "What's wrong? What is it? Where's Ma? Is she okay?"

He stood about three feet away, with a folded sheet of paper flapping in one hand. "Oh, God," he said, coming quickly to my childish side. "She's fine. She's at work. I'm sorry for scaring you like that. . . . Is that how bad it seems when I wake you up on the odd morning?"

"Yes," I said relieved, concerned, still in the dark about it all. "Sorry, but any weekday morning I see you, Dad, you might as well come at me in a black cloak swinging a scythe. And I *still* don't know what the problem is, so could you please tell me what's in the letter?"

He handed me the letter. "It's from the school. Your mother hasn't seen it."

"Yeah . . . ," I said, wary.

"I thought you liked school, Arlo?" There was a shimmering sadness to him, where I might have expected anger.

"I do, Dad. I like it fine."

He looked at his watch pointedly, then back at me. "And yet . . ."

"Oh, you know, perks of the football job. It'll wind down after the season's over."

He gestured at the letter. "I think it needs to wind down sooner than that. It's an early warning on overall attendance and two subjects. Biology? Son, you've always loved biology."

I finally looked at the letter, and the surprise number of absent days.

"No way, Dad. They're wrong. I haven't been absent one single time so far."

"Read it all. If you haven't signed in for homeroom, you haven't officially been to school that day."

257

"But . . . ," I started my protest, but Dad wasn't having it.

"Remember when you loved the beginning of the school year?" he said, ignoring my demonstration. "The new subjects, new shoes . . ."

"I know, I'm sorry," I said, hoping he'd just go away.

He still wasn't having it.

"You'd even get all worked up about the new fall TV schedule. Remember that?" he said.

"No," I said with a dramatic sigh that made it embarrassingly plain I was just waiting for him to give up and go.

With his usual composure, which probably masked more than the usual effort to hold it, he nodded, held out his hand to take the letter back. I offered it, and somehow that was the move that did it. He reached out and snatched the letter from me, crumpled it in his fist. He looked at it, then jammed it all scrunched into his pocket. "This is the only one of these I will ever keep from your mother," he snarled. "Just so you know."

"So I know," I said. He was apparently cutting me a break here. He wasn't trying a sneaky guilt lecture or bringing in Ma, who surely would. And still, he was making me so mad . . . for daring to even be in my room. For daring to get angry at *me*, for whatever reason. I could control my own situation. I never failed at anything before, and the idea that I might start *now* was a joke.

My father and the school with their stupid letter could just butt out and leave me to me.

I knew better, of course, than to say that kind of thing to him.

But I didn't know how to keep my face from saying it for me.

"Everyone is only trying to help you, son," he said. "Maybe you should try to accept that, while it can still do you some good." He nodded hard at that, at me, and walked out.

"I'll help myself," I said after he had gone.

And I immediately went to work doing exactly that. I grabbed my phone before even getting out of bed. I texted Sandy. *I sent you a card. I never sent a card before. Did you not get it?*

I got up and got dressed for school, thinking about her every second and trying to force myself not to.

I was eating bananas and toast and drinking a protein shake when my phone signaled a text.

I dropped the shake right out of my hand. It thumped onto the table and tipped over, coating the surface in gritty, milky ooze while I picked up the phone and walked away from the mess.

*It was very sweet. I know you are not really that awful but there is some awfulness. I think the break last season was a good idea and good for us. I think it is a good idea again. Don't write back cuz I don't want to talk about it now. Good luck with the season. Don't get hurt. Don't be a jerk. I will miss you. Call me when it's over.*

I just stared at the text for a while, rereading for something better that I might have missed. But it kept saying the same thing no matter what I tried to force it to say.

It sucked. But it was something. It was better than it was before. At least we had a kind of understanding. A structure, a goal, a game plan. I could work with it anyway.

So I worked. At my football, at my grades, at controlling the only things I could control because that would not include Sandy. Not until December anyway.

It was simple enough to fix the attendance thing, but when I tried to bear down on the schoolwork, it was suddenly hard. *Hard.* I reached for it and it wasn't there. I couldn't concentrate. I couldn't remember. In a biology quiz that required us to arrange thirty different animals into their kingdom, phylum, class, order, family, genus, and species, I got a D. *I got a D.* When I was eleven I used to do that for *fun,* writing it all out as fast as I could as soon as Animal Planet or Discovery or National Geographic identified the star of the show at the beginning of the program.

It bothered me, that D. Then it didn't.

The thing about football was this: that you could *always* understand it, not just sometimes. The grid. The objective, the gaining and relinquishing of territory. The controlled aggression that gave it honor and nobility that supposedly related games like chess didn't. Offensive and defensive strategies, game plans tailored around personnel, the array of different positions, their functions, and the amazingly varied skill sets and body types required to make all the modules of the great organism function. And of course, how the flawlessly delivered, devastating hit was the ultimate answer to everything.

It was there, in its perfect form, even when nothing else was. And the more I understood the simple genius of the game, the more the sloppiness and complication of everything else made me angry. So I stopped caring about everything else, and concentrated on the one place where I felt like trying, always. Football made me calm, even when everything else was nuts.

The first week in November we played a nonleague game against one of the powerhouse schools that go to the state Division 2 super bowl more years than not. It was our ninth game, we were 6–2, better than the team had been in years. This opponent was a tall order, a measure of how far we had actually come in relation to schools outside our conference. We liked our chances.

By the end of the first quarter we were down 21–0, and that didn't fully reflect the extent of our humbling. Their second string quarterback was in by the second quarter, and defensive replacements were coming in each time the unit came back onto the field. Which wasn't a lot, since even their backup offense was having their way with us.

It was 35–0 late in the second quarter when I first heard one of our defensive line starters ask out of the game. He claimed a sore groin or some crap, and Coach took him off with a groan. One running play later, another of our guys pulled the same thing—this time it was Dinos.

I screamed at him as he limped off. "Are you kidding me!" I shouted, storming after him as if I were pursuing one of the other team's runners. "You get in like one out of every ten plays as it is, and you're asking *out*?" He halfway turned in my direction and gave a *whatever* shrug.

I kept coming, enraged at him, until Coach took several steps in my direction, pointing at me with his arm fully extended and his voice definitive. "Get out to your position, Captain. Now."

261

"Oh, I will," I said, arms waving and feet stomping. "*Somebody's* got to have the balls to play these guys, right?"

Back on the field I had to force myself to let go of it all. Focus. The only thing left in a game like this—especially one that still had a lot of humility ahead—was to do yourself proud. Do your job, hold your ground, don't quit.

And if you can make those other guys *feel* it a few times, that's something.

I would make them feel it.

I was so deep in my game, in my world within world within world, that the whole game began to feel like it was being played in a tube that only included the central one-third of the field. A pass play evolved perfectly formed in front of my eyes. The big fullback hesitated, held off like he'd be blocking for the quarterback, then suddenly released. He sprinted out of the backfield and, six yards up, turned, timing the play brilliantly with the QB. He reached up and the ball was there in his hands.

Except that I was like the third partner in that play because I timed it just as perfectly. The instant he turned to go upfield, he barreled point-blank into the tackle I had been building to all my life.

It was close to spontaneous combustion as we cracked heads and everything else as hard as humanly possible. The ball shot straight up into the air while the fullback dropped to the ground like he had been bazooka'd.

I never even went down. I stood over the guy, probably looking like one of those showboat jerks I would never be, but I was kind of stunned and stuck there. It was quite a crack.

"Okay, dude?" I said as he rolled slowly from his back to all fours and I saw him shake his head around a little.

"Think so," he said. "Helluva pop."

"Yeah," I said, patting him lightly on the helmet as I turned toward our bench.

Only when I did, the effect was stringy, whirly. Everything bright in my vision kind of strobed out with the movement of my head. I shook it a couple of times, back and forth, and it kept happening. I bent a little at the waist. Worse.

One of our guys ran past me and pounded my shoulder pad.

"Hellacious hit!" he yelled, running on.

Pain shot through my head from the shoulder smack or the shout, or both. I didn't move. The ground looked fine, gridded like it should look. It was only a bit of a shock to the system. I would just stand still for a few seconds.

Then there was a tugging at both of my elbows, and a couple of teammates were easing me off the field.

"I mean, it was a great hit and everything," one of the guys said, "but the bow was a little excessive. They need the field for a football game."

I laughed when they did, a little embarrassed at how that must have looked. I wondered how long I had been out there.

"Are you sure?" was the next thing I heard.

"What?" I said.

The skinny guy who was apparently qualified to be team trainer because he was a phys ed major at the college and this was his internship was leaning into my face.

I was sitting on the bench with no idea of how I got there.

"Really? Because in a blowout like this there's no reason to go on risking your neck when you've already done your part."

"What are you asking, do I want out? Of course not. I mean, thanks, but I'm fine. Day at the office, that's all."

I was already feeling better. That's how it worked. And no way was I asking out. No way. This is where a man shows his stuff. Right here.

"All right," the trainer said. "But just keep in mind, these things matter. They add up. There is a limit to what the human head can tolerate."

Thanks, Ma. I saw her then, waving that foolish file at me, and I wondered how much of *that* a human head could tolerate.

"Not a linebacker's head," I said, feeling like I had definitively settled *that* little wits-test.

If nothing else, I frustrated him enough to make him go away.

But I wasn't heartbroken when the whistle blew just then to end the first half.

I played every last defensive snap of the second half. I made a bunch of tackles and every one made my head hurt.

# RANDOM ACCESS MEMORY

"Ya, right," Dinos said when he finally noticed that I hadn't noticed that he wasn't talking to me. It was our last pre-Thanksgiving practice, mostly a walk-through and some easy running. I was doing laps on the oval, and he came alongside me looking for an apology of some kind.

"Seriously, man, I don't know what you're talking about. I don't remember it like that at all."

"Arlo, you were screaming at me, in front of the whole place, humiliating me for coming off the field. The guys on the other team were laughing their heads off. I don't need to get slaughtered on the field at this point in my football life, and I don't need shit from you about it, either. My life is out *there*," he said, pointing at a lovely cloud that looked a lot like himself. "Yours is here," he said, pointing at the field. "So don't be a jerk to me ever again."

"You're exaggerating," I said.

"I am *not*." He started laughing, which made me feel better. So even though I still did not remember the incident, I was happy to apologize.

"Sorry, man. Sometimes when I get in the heat of battle . . . I don't even know what comes out of my mouth. Won't happen again." If it even happened that time.

I'm not sure I was even supposed to remember that kind of thing anyway. I didn't remember the seventy-two million miles of road running or the seventy-two million push-ups, sit-ups, stretches, biceps curls, triceps extensions, bench presses, and shoulder presses or the seventy-two million whatnots that put me in position to blast lights-out hard into another guy who was just as built as me but who maybe only did sixty-eight million of each of those things.

I remembered the *events*, as opposed to all the connective tissue between them.

I remembered the hits.

I remembered the get-ups, when I got up, from those hits.

And I remembered the times when the other guy didn't get up, not right away anyway, or not so steady on his feet anyway.

Which was why I needed more *events*. I was homicidally bored standing on the sidelines. I needed to get myself onto the field more. So for the last couple of weeks of the season, I convinced Coach to let me also work out with the offensive unit, as a tight end. Partly due to the fact that we had crap tight ends, he went for it. We knew I could be a good blocker and could read defensive schemes as well as anybody, so when it turned out I also had decent hands and even enjoyed the job, I was in.

It wasn't linebacking. Because nothing else is. But it wasn't half bad.

The problem of being on the sideline for half the time—seeing the action without being able to *feel* it, hearing the pop of pads, the crack of helmet on helmet—that problem was solved, and I was complete.

And that game, on Thanksgiving, provided the extra bonus of Burgoyne. Even Dad decided he had more important things to do than come this year, and that was fine. I knew I was good at this point, and didn't need to be watched, to be told by people in the stands. The only people I needed to measure myself by were right there on the field with me.

Kind of my mirror image, Burgoyne was a tight end who also moonlighted as a linebacker, so we would be facing off *all day long*. He was a half-decent player, but when I'd gone up against him before I thought he was a fake. Intimidation and cheap shots but no real guts. Guys let his reputation beat them. If you took him on, it was another story.

I didn't like Burgoyne, or the undeserved attention he had been getting in the *Citizen* since I had become a regular reader of the sports page.

We were trying to grind them down with our running game, so both of our backs were getting a lot of work. Tyrone, our fullback, was a horse, but because of the size of their line and the stupidity of our scheme, he was getting only a yard or two at a time. Because of a quad injury to McCallum, we had to play our backup halfback, Rafferty, who sucked.

The point, anyway, was to draw them in, and set them up for a deep throw at the right time.

It wasn't working.

Tyrone was gang tackled by five guys almost as soon as he touched the ball. Just about every linebacker. But not every linebacker. All-conference Burgoyne wanted no part of Tyrone, even with half his team already riding on his back. He had no problem going after Rafferty, though. He leveled him twice. That's what he would do. Clothesline a guy, blindside him, chop him, spear him, pile on, as long as the guy was a certain type of guy—and little Rafferty was that kind of guy.

Blood-boiling stuff to see.

The score was tied. Fourth quarter. Late. Possibly.

I was a capable tight end. An outstanding linebacker, a capable tight end.

So I was surprised when our scrambling and terror-stricken quarterback saw me just before the pack swallowed him. He threw me a dying quail that managed to flutter into my hands right over the middle about eight yards upfield.

Once I gathered the ball and turned, I almost squealed with joy.

Because of the blitzing and too much Tyrone, most of their defenders were behind me, and the one big, bad inside linebacker I had in isolation.

He was not even strictly in my path, if I wanted to get to the end zone, and he didn't seem to be in any rush to get into my path, either.

So I helped him.

I would replay this one in my head, in the future, on my good days and on my bad ones. The look of shock on Burgoyne's face when I ran straight at him, which was nothing like a straight line to six points. Then, just before contact, I saw the other thing, the *lean* in my direction, the look of determination that I thought was mine alone.

*Bam!*

I knew for certain I never hit anybody that hard. It was similar to how a car must feel when it meets a pedestrian at a good clip. The first crack, of his helmet into my chin. Right up under the face mask and driving it backward. Torquing. I counted the crunching clacking of individual vertebrae. Six.

People would talk about hearing that stuff. After injuries. *Heard a pop. A crack. A snap.* Always sounded like cereal crunching to me. Stupid. Lying. You don't hear those things. Drama. Just shut up and play the game. The game is killer enough. You don't need to big it up, put bells on it. No rocket bursts, no snap-crackle-or-for-God's-sake-pop.

Until it happens. Rib cartilage, jaw, spine, shoulder—all spoke. Raspy, devilish. So loud, so loud. Screaming inside me and out. New pains splintered nuclear over the whole trip—up, then horizontal, then very, very down—and it seemed so long, so torture-like, it would just go on dividing pains into pains until I hit the turf.

# COACH

"Next year, son," Coach Fisk said to me as I sat on the bench in the locker room after everybody else had gone.

I didn't know how else to play, though. And Burgoyne responded exactly the way he should have.

We were both playing *football*. Playing it the way we had been taught at every level, by every coach, like the one right in front of me at this moment. Why be on the field if you don't like to crash into other crashers?

"That's three serious collisions in the last four weeks, Arlo," Coach said while the twerp of a trainer went through the tests again. The flashlight in the eyes, look here, look here, eyes up, eyes over, etc. I could pretty much give myself the tests by this point. But I thought it was just the routine. Thought it was just like stretching after the game, just what you did. Who knew they were keeping a tally? Who would have thought that weedy intern-trainer's clipboard had a purpose, and that he was watching everything we did and counting the hits, even in practice?

"It's time to shut it down, for your own good. Not sure how much of it is bad luck but, my man, you are snakebit. If trouble doesn't come to you, you go find it—none of which is helped by your admirable but dangerous ability to play to contact on every single play. Are you listening? Do you understand me?"

We finished the season in the second slot of our league table. That meant we had a conference championship game to look forward to the next week, and the chance to go on to the Eastern state tournament.

"I'll take the rest of the week off," I said. "Then I'll be ready for the—"

"You will take the rest of the season off," Coach said. "There will be other seasons, other years, other goals in your life, young man. You need to look out for yourself now. Arlo, I think you and I both know how good you could be. You could play this game at a high level. But right now, you just have to play it smart."

I found myself staring up into Coach's concerned eyes. I was still wet from my shower, but my stuff was packed up for me by the little weedy traitor trainer himself, and my bag was in my lap and somehow my jacket was on me and zipped up.

"Where's your hat, Arlo?"

It was cold outside. I had wet hair on my sore head.

"Hats are for managers and trainers, not linebackers," I said, thinking through my fog that this was not only funny but also likely to remind the coach of my toughness and commitment.

He took off his own thick wool ski cap, the distinctive teal blue of the Miami Dolphins, and pulled it snugly down over my ears. His wispy fringe of sandy hair stood up all around the perimeter of his head like a sort of sad angel halo.

"Take care of this," he said, gently tapping the blue leaping dolphin patch at the front of the hat.

"I'll get it back to you, Coach," I said.

"Not the hat, dum-dum," he said.

When I got home, in that lonely deep cold of the rawest evenings, I was surprised to find only Lloyd there. Then I remembered it was movie night for the parents.

He was drunk and whatever else, multiple elses it seemed. Movie night was an opportunity for Ma and Dad to unwind and treat themselves in the middle of the week. It was Lloyd's opportunity to do his version of the same thing, without them noticing.

I was just stupid. I went to talk to him because he was my brother and he was there and my head hurt. My head really hurt.

"What the hell is that?" he said as I stood in the doorway of his bedroom. He was messing with his stereo. When he was at a certain chemical balance, he could be messing with his stereo for hours. "Miami Dolphins?" he said, coming over and ripping the cap off my head in that signature big-brother move that was simultaneously dehatting and a good hard smack. He tossed the hat into the hallway.

I stood there. The smack hurt me enough to make my eyes bulge, wet and pulsing.

Then I told him about my day and the collision and practice and what happened after. Because he was my brother, and they had taken football away from me like they had from him.

"You got kicked off the football team? Because you hit your *head*?"

I opened my mouth to speak, even as I lost the will to do so.

"Well," he said, backing me out the door, "welcome to the shit heap, big man." He didn't even have me all the way out when he slammed the door right in my face.

I got my hand up—my hand absorbed the door, and my nose absorbed my hand.

I bent down to pick up the Miami Dolphins hat that Coach was kind enough to loan me. The blood rushed to my head and I got back up before it flooded me. I didn't feel well, on any level at all, as I shuffled toward my room.

As I crossed the threshold to the bedroom, I flipped on the light. Everything went bright for a second until everything went black.

\* \* \*

I woke up in an awkward heap on the floor, my arms under me, my face propped some against a footpost of the bed. My head felt like someone was actually turning a big screw, driving it into the bone and brain with a turn, then a turn, then a turn.

Eventually, through inch-worming along the floor, I made it to the head of my bed without pulling any attention from anybody. I assumed hours had passed and my parents were in bed, but I had no interest in confirming that in the state I was in.

I could not make it up onto the soft mattress, and just pawed at it a few times before giving up and laying my head on the rug.

* * *

"I'm sorry," my brother said, a desperate whisper in my ear. "I'm sorry. I went to the bathroom. Your door was open. I'm sorry they did this to you. Sorry, here you go." He heaved and strained, getting me up off the floor, struggled, but then between the two of us we got me up and into the bed.

"Be careful now," he said while backing away, which even at the end of my horrendous day, my football life, my wits, and maybe my rope, I managed to find funny enough to laugh at.

# GROUND ZERO

For three days I told everybody it was some nasty bad flu, and I was just bitchy enough that I was left mostly alone to be miserable in my room. And I was miserable with the lingering headache, jumpy vision, and a Dracula-level reaction to strong bright light.

But when those things started gradually lifting on day four, and five, and six, I didn't actually feel *better*.

In a way, I felt even worse.

Because without the symptoms I had the clarity. The realization of the gaping empty in front of me. Football and I had been forcibly separated, and I'd bet football didn't like it any more than I did.

Okay then. So, Coach said clean slate next September. Regardless of right then, I had no choice but to set sights on that slate, that month.

Even if right then, that seemed near impossible. I hadn't been able to bring myself to watch the conference championship game, which we lost. Which *they* lost. So then nobody was playing for the rest of the year, which should have been a consolation since I wasn't actually missing anything. It wasn't.

On Wednesday, about a week and a half after getting fired from the team, I sat down on the wall in front of the school and just occupied space there. Vacant, stupid, useless. I still kept feeling like I wanted to cry, and that made me want to punch myself in the face. If I did either or both of those things, there on the front wall of the school, I could safely expect things to deteriorate further for me.

And then I remembered. Football season was over. For me it was already over a week before then. I took out my phone and started punching at it furiously with my big, stupid finger.

*I don't play football anymore*, I texted Sandy. We hadn't communicated in *how* long?

Thirty seconds later my phone rang.

A five-year-old would have been embarrassed by the sad, cracking little laugh that came out of me at the mere sight of her name on the screen.

* * *

"You can hardly expect me to celebrate," I said.

It was Friday, and we were in that same old place in front of that same old pizza because Sandy said the same old place was a good place for a new start. It had been almost too easy for us to get it together again, for apologies—okay, *apology*—to be offered and accepted, for us to resume us-ing. I was so pleased about that outcome that I was happy to ignore that it seemed to be connected in Sandy's mind to the idea that football was over *forever*.

"Not at all," she said. But she slurped her drink quite dramatically. Sandy was no slurper. This was her victory dance, her

**276**

touchdown spike, not over me but over the game itself. "God, your mom must be over the moon! I mean, not that you got hurt, of course. But that you won't be getting hurt like that anymore. Oh my, she must be just . . ."

Sandy's voice trailed off as she read the clearly defined rotten *son*ness on my facial features. I had not, in fact, told my mother. I wasn't planning to, either. It was just a temporary suspension—no need to worry her.

"You have got to be kidding me, Arlo."

"I guess I was waiting for the right time?"

Sandy could combine a slightly tilted head, an arched eyebrow, and pursed lips in such a way it amounted to a brutal and sustained face-slapping.

"Y'know, Arlo, you just get more attractive by the syllable."

"I'll tell her, I'll tell her." I wouldn't.

"What's stopping you? If you don't call her, I just might. We did exchange numbers, you know."

"No, please. I really want to do it in person. I want to see her smile." I knew I wouldn't do it, though.

She picked up another slice of pizza and then aimed the sharp end at me. "So the possibility remains that you might be a human somethingorother after all."

"Now there's something to celebrate," I said, pointing a slice right back at her. I felt like a rat. I felt like I was making the right decision.

# BAM!

It started a few weeks after the season ended. By early spring the fear had taken over. The fear that I might not ultimately be able to prove I was sound enough of mind and body to ever be allowed to take the field again. That I had already delivered my last ferocious tackle. That I would be forbidden to do what I do best. What I do better than anybody. The thing I was *born* to do.

That was not the way this was supposed to play out.

It was unreal, was what it was.

Except my fear was real.

So if I was going to put things right again and get back in the game, job one was going to be dealing with this fear. And the only way I ever knew for dealing with fear was to break its friggin' head.

I needed contact. I needed smash. I needed *Bam!*

* * *

"I think your brains are even more scrambled than anybody knows," Dinos said as he followed me, uninvited, out toward the lacrosse field.

"And I think you should mind your own business," I said.

"I am. My friends are my business and you're my friend, so I'm minding *you*. You need minding. Why are they even letting you play anyway?"

"Because I'm Starlo," I said, turning to face him just as we reached the running track. I put my hand flat on his chest.

"No, you're not. You're a regular human earthling with a brain box that needs protecting—from yourself, mostly."

"Dinos," I said, bringing my second hand up alongside the one already gently pushing him away, "I appreciate your unnecessary concern. Now go away."

And, kind of surprisingly, he did just that. But when he spun away and all I had of him was his angry back, I felt a little jolt of something that was almost like regret.

So I spun away in the other direction, just as quickly, and concentrated on the crazy excited feeling I had in my gut.

The idea started forming when I ran into some of the defensive backfield guys from the football team in the weight room. They were hitting it like the season was starting up again in a week. Only it had nothing to do with football. They were getting into lacrosse shape. I saw them dashing between strength workouts out on the field and then back to the weights without pausing, and I caught a rush of the same adrenaline and asked if I could join.

Just for the conditioning. Those boys were into harsh conditioning, and that looked very attractive to me.

Bit by bit they let me in. I was never a real part of the team, just a kind of unofficial associate, training partner—all under-the-radar stuff.

Then I started playing a little. Just a little. No contact. Coach Carey made that clear. No contact for me, but as long as I wanted to be an enthusiastic supporter of what his team was doing—well, the old Starlo glow wasn't completely gone yet, so it was win-win. Even my mother and Sandy were okay with it because of the no contact.

Except me. I wanted to play so badly. I knew I could play, and play well, and so did the guys on the team. But rules were rules.

It was an intrasquad game, a Captain's Practice, run by the players while the coach was away for the afternoon. In other words, an open door.

It was one of the best days I ever had. The conditioning paid off, and I was faster and more flexible than I had ever been, less bulked but just as hard. The old football adrenaline came flooding back—and even better, it was like the beginning of football all over again, the newness, the something to prove. I would show them all they were wrong.

I spent the whole time flying up the left side, cutting in and across the front of the goal. I did it with the ball, without the ball—no matter. Guys were hacking on my arms, cross-checking me on my back, my face.

It was heaven. This was going to be my new home, my beloved foster home, until football was ready to take me back. It was coming to me so naturally, so easily, it was as if everything had been set up perfectly to help me get back to where I wanted to be.

Until, of course, it wasn't set up that way at all.

I saw a guy on my team get absolutely crumpled as he carried the ball across the middle of the field. A beautiful crunch that left him flat and the ball bouncing. Until I collected it up and barreled like a thoroughbred toward the goal. There was nobody between me and the goalie, who I saw coming out, coming out toward me.

I was looking right at him. He was in his squat, deep inside his protective padding. I actually felt a little sorry for him. A little. He had no chance.

Other than the big chance.

I honestly didn't know they could do that.

He played me some possum, stayed down low but came forward, until I was about two yards in front of him. Then . . . man, the squat bastard nailed me. Up out of the crouch like a dwarf being fired from a cannon. Clever and nasty, he caught me with both forearms in my face mask, elbows right in my collarbones.

My lower half kept travelling forward, while my head whipped backward right into the ground like a pile driver.

I don't know how long I was out, but by the time my vision had just about cleared, my eyes were bringing me the most unwelcome sight.

"The thing is," I said to Coach Carey, "I was just caught off guard. That won't happen again."

"No, son, it won't," he said sternly from the wrong end of a flashlight.

* * *

"How am I ever supposed to leave you here without me next year?" Dinos asked. "You're a hazard to yourself."

We were in the stands at the rink, watching a scrimmage between our school's varsity and jayvee hockey teams. The style of play was physical, almost as thumping as our football games.

"I don't need you," I said, mock-laughing. It was a rare occurrence when one of us was laughing and it wasn't Dinos. It was real concern I was seeing. I hated real concern. "I'm fine."

"You're not fine, Arlo, you're insane."

I wasn't insane. My plan had a totally reasonable goal. Even if it was a little crazy.

"I just want to play football again, man," I said.

"So wait for football season to come around again. Let yourself heal up. Train through the summer like always. Then August will be here before you know it, then you can let the staff check you out and take it from there."

I was already facing away from him, watching the action. There was a fantastic three-man crack-up in the corner where two ballsy jayvee defensemen *rocked* the big varsity left winger into the corner boards. They smashed into the glass and made such a racket I had to jump out of my seat and roar.

"How great was that?" I said as I took my seat again. There were only maybe a half dozen of us in the arena, making all the sounds echo around at ten times the decibels. I noticed several of the skaters looking up in our direction and then realized that applied to my noise as well. I waved.

"It was a big bang," Dinos said flatly.

"I know a few of these guys," I said. "I've been talking to them."

He let out a long blast of exhale. "Yeah, Arlo. Your ambitions are kind of obvious at this point. You've got to stop, man, you really do."

"What? Stop what?"

I looked at him, but he was looking off, at something or somebody else, and made a big thumbs-up. I turned to see Coach Fisk and Coach Carey climbing the arena steps toward us.

"What did you do, ya rat?" I said to Dinos while smiling politely at the grim reapers coming my way.

"I did what anybody who really cares should do."

"Fink."

"Friend."

Just as the two were reaching us, Mr. Grant, the hockey coach, turned from behind the bench and threw his own big hearty wave at us. He was adding his endorsement to whatever was going to happen here before turning back to the job before him.

The two coaches sat down on the seatbacks one row down from the chairs occupied by me and Dinos the fink.

"There's been a lot of talk about you, Arlo," Coach Carey said.

"Which is, of course, nothing new for you," Coach Fisk added. "Although, I suppose it's a little different from what you've been used to. For once, people aren't wanting more from you but less."

"A lot less," Dinos chirped.

"A lot less of you right now wouldn't be a bad thing," I snapped.

"Easy there, son," Coach Fisk said. "You haven't got a better friend in the world than that guy right there, as far as I can see.

Horsefeathers as a football player at this point but a four-star friend."

"Thanks there, Coach," Dinos said. "Way to keep me from getting a big head."

Everybody automatically looked at Dinos's epic skull.

"That horse appears to have left the barn already," Coach Fisk said. Everybody chuckled, and I forced myself to join in.

There was another loud crash into the boards just below us, a whistle, and a lot of stick-clashing and bellowing sounds.

"We're not here to talk about Dinos's dome, are we?" I said when the noise died down.

"No, Arlo," Coach Carey said, "we're not. Are you familiar with the concept of Hit Count?"

"No, sir. But whatever it is, it sounds like I'm your man."

"What?" he said. "Wait, oh, that was a good one. Only . . . you're not joking, are you?"

"Okay, let's get to the point," Coach Fisk said before I had to answer. "We have to take this kind of thing seriously, Arlo. There are only so many blows to the head anyone, even a strapping young anyone like yourself, can withstand without risking permanent—"

"I don't mind, really, Mr. Fisk. I swear, I hardly even feel it most of the time."

"Arlo," he said, holding both hands out in front of him as if I might come bursting up out of my seat. "You are at the limit for Hit Count this year. We are shutting you down, at least until next fall. You are not going to be allowed to so much as train alongside any school teams this year, for your own good. You will be evaluated

**284**

at the beginning of football season, and we'll take it from there. If you are caught sneaking into any more banned activities, then we'll have to disqualify you for next year as well. Is that clear?"

Even as he was speaking to me I was leaning over slightly to get a glimpse of the action on the ice as it seemed to be really heating up. He put his face in mine and made a close-up effort to get eye contact, reminding me of some of those postimpact exams he'd put me through.

I focused my eyes on his. "It's clear, sir."

"Good stuff. Just concentrate on your studies, your extracurricular things, your love life. Enjoy yourself."

"That's what I was trying to do until you guys stopped me," I said, grinning like maybe a joke between us would clear everything up and they'd remove all my restrictions just like that.

He grinned right back, stuck out his hand. We shook.

Mr. Carey stuck out his hand. We shook.

And that was that.

And the fear came flooding back.

"So you going to spend the rest of your senior year following me around and reporting any suspicious activities back to the administration?" I said to Dinos. I couldn't look at him.

"No," he said. "But I would if I thought it was necessary."

"Why don't you just leave me alone?" Before I throw you down the damn stairs already.

"Why? Because *alone* you're making bizarre decisions. I mean, what are we even doing here? You can't even skate."

"I can skate."

"Yeah, like a guy who takes his girlfriend to the rink once a year around Christmas. But not like a *hockey player* can skate. Arlo, man it's like you've got some kind of disease, like you're the town drunk getting thrown out of one dive bar after another until there are none left that'll let you in. You have to listen to what people are saying, and stop taking stupid risks."

The sound between us now was beautiful. It was all steel-blades-slicing-ice on a three-on-one break. It was sticks cracking sticks, of a wicked wrist shot deflecting off the goalie's blocker and then banging high off the plexiglass behind him. Of a defenseman smacking the loose puck around the boards and out of the zone. Such better sounds than listening to Dinos's crap theories about me.

"Where are you going?" he said as I abruptly got up and went down the stairs. Since he would not back off, *one* of us was going down the stairs, one way or another.

"Not going anywhere, pal. Just keep on talking. . . ."

**\* \* \***

"It's probably terrible of me to feel this way," Sandy said after I had apparently done some moaning, "but I think it's kind of sweet to find you feeling sorry for yourself."

I didn't fill her in on all the details, obviously, but I had let her know that my football ban was now extended across all official school sports activities.

"Well, that would at least make it one of us feeling sorry for me," I said.

"I am sorry, Arlo," she said, lifting up my arm and draping it

**286**

over her shoulders, which I would normally have done myself at this point, except I wasn't feeling the sympathy I wanted. "But I'm also not sorry. For once the school sports machine seems to be looking out for the vulnerable individual."

Bad. Bad words. Bad timing.

"I am not a *vulnerable individual*," I snapped at her, very unlike my normal Sandy tone.

"I'm sorry," she said, soothingly. "I didn't mean anything by it, you know that."

"Okay," I said. I removed my dead-weight arm and got up from the porch. "I'll talk to you later," and for the second time in the past hour I found myself walking away from somebody I knew I shouldn't want to walk away from.

# TOXIC SPACE

Fine.

At the end of the day you've only got yourself anyway. Even in a team game, *you* are the only person you are ever going to be able to fully, absolutely count on. Anybody else could screw up or fall down and leave you exposed, but you are not going to do that to you, ever.

So I powered up on my training one more time. By myself. By myself I was clearly focused, and could tailor workouts to my own needs, desires, goals.

I was a linebacker. I am a linebacker.

I hit the weights harder than I have ever hit them before. For three weeks I did almost nothing but lift and lift some more. Some sprints on the track, but mostly those were just to break things up, and to give the oxygen a chance to return to my upper body again. As soon as I felt it coming on, I stopped the running and got my hungry self back pumping the iron. Felt good, too. Like a bull sea lion hobbling off the rocks and back into the ocean where he was a *force*.

"I know it's old habits and all that, Arlo," Sandy said as we jogged along together the following week, "but you probably want to think about writing yourself a new program. Without football, is there really a lot of use for the big muscle workout? Older gentlemen like yourself have to gear down and streamline sometime. There's no shame in it, you know. I promise the rest of us mere mortals won't think any less of you."

"Har," I said, "har . . . har." The great gaps of time between *hars* weren't helping me in the debate. But at least they helped me put up a front of good humor. Because the honest first reaction I had to that, deep inside and stabbing sharply, was, Yes you will. Of course you will. Gear down and streamline? Never mind the mere mortals, I'd think less of myself. And we'd all be right.

"You know," Sandy said, giving me a merciless unamused stare, "I'm not loving that weird expression on your face. I think I'll run ahead."

"Sure," I said to her speedy backside after it was obvious that she was not seeking my approval. "I'll catch up."

She may have been spitting, like runners do, or she may have been commenting, when she made the sharp hacking noise. "Bet you won't," she said boldly.

She had every right to be bold. Whether she meant that as a challenge or a taunt or a complaint, she knew she was winning that bet.

I was not catching up.

* * *

It was way before my wake-up time, so I didn't really stir at the first few rings of the house phone. Four. Probably five. But when I heard my father's voice, as full of fury as I could remember it ever being, I shot up.

"What? Hello . . . *what*? Are you fucking serious?" Nothing and nobody could ever whip that wildness out of Dad.

Well, not nobody, exactly, but it took a special somebody.

"No!" Dad bellowed. "Not a chance, not for a minute, not one single dollar, no. I had my chance, and it was no good. You keep him. And may you have better luck than I did."

I was at the door now, straining to hear more. My father was quiet and I wasn't sure at first if he'd hung up. But then small, reasoned *unnh* and *huhh* sounds came out of him as if somebody on the other end had presented him the kind of cost-benefit analysis of choices he could appreciate. Things he might want to think about before hanging up and giving up.

"Right, of course. I agree," Dad said in a tone that said a whole lot of things were not right and not agreeable.

He bashed the phone down and growled words that I didn't have to hear to understand. He was already stamping back to their room, then all around their room, as Ma talked calmness and sense. "No, Emma, no, no. It's humiliating enough already. I won't let you be degraded by going to that place in the middle of the night." The conversation halted right there, and he stamped back out and toward the door to find me right there and ready.

"What?" he said. "Go back to bed, Arlo, this doesn't have to concern you."

"Oh, it absolutely does have to," I said. "I know when a situation demands a referee."

* * *

"We found him asleep, on his motorbike, at a stoplight," the sergeant at the desk said. "He was like a flamingo, one foot up, resting, the other one on the street for balance. More importantly, his saddlebags were loaded with a fair amount of weed broken up into a lot of small baggies. Not good."

"No," Dad said at a lower volume but a higher level of disgust, "not good at all."

Paperwork filled out, bond arrangement settled, Lloyd appeared almost instantly, like we'd just purchased him out of a loser candy machine. He looked like they had had to wake him up all over again. Out of a refrigerator box.

"There's your court date right there," the sergeant said, looking at Dad instead of Lloyd. Fair enough, since this was a lot more than one guy's problem. "I would strongly advise you not to miss it."

"What's going to happen to him?" I asked when Lloyd slinked away without bothering to ask.

The sergeant shrugged his shoulders all the way up to his fleshy earlobes. "Impossible to tell, kid. No priors, very helpful. Quantity of dope, packaged for distribution, very unhelpful."

The three of us walked down the wide concrete steps of the police station under bright lights that showcased the awfulness of all this. Dad was first, followed by Lloyd, followed by me.

"Sorry," Lloyd just barely said as he reached the pavement. But just barely was enough to get my father started.

"*We*," Dad said, whipping around and stabbing his number one son in the chest with his finger, "were not the type of people this was supposed to happen to. You have no reason to be this way, Lloyd, none. You have no *right* to be this way." He spoke in a sort of desperate, cracking voice I had never heard before.

Lloyd stood rigid, like a soldier being inspected, as Dad inched closer and made a frightening two-handed claw gesture inches away from his face. "I swear, I could . . ."

"Do it," Lloyd said calmly. "Go for it, Dad. You've earned it. I won't fight back. Might do us both some good."

I gave it a second just to see. Then I saw Dad going for him, and I just couldn't let it happen, especially with Lloyd so weak and pathetic. I banged into the toxic space between them, surprising myself by giving Lloyd a bit of a shove toward the curb.

Not that my brother didn't deserve an ass whipping. He'd get it, when he was ready. And when I was.

"Do you *both* some good?" I shouted at Lloyd. "Count again, there are three of us. Let's just get away from here, huh?"

Without a word, I headed after Lloyd and my father followed. As I reached him, two cars came heading down the street at a fast enough clip that they must have been taunting the desk sergeant. I stopped just as they were about to barrel past us.

But Lloyd didn't. He stepped right off the curb without even pausing. My right arm shot out and grabbed him by the back of his shirt collar, and I pulled him back with almost enough force to pull his stupid head off but definitely enough to fling him sprawling across the sidewalk back toward the steps of the station.

Everything stopped. All traffic had vanished, all sound snuffed. As I looked down at my brother, who lay there in a heap, bathed in hard light, the thought I had above all the others was how easy that had been, to throw him. He was so . . . insubstantial.

Eventually my brother got back to his feet. My father did not give him a hand. I did not give him a hand. The three of us negotiated our way across the road in an eerie vacuum of almost any sensation at all.

The sounds of the engine and the talk radio blah-blah-blah got us home. The door opened and Ma shot through the stillness like a greyhound out of the gate. She slammed into Lloyd and hugged him tight enough that they would possibly meld into one organism if they held the hug just long enough. Dad drifted away to his room, and I floated off to mine, so numb I didn't even call Sandy.

\* \* \*

It was probably not an exaggeration to say that my mother saved my brother from prison. She wrote a letter to the court on his behalf, detailing Lloyd's history of mental instability, of substance abuse issues that she maintained were both exacerbated by and resulted from a succession of head injuries. All the homework she had put into compiling The File paid off here as she pumped in equal shots of hard data and mother love. She had even contacted Coach Fisk, and he showed up at the hearing, and spoke privately with two separate court officers.

Between Ma and the Coach, they did twice as much as Lloyd's lawyer, who mostly just sat slumped in his chair as if he was just a leftover from the hearing before this one. With the two of them side by side, it would have been tough to tell who was who if Lloyd had worn a suit like he should have.

The judge's verdict: probation, mandatory counseling, and community service.

Arlo's verdict: everybody in the room would probably have benefited from sending the accused to jail for a few months.

Lloyd was not grateful.

"Look what you did to me, Ma," he whined after we left the courtroom, pointing at details of the judgment here, here, and here on the pages. "I mean, okay, I'm not going to jail, but look at all the shit I gotta do. Ma, I know your heart was in the right place, but y'know, you went a little overboard with all the storytelling. What am I gonna do with *counseling*, for cryin' out loud?"

Ma was already absolutely spent by the ordeal and all she had put into rescuing the ungrateful rodent, so said absolutely nothing back to him.

But I did.

"I am going to kill you," I said, leaning into him and banging the bridge of my nose on his. I knew how genuine I was in that threat when I saw Lloyd's eyes try to smile but stay wide with fear instead. In a building that knew killers when they spoke, I did not feel one bit of a faker at this moment.

"Good result, I'd say," Coach Fisk said then, squeezing my upper arm firmly.

"Thank you so much for coming," Ma said, spontaneously hugging him and then retreating shyly.

"It was my pleasure, for sure," Coach said. He shook Lloyd's hand and then introduced us all to a friend he'd brought along. "Folks, this is an old, old pal of mine, Jamie McAlpine."

"What do you mean, old, old . . . ?" Jamie said, and everybody laughed more than the joke probably deserved. He shook hands with Ma first, then with me, firmly. It was like shaking a glove full of rocks. Finally he gripped Lloyd's hand and shook it vigorously, for a long time. I could tell by the expression on Lloyd's face that Jamie wasn't letting him release, but also that Jamie McAlpine could just do whatever it was Jamie McAlpine wanted to do and for as long as he wanted to do it.

"Could Lloyd and I have a private word just for a minute?" Jamie said. He kept squeezing and shaking Lloyd's hand while looking at Ma for permission.

"Certainly, by all means," Ma said.

Jamie finally let go and led the way to a bench in the far corner of the black-and-white marble floor. Lloyd slouched after him.

As they went off, Ma said, hushed-like, "Well, he looks better than I would have thought, all things considered."

"He takes good care of himself now," Coach Fisk said.

Jamie McAlpine. If our town had one legitimate legend, it was probably Jamie. He had been a tenacious, rock-hard middleweight, then a bulky but still fearsome light-heavyweight boxer who never got the big fight because it was said even in defeat he was hell to tangle with and made everybody suffer and look bad in the process.

I only saw him fight one time, toward the end of his career. He was the headliner on a card of local guys who were never going anyplace. But the whole afternoon, at the old Memorial Auditorium that got torn down a month later, was spoiled because the young guy Jamie fought turned out to be a lot more of a legitimate prospect than he was supposed to be. The kid wasn't a power puncher but he was fast and precise, with that twisting snapper type of a jab that produced cuts as if his gloves were covered in coarse sandpaper. I remember, as a twelve-year-old soft kid, wincing and turning away as the kid made Jamie's face into something you'd see in a butcher's shop window. It was only when the referee stepped in and warned Jamie that he was going to stop the fight soon that desperation took over and restored order. Everybody could hear the conversation, that's how stunned silent we were. After that the old slugger went all raging bull and finally landed three straight bombs right on the kid's button nose and dropped him like a big dead tuna bouncing on the ring mat. Jamie retired a couple of months later to open his own gym—and to close a lot of bars. According to the local paper.

Ma was completely right, that he could have looked a lot worse. And as he guided my misguided brother into that far corner of the courthouse, I thought he was possibly the one person with the *weight* to get him to listen.

I mean, I couldn't even hear what he was saying and I found myself nodding agreement to every bit of it from all the way across the lobby.

Nodding right along with Lloyd, until I realized that and I stopped.

# HELLO GOOD-BYE

It was a long way to go before the August day when Coach Fisk was going to reinstate me and I was going to begin the kind of senior season folks around here would still be talking about for years. I thought about it every single day, even though the school year had just ended and the whole summer stretched ahead. It was all consuming, and as I had gotten more intense about my solo workout program, I got less interested in what anybody else was doing, even if Sandy was that anybody. Even Dinos. Especially Dinos.

"Yes, Arlo, the graduation. You know, where they give out diplomas? Like the one they will be giving out to your best friend today?"

"You're my best friend, Sandy."

We were talking on the phone as I walked home after my longest run ever. I woke up to such a crazy gorgeous morning, the kind of air that makes you just have to get outside and do something with it even if you were not planning to run at all. It must have been twelve hard miles, and I felt so good about it I had to call my best girl and the best runner I knew to tell her about it before I even reached home.

"Not right now, I'm not. How could you blow that off?"

She was ruining the day's perfection, and I already regretted calling her.

"I never said I was going to the graduation. Anyway, it's for family."

"Yes, you did say you were going. Dinos *asked* you to go."

Dinos and I had been just barely on speaking terms since he called in the big guns to shut down my multidiscipline training plans. So on one hand, you could say it was easy for me to space out on his graduation day. But on another, bigger hand, you could say the effort he made in personally inviting me in the middle of the cafeteria on bacon burger day should have damn well stuck out in my mind.

"All right, all right, all right, Sandy, I'm on it."

"Ceremony is starting right about now."

"I said all *right*," I said and hung up on her. I would have to make up for that social screwup after I took care of this one.

My sweat was almost dried up by then, in the perfect late-spring sunshine, but I'd have to get it going again from a cold start. I burst into sprint mode, and felt none of the easy fluidity of my earlier run. That was to be expected. Different stride, no warning, I'd loosen up again in no time.

I owed him, after all.

He was my friend. Since freshman year, Dinos was my one great friend, and as an upperclassman he pulled me along in his wake and made my journey easier and a whole lot more fun than it might have been. Yes, he was an ass for ratting me out, and he was wrong. But he was a wrong ass for his own right reasons.

My stride was not coming along. I pushed harder.

He did what he did. He did what he did for reasons he thought were noble, and because he was Dinos there was no reason to question that no matter how wrong he might have been.

He asked me to come.

I pushed harder, and got nothing for my effort. My sweat was not returning, either. The sun now felt like late summer mean, and that was not helping things.

I was going to be so late. Felt like a rat. *Was* a rat. Sandy was right to be disgusted with me. I was disgusted with me. How does she always know when to be disgusted with me before I do?

Every workout, every game, every time Dinos pounded on my shoulder pads came to my mind now as my legs flatly refused to do what they were well trained to do.

I got dizzy. Lightning strikes of pain cracked across the entire surface of my skull. I veered off the pavement, the wrong way, almost right into traffic. A car horn wailed in my ear, making everything happening in my head happen harder. I staggered back on the pavement, weaved and stumbled until I fell and found myself lying up against somebody's dense and prickly hedge.

I felt like the hedge was inside my head, working its thorny way through the cracks the way roots get into a house's foundation.

I had to close my eyes. The sun didn't care and came right on inside with me.

\* \* \*

I was certain that I never lost consciousness. I sat, composing myself, eyes closed, thinking about getting to Dinos. First I would rest, lose the dizzies, get up the strength to rise. Then I'd get something to drink, because this was dehydration, was all it was. I had drunk plenty of fluids but obviously not enough. Didn't plan for twelve miles. Didn't plan for a crap conversation with Sandy. Didn't plan for Dinos.

"Are you all right?" a lady's voice asked me.

I slowly blink-blinked up until I could make out the figure of a woman, possibly in her seventies, but looking a lot fitter than I felt. She had on a flowered hat and a matching pair of gardening gloves.

"I am, ma'am, thanks. Just got a little dizzy, thought I should sit for a little bit. I'll get out of your hedge now. Nice hedge you have. Firm."

"Thank you," she said as I started up. I got halfway upright before I went to my knees, grabbing my head with both hands to squeeze the pain away.

"Do you have a hose . . . handy by any chance . . . ma'am?" I looked at the pavement while I choke-spoke. She made some kind of worried sound in response, and in a few seconds I heard the scrape and splash of a live hose being dragged my way, the most delicious sound ever. "Thank you so much," I said, and took a huge drink, bloating my belly before turning the water on my head, my face, my chest my shoulders, my head. My head. Dear God, my head.

"You are a true lifesaver, ma'am," I said after I had emptied half the town's water supply over myself. "I can't thank you enough."

She took her hose back and started dragging it into her garden again. "You can thank me by respecting the strength of that sun from now on. Wear a hat next time."

"I will," I said. "I promise."

I was feeling much better. Until I checked my watch.

Between being lodged in the hedge and hosing myself back to viability, I had lost fifty minutes.

I broke into a run once more.

And once more the headache screamed, the landscape wobbled, and I stopped trying to do anything more ambitious than gently walking myself home.

The cool shower felt fantastic enough that I could have stayed in there for a couple of days. But as I relaxed into it I became more aware of the time getting away, which made me anxious, which made me hurry, which made me queasy, which made me slow down again. It was one cycle that truly did deserve to be called vicious because the more I wanted to make things right for Dinos the less able I was to actually do it.

As I lay down on the bed I still held some hope that this could work out. I'd go to his house once I felt right. I'd have missed the ceremony, but once I saw him and told him face-to-face how it was an accident we would be good again. I closed my eyes. Just for a few minutes. To finish the job, charge my battery, get me right.

My phone beeped me a message.

I opened my eyes, getting my bearings yet again. I had the

fogginess of having slept for a day and a half straight, though I was sure I hadn't slept at all. I got my phone off the night table.

It was from Dinos. *Best thing about being a hs grad? Do not have to hang with jerk punks anymore. Sorry not to see you today. Have a great summer. Cuz I sure will. STINYGIASOU! That's good health. Or maybe screw yourself in Greek. Let's say it's both.*

His trip. He was leaving right away. His Greek trip. As a graduation present his folks expanded it to include Portugal, Spain, France, and Italy. How could I forget that? He *told* me. When he *invited* me. To the graduation.

I hit the call back button immediately. "Pick it up," I insisted to the phone. "Don't leave me twisting." It rang. I twisted. It rang. I deserved it. It stopped ringing and invited me to leave a message. I opened my mouth to start, heard in my mind how weaselly I sounded, and hung up on my sorry self.

# STINYGIASOU

Have a good summer. Good health.

As it turned out, I think it must have meant to screw myself. As I drove myself harder and harder through the long solitary summer, I had to get used to the fact that I was never going to be completely alone because pain was going to be my workout partner now. Muscle tweaks and aches were par for the course when you upped the intensity like I did. Fine.

And if near constant headaches were part of the price, too, well bring them on. Can't be a linebacker if you can't live with a ringing head anyway, so I was already on top of things.

I had no real summer to speak of, apart from the gym. Sandy left shortly after Dinos, and there would be no visiting her on Nantucket this year because she wouldn't be there. Her family decided for a change to go to a place called Half Moon Bay. In Northern California. For the whole summer. I wouldn't say that they decided to put a whole country between us this year, and to stay even longer, because of anything to do with me. But since I couldn't concentrate on anything else except getting lean and strong, I think Sandy's great escape actually saved us. Saved us, from me.

Lloyd and I passed each other during our comings and goings, and while we were mostly just taking care of our own business, I had to say he looked good. Not just sober-good but also with a humanness that came across in little things like "Hello, Arlo," which for the first time in some time didn't sound like I should be waiting for a punch line, or a punch.

By the third week of August I was ripped. I was lean and strong, and furious. I wanted to hit more than I had ever wanted to hit, and if football camp didn't get here quick, I was ready to just go out into the street and start taking on moving cars like they were tackling sleds. It was good Sandy was far away, and Lloyd was doing his thing, and Ma and Dad were taking a hands-off approach to a household that was finally allowing them to do that for a while.

Because every day I felt a little less able to talk to people. I was angry and anxious and counting on the idea that getting back to football would make me right again, since the end of football was really the beginning of *this*.

* * *

"You're really going for it?" Lloyd asked me on the morning of the day that had taken so long to arrive. Just when I thought we'd all settled into a permanent pattern of quiet coexistence with everyone functioning independently and inconspicuously, Lloyd showed something else. He was tuned in to what I was doing, and merely picked his moment when he had something to say.

"Of course I'm going for it," I said. "Did you ever really think otherwise?"

"Can I come in?" he asked from the doorway while I did a few last torques with the medicine ball.

"Who are you, Dracula now, needing to be invited? Come in."

"Thanks," he said. It was all condensed right there, in the asking and thanking, how the Life of Lloyd was becoming something very different from what it had been. It was about the difference courts and counseling and community service under the supervision of Mr. McAlpine could make to the evolution of one hardcore knucklehead punk like him.

"You look good," I said, only really noticing for the first time. Four months clean combined with his court-ordered slaving for Jamie—performing janitorial services as well as leading training sessions for groups of even younger hard-core knucklehead punks—had done him good. Enough good so that he at least didn't look like the diminished, withered version of himself he had become. He wasn't the *force* he once was, but this was progress for sure.

"Thanks," he said. "I try and work out as much as I can at the gym, whenever Jamie doesn't have stuff for me to do. You should come down sometime."

"Thanks, but no," I said, and dropped the medicine ball from too high. It made a loud, awful thump on the wood floor, and I felt like I was one of the blowhard grunting jerks who make far too much unnecessary noise in the weight room. If Ma were home, I would have to be apologizing big time. "Nothing personal, but isn't McAlpine's basically the bottom rung on the loser ladder at this point? I mean, doesn't a person have to be *sentenced* to time at 'Pine's?"

Lloyd, being slow and thoughtful in another change from the past, frowned and nodded before answering. "Harsh, Arlo."

He was correct, too. I heard it as it was coming out, and yeah, I kind of surprised myself. Surprised but not bothered. Sometimes harsh is just the way it is.

* * *

Coach Fisk looked almost surprised to see me when I walked across the field to shake his hand. If he ever seriously considered the possibility that I would pack it in without a fight for my football life, then he had forgotten everything he ever knew about me.

"Arlo," he said, shaking my hand hard, "good to see you. How was your summer, son?"

"Excellent, Coach. Super. Rarin' to go now."

He hesitated. "Well, now, you remember, there are hurdles—"

"Let's get to hurdling, then."

"Easy, easy there, big boy. Great to have your enthusiasm on the field again, but it will take a little more time to get all that sorted out. It's not going to be just me making this call, Arlo. There's a procedure. Medical folks have to be involved. Very specific examinations you are going to have to pass."

Even this conversation was making me anxious. I bounced up and down and then side to side on the balls of my feet, just the way I would when I anticipated a running play coming my way and needing to be stuffed. "Whatever you need me to do, Coach, let's just get it done."

He reached out and grabbed my shoulders. He exerted substantial downward pressure to get me to keep still. "It's not going to happen right now, okay? Things have to be arranged. To be honest, I wasn't exactly prepared. . . ."

"Why? That doesn't make any sense. There's no way I'm not gonna play. . . . Anyway, fine, whatever, just arrange it."

"In due time. Today it's all just conditioning, assessing who's in what kind of shape, you know the drill by now, you're a vet. So just get in there, go through your paces. There'll be no contact. I can clear you for that. Then we'll take it from—"

"Thanks, Coach," I said, bolting for the far end of the field, where the entire squad of players and hopefuls were stretching for the full-field, half-speed sprints that always kicked things off. I had not been this excited for the beginning of camp since . . . ever. Never, ever.

"Do my eyes deceive me?" McCallum said as he pulled me into a big slapping hug.

"They do not," I said.

"It walks, it talks," Jerome said raising both hands high, slapping them into my hands, and holding on before I could even get out of McCallum's grip.

"It does a lot more than that, pal, I'll tell you that," I said, and the laughs all around were only quieted by the assistant coach's whistle calling us into formations for the sprints.

There were probably eighty guys, maybe a few more, and we

lined up in groups of ten across. "Go!" the coach yelled, and the first group set off for the goal line. "Go!" he said, and the second group went off. It was a completely mixed bunch, fast guys and bulky guys, seniors and rooks all running along side by side by side. "Go!" the coach called to the fifth group, my group, with McCallum on my right and Jerome on my left.

We were running at half speed, an arm's distance between us. It was August hot, the kind of heat you can feel coming down from the sun and up from the ground at the same time. I felt the first drops of sweat rolling down from my scalp before I hit the fifty-yard line. A little early, but I always liked sweat. We had just run through the first, then the second line of players coming back the other way, each group passing through the other with marching-band precision.

"You gonna be all right?" Jerome asked me.

"What are you talking about, man? Of course I'm gonna be all right."

We passed through the third group.

"Okay, okay, it's just, wantin' to make sure, is all."

I felt a small bump as I shouldered through the fourth group.

"Better watch where you're going there," McCallum said as we reached the far end and stopped for our short breather. "Football field can be a dangerous place, if you recall, Mr. Brodie."

"Nah," I said, "somehow I forgot all that stuff. Probably for the best anyway."

Before we stopped goofing, it was time for us to head upfield again. "Go!" yelled the second assistant coach at this end.

We went, and the excitement was making our whole line move

faster than we had the first time. Guys started yelling as we gained ground on the bunch just ahead of us. We were laughing and taunting them and they picked up speed as the first, then the second group passed through us in the other direction again, and I turned to Jerome, who was smiling broadly, just like I was feeling inside, just like I always knew this was going to be, for senior starters on a great football team and who knows what all in front of us.

"Heads up!" I heard, just before the impact.

It wasn't stars, it was rockets, and it was drums in my head as I lay there on my back, then up on my elbow, feeling around my face for broken bones or blood. Around me there was hell kicking off, Jerome going crazy, bellowing and launching himself at somebody.

"Anderson, chicken-shit scumbag . . . that was on purpose, goddammit!" Jerome yelled, grabbing big Anderson around the neck and driving him backward.

McCallum and several other guys jumped in and started pulling them apart, while Anderson yelled back, "No, no, no, he wasn't looking, he ran into me, it was his fault. I didn't do nothin'."

"I can fight my own battles," I said as I got halfway up, then fell back down. I immediately attempted to get up once more, but there were many hands suddenly keeping me seated until I stopped trying.

The fight was broken up, and the players dispersed to other parts of the field. One of the assistant coaches was down on the turf with me, waving an ammonia capsule under my nose. My head cleared, quickly but partially, stars now, not rockets, and I pushed the capsule away.

"I'm fine, thanks," I said.

"Okay, Arlo," he said.

"It was just, the guy weighs about a million pounds, y'know, and I ran into him, totally blindsided. He's probably right, my own fault. Live and learn, right?"

"Right," the assistant said without a lot of enthusiasm.

I put out my hand, and he helped me to my feet. We got me successfully up, where I stood, a little unsteadily, looking at the ground for several seconds before he let me go to stand on my own.

"See?" I said. "Fine. Good to go." I took a step forward, still looking down, so I bumped right into him. "Ha," I laughed. "I really do have to look where I'm going."

Then he grabbed me. In a hug, that was such a hug, it scared me with what it was all about. Then as I looked up I found out what it was all about, even as it became a new kind of hug entirely.

It wasn't any assistant.

"It's all over, son," Coach Fisk said. He was holding me close to him, with one hand cupping the back of my head. The side of his face pressed right up to the side of my face while he spoke softly right down my ear. "There won't be any assessments. I wouldn't care what they said. You're a brave kid, Arlo, but I won't watch this happen. I won't *allow* it to happen. That's that."

That's that.

I was so weak, I didn't even try to answer him back. Already, I couldn't even *act* like a football player anymore. I felt it all over my stupid face as I just went and cried. And cried. Like a damn baby.

# BRAND-NEW MAN

I had to tell my mother, of course.

"I didn't expect you to *cry*, Ma," I said, muffled though I was by her arms wrapped around my big healthy, mostly pain-free head.

"I'm not crying," she said while clearly crying. She let go of me and occupied herself flapping all around the kitchen, getting dinner ready. Then I got the sunburst smile, which made me wish that I could laugh.

"I figured if anybody was going to cry, it would be you," I said to my dad who was sitting across the table from me.

"I thought about it," he said dryly, winking at me. "I still might. I'm working through it. I don't like to rush into things."

"Good, sound reasoning there, Dad." He was trying, and I was glad he was trying. Because I was sick when I thought how I had let him down. He had to feel that way, at least a little.

Pasta now doing its thing on the stove, jumbo shrimp defrosting in the microwave, my mother came back at me.

By the time she reached me she was crying again.

"So you had a concussion," she said kind of quavery and feeling all around my skull as if she thought concussions were something she could locate and examine for herself.

"No, I didn't. Never had a concussion. Not one." There was no way I was going to say anything about hit counts.

"Never had one diagnosed, you mean," Dad said with extraordinary unhelpfulness.

"Didn't you have some emotions to process or something over there?"

"Well, that's true, isn't it?" Ma said, plunking down in the worry chair with worry hands framing her worry frown.

"Subconcussive hits, that's what they concluded. Listen, the coaches have a lot of this kind of experience. They know what they're doing. I'm fine. Fine, okay?"

She kept me locked in her laser stare.

"That poor boy from Kansas," she said. "They talked about something called Second Impact Syndrome as maybe being a factor in his death. That's very scary to me, Arlo. Second impact syndrome, do you know what I'm talking about?"

I mean, God rest his soul and everything, the poor guy. But I was sure if he knew the headaches he had caused me, he would not be happy about it.

"Yeah, Ma, I know. But since I never even had a concussion, you don't have to worry about it at all. And, as a matter of fact, since nobody around here plays football anymore, you can probably give up that morbid hobby of yours now and start reading, like *Better Homes and Gardens* or something like normal mothers do." At least I could give her back The File.

She locked the stare on me again.

"Does second impact syndrome need to involve an actual concussion, necessarily? Couldn't this subconcussive thing—"

"Ma," I reached over to her, completely encased her small-boned hands in my big-boned ones. "I was kind of hoping the one real upside to my shortened career would be that we could enjoy this part. The coach shut me down *for my own good*, just like you would have. That's one in the win column for you, isn't it?"

She looked at me, nodded, looked at me again. Then she got up and did a hip swivel half turn in my direction, poured on the full wattage of the happiness she was allowing herself, and just as quickly swished away again.

It lit the joint right up, which was sweet. Except for it being a big fat diversion. I had too much to do, too much at stake, to be fighting battles every day with the well-intentioned people who didn't want me doing it.

It was plain that she was celebrating a finality.

There is no finality. Not when you have to hit, regardless.

# SENIOR YEAR

# BRUTUS

My hands hurt.

Doesn't stop me punching, though. And I'm doing it right, I know I am because my lats are killing me even more than my hands. The torque is the thing. Grinding, grinding left hooks, right hooks one-two-one-two until my entire core feels as if I've been rung like a sweaty, ratty wet towel. That, once you get it going, is an irresistible force. Nobody can stand up to it.

Except Brutus. Brutus can stand up to anything. I can punch Brutus till the cows come home—meaning forever, since we never had any cows so they won't be coming home—and he'd love me for it.

I could be good at this. I could be great at this, I'm thinking as I roll smoothly from one foot to the other, from hard rights to hard lefts that have equal power and precision. Yes, I'm thinking, hitting harder, like I'm breaking out of chains and smashing down walls. Perfect sport. A man alone. Pure power. This is what a man does. Punch. A man does. Punch. A *man. Does.*

"What?"

"What yourself, Ma. Leave me alone, huh?"

"Excuse me?"

"Excuse *yourself*," I say. "Barging in like that."

"Barging? Do you have any idea how much noise you're making?"

She has entered my room unannounced because she's heard me hammering away boxing. I am sweaty and wearing my padded training gloves as I stand in front of her.

"I'll punch quieter. I'm just trying any way I can to keep in shape."

"Uh-huh. Like a *man* does, you mean?"

Ah, hell. I must have been talking out loud. Just shut up and punch, Arlo. That's the key to everything from now on, just shut up and punch.

"Sorry, Ma. I promise I'll be quieter."

"Fine, but if you just want to get in shape—by the way, what is this I'm looking at right now, *out* of shape?" She is gesturing at me with that up-and-down hand gesture, like a model at an auto show calling attention to a shiny new car.

For the record, I'm six foot two, two hundred and twenty pounds, waist thirty, chest forty, inseam thirty-five. For the record. It's okay shape. Could be better, though. I'd like it to be better.

"If you just want to get in shape," she continues, "what is *he* doing here?"

He is my training partner, a Slam Man, Brutus, the bottom-heavy, man-shaped, molded-plastic opponent who takes punches forever and never asks questions. In a less complicated world, a

Slam Man wouldn't necessarily get Ma's hackles up this high. But ever since I rescued him from McAlpine's scrap heap, Ma's been on edge a little.

Lloyd came home from the gym one day and told me Jamie was going to be putting this *thing* out for the weekly trash pickup and Lloyd thought maybe it'd be of interest to me. A little beat-up, he said, but good exercise, didn't take much room, and I could pound the daylights out of him without him ever hitting me back. So naturally I went down to see.

"He is a piece of exercise equipment. Like my bike."

"Like your bike? Does your bike get to live in the house? Have I heard you talking, in depth, to your bike like you have to him? Does your bike have a *name* for the love of—?"

"Bike's name is Raleigh," I say, jabbing her in the ribs.

She slaps my glove. "*You* didn't give it that name, unlike this brute."

I didn't name him Brutus. He revealed his identity to me, once I had earned his trust and respect. I considered sharing this information with Ma, but couldn't see it helping the situation a whole lot.

"If I ride him around the neighborhood, will you relax some?"

She sighs. This is almost good. Like with any quicker and more technically skilled adversary, wearing her down is usually my only hope. "McAlpine's, though?" she says.

Thing is, when I found Brutus, I also found McAlpine's. As soon as I pushed through the heavy, groaning metal door, I was hooked. So weathered even the walls seemed rusty, and aromatic as onions, the building had more real atmosphere than fifty Rocky movies could ever manage. It was not part of any school system, which could tell me what to do with my own head, and it had the most incredible sound going on, that spoke to me like the guys had been waiting for me here forever. There were maybe sixteen of them in the whole place, but it might as well have been three basketball teams dribbling and driving and jamming, and the whole rhythm section of a marching band wedged into the grungy, echoey, sweaty, bloody concrete box of a joint. How did they get the rhythm so right, so that it was driven straight into a guy's own heart the minute he stepped inside? The sound and the scent and the thrump of this place were absolutely *it*. You could not draw a breath in McAlpine's Gym and not sense everything you needed contained within it. At least I couldn't.

"Hey, it's been all great for Lloyd," I say. "You said so yourself."

"There's a difference," she says, a glance at Lloyd's open door. "He's working to get *better*."

"What do you mean by that?" I snap. "What, that I'm going some other way? That I'm going downhill into something anything at all like what he did to himself? No comparison, Ma, none. If he gets himself straight and you want to be proud about it, then that's great, but don't pull me down just to pull him up, okay?"

Dad ambles in, making this an almost unheard-of family meeting in my room. This does not fill me with hope.

"What am I missing?" he says, as if there were any mystery.

"Our son is training for fighting now," Ma says caustically. It doesn't sound good and doesn't sound right coming out of her.

"I'm not training to fight, I'm just training to train. It's the best training there is, millions of people do it now, even old ladies and everything with boxercise or whatever they call it. It's really, really common, what I'm doing, so just don't sweat it, all right?"

"Boxercise," Dad says so flatly I can't tell if he's teasing or believing.

"I can take care of myself, guys, honestly. I'm fine. And I will be fine."

She's not buying a bit of it. I've upset her now truly, and she's laying another one of her devastating looks on me. The one that makes me feel sorry or angry for whatever chump she's looking at like that. Who is he anyway, this chump?

I know who it *used* to be. Used to be the chump right down the hall from me. The thought of her looking at me now like *that* . . .

I will myself to stay calm, blink slowly, but this whole thing must be raising my blood pressure or something, because I'm suddenly getting a little woozy. Not sure if she could appreciate it or not, the fact that her intensity probably rocks me more than any supposed head shots. Don't think I'll ask her right now, though.

I am still standing, my weight shifting from foot to foot, trying to match the internal swaying motion. I shake my head slightly, checking, the way I do, the way I didn't used to do, like a dog shakes his head coming out of the water but not like that, either. This dog is not in the water, the water is in the dog. I can actually feel it. Somewhere in there I find a kind of comfort, my consciousness of what is not right meaning I must be all right at the core. "If it's done so much good for Lloyd," I say, "it'll do twice as much for me."

I can feel the fluid surrounding my brain, separating my brain from the inner wall of my skull. I can feel that fluid buffer failing a little as I shake my head slightly and sense the movement of the gray vital meat, feel it bash into its walls like a mental patient trying to break out of his cell. But I'm aware, so I'm good.

"The difference," Ma says again, "is that Lloyd accepts now that it's all over regarding fighting and contact sports and that whole nonsense part of life."

"And," Dad adds, "that whether he accepted it or not, there is nothing much he could do about it."

There is always something you can do about it. I have learned this, even if Lloyd didn't.

I push past my parents. I don't say good-bye.

# CONTACT

I like contact. I'll make no apologies for that. I love it, in fact. That's what we do it for. Nothing compares. Nothing. Nothing fills, thrills, moves, removes, satisfies, rewards, revives, relieves . . . hell. Anyway. Nothing. I'm not the guy to describe it, maybe. But I am the guy to carry it out.

It's just that the price of contact is contact. I am more than happy to pay it. More than.

I don't mind getting punched and kicked in the head. No bragging, just true. Does that count as some sort of abnormality? I don't think so.

You show me a guy who has no fear of getting his bell rung, and I'll show you a dangerous guy.

I like to think of myself as a dangerous guy. You don't have to be a bad guy to be a dangerous one.

And you don't have to be a bad guy to be a fighter. I am a fighter. I know this because I have to fight. Because I can't not fight. I know what the stakes are, and that the stakes are fairly high.

But I am willing, that's the thing. I'm the one taking the shots, so I should be the one calling the shots.

I have bided my time at McAlpine's. I work out on the weights, on the speed and heavy bags most mornings before school, most afternoons after school. When Lloyd is in the place and not doing flunky work, we take turns punching the daylights out of the big hand pads that we wear for each other to wail on. It feels really good, like the days he was training for the army, and we're both in good shape for it.

I was born to do this.

# COACH

Mr. Fisk and I don't talk about much these days beyond Twentieth-Century American History. He's my teacher for the subject, and I really almost enjoy the class because of him and his robust way of conveying his personal enthusiasms. From the first week of school, he made it clear that football was behind me now, so there was no stress between us.

Until now.

"You are failing, by a comfortable margin," he says after class.

This is news. Ish.

"Sorry, sir," which I calculate as being the correct response. I'm so disconnected from the magic footprints that get a guy out through the other end of high school, it's kind of guesswork at this point. Academics has been collateral damage to my so-called sports retirement this year.

"You're not stupid, Mr. Brodie," he says to me now.

"Thank you, Mr. Fisk."

"I know of no reason for you to be failing. Are you not concerned?"

"To tell you the truth, sir, probably not as concerned as I should be."

"Are you aware that you have to pass this class to graduate?"

"*Wwwhat?*"

"Arlo, I'm going to make a wild guess that means you were not cognizant of this fact."

"But, I've passed all the other—"

"This is not an elective, Arlo. This is core. No pass, no graduation. Until after summer school, of course."

"*Summer . . . Jeezuz H.—*"

"Hey," he snaps.

"Sorry, sir. But, you just have no idea what all else I've—"

"Right. I have no idea. Sure."

I realize. I know better than this.

Up go the hands in surrender. "Of course, you have every idea, Mr. Fisk. I didn't mean that."

He snorts a laugh. "Heh, of course you mean it. All you young bucks mean it when you tell me, in one way or another, that I simply don't understand. Even the kids who love me—which means the kids with any discernible brain wave—usually get around to pointing out the inherent cluelessness that comes with my job. They mean it, temporarily, then they get over themselves, then they listen to about half of what I have to say, which is an acceptable success rate as far as I'm concerned."

He's going too fast.

"Right," he says, more deliberately, when it's clear I have nothing to say. "When did you quit?"

"Huh?"

"On the academics. Come on, Arlo, I'm pretty sure you were a decent student at some point, and even without trying you're fairly bright in class. At what point did you punch out?"

"End of first term, sophomore year." I didn't even have to dig for that.

"Well," he says, clapping once and leaning way back in his chair, "that was quick and specific."

It was, wasn't it. Huh.

We smile at each other, sweetly and kind of stupidly, for a few seconds over this.

Extra stupid on my part, because I am feeling almost overcome. With good stuff, warmth, appreciation. Jesus, over nothing. I could just about slap myself.

His smile vanishes and he holds out his hand to me like a bully demanding lunch money.

"My hat," he says.

"Your what?"

"My hat. What did you do with my hat? My Dolphins hat? I want it back now."

Pass Twentieth-Century American History? I can't even pass the conversation.

"I forgot all about it."

"There is no statute of limitations on betrayals of kindness or stealing hats."

"I'll look for it." I have no idea where it is. "Or I'll buy you another one."

"No. The original."

"Okay." I hope I remember to look.

"What are we going to do about your history grade then, Arlo?"

It takes me a second to register the sudden change in topic again. "I don't know. Try harder?"

He laughs. He laughs so barky and infectious that I can't help but join in.

"Ah, you kids," he says when he's composed himself.

"Well, I have a couple of months to—"

"Weeks."

*What?*

"Months are gone, son, leaving us with weeks. And if you fail, it's automatic summer school. Leaving us with extra credit. In your case, a lot of extra credit."

"What kind of extra credit?"

"My car needs new break pads, for starters."

"Oh. Oh, I know nothing about—"

He looks at me sharply. "I'm kidding, Arlo. I will come up with some research papers you can do. You're also going to have to pass the final, which is not going to be a breeze. You'll need some extra tutoring. I'll fix something up."

Or I could just quit. Which would destroy my parents once and for all, and who really wants to see what *that* looks like at this stage? It might be nice if I could at least provide them one high school graduate son. At least that.

"All right, Mr. Fisk. Whatever it takes. But you mind my asking, how come you're going out of your way to help me? After I let it happen in the first place and everything?"

"What, you think you're special or something? I do this all the time. If I had a *real* title, one that reflected my true calling around here, it would be something like Vice President in Charge of Walking Wounded."

It is funny. I laugh. I don't like it.

I rise from my chair, nod, and shake his hand.

"I'm not wounded, sir," I say, and I look him in the eye in a full-on way I only now realize I was not doing before. In his expression I see he notices. He keeps shaking my hand, very firmly, refusing to release until he's done talking.

"I played football in high school," he says. "Varsity all four years. I was exceptional. Defensive end. Till I shattered my thigh bone midseason senior year. I mean *shattered*. I'm pretty much cyborg down there now. That was the end. Shut me right down, stopped me right in my tracks. Miss it still. Missed out on a lot, I feel."

"Sorry to hear that," I say, gently easing out of the shake. "Really sorry, sir."

"Still be playing today, I figure. Probably playing for the Dolphins. . . ."

I'm walking to the door now.

"I will look for the hat, for cryin' out loud."

I reach the door, open it, and hear, "Do you ever feel like you were ripped off, Arlo? That I should have cleared you, let you be the star you were supposed to be?"

I don't look at him. "Just moved on," I say. "World keeps moving, Mr. Fisk."

"And so it does," he says. "How's the head?"

"Head's fine. See you tomorrow." I exit rapidly before he can see I'm misting up and I cannot get it under control.

# IMPERVIOUS

Thing is, you're a fighter if you feel like you're a fighter. Even if you have a reason or reasons not to fight, that just makes you a fighter who doesn't fight. Which would be a very hard thing to be.

I am nearing the end of a routine workout before heading off to school. I haven't even done enough to require a shower, so I'm using that extra time to have some fun showing off my balance and technique on the speed bag.

What a thing, the speed bag, *bubbada-bubbada-bubbada-bubbada*, the way it tells you loudly and instantly whether you are getting it right or wrong, and wrong is humiliating and right is this, *bubbada-bubbada-bubbada-bubbada*. Light as a cloud, up on the toes, right foot, left foot, right foot, left.

"You got it, boy," I hear just before taking a light thump from behind in my left side ribs.

"Har," I say, pulling my elbows in quick, turning and backpedaling.

It's Jason, a light heavyweight banger of anyone's-guess age who works out every day. An old school pug, Jason is just happy to get in and exchange punches with anyone.

"Thanks, man," I say, and the two of us do a bit of shadow-dance sparring, short-arm punching, blocking, ducking, faking.

"Why don't you come on up in the ring and learn something?" He catches me with a playful slap on my left cheek.

"Or teach you something," I say. I attempt the same slap, which he catches and holds on to and then slaps me again.

I have light training gloves on, but Jason has his hands lightly taped, so he's preparing to spar with somebody, regardless.

"Ha," he says, "let's go then."

"Can't," I say as our session gets a little feistier. "Not quite ready yet for that. And I have to get to school." I snap a light flick-jab that catches him on the chin. My heart jumps with the thrill of it.

"Well, that's what I'm sayin'," he says. "I'm offerin' to take you to *school* myself."

"Ha!" I say, and the instant I say it he proves good to his word. He catches me right in the mouth with a crisp untouchable pop that would have done me great damage if he had thrown it with full bad intentions.

"Hey, hey, sorry, man," Jason says, walking up close and grabbing my shoulders as he takes a good look.

"Nah, man, Jason, it's nothing at all," I say, looking at the blood painting the palm of my glove. "I didn't even feel it."

And I didn't. There was no pain to it at all, and if anything, it made me kind of excited to do it all over again, take another shot in the mouth right now just to have it happen, to be in that moment once more.

My tongue feels around, pushing at an eye tooth that is a little bit wiggly, running over a top lip that has a little bit of a split and a lot of swelling already.

"Took me to school, Jason," I say when he retrieves a cold cloth for me.

"True that. Now take yourself to the other school."

* * *

By the time I turn down Baker Street to the other school, the bleeding has stopped, and the swelling has reached lobster tail proportions, so I dump the cloth in a trash can and just savor the lip that it is. I smile a little until I feel the lip tear a tiny bit and force myself to stop.

And I stop again, when I see Sandy.

I have been dodging her with every trick and excuse I can think of lately because . . . Why? I know right this instant that it isn't that I don't want to see her, because the sight of her here is making me ache so bad I want to run to her like a big oaf right in front of the whole school crowd milling about.

I take two quick anxious steps toward her and I stop short again when a whole new smile splits the lip once again and I do know why I've been sneaking. I feel like I have had ten other girlfriends, and a drug addiction, and an international arrest warrant out on me. Because I know how she would feel, about what I'm doing, where I'm doing it, what I'm thinking about.

I stand there frozen, stupid, cowardly, and I notice next to her as she sits on the low wall. On our low wall. Two tall coffees sitting, waiting for me. Like they waited for her all the way back when we started being us.

She looks up in my direction and I take off, back in the direction I came from.

# THE FIGHT THING

I wake up, well before dawn, feeling it. It's so powerful. It is irresistibly powerful.

I lie here, in the darkness slashed with yellow streetlight, looking at my hands. I have big, strong, gnarly hands. I flex and flex and watch them like they just grew there overnight. I am utterly fascinated. They are so strong. I'm so proud of my hands.

And I have good bones. I've always known that much.

The fight thing. It's so, so powerful.

Brutus and I are touching noses. When did I get up?

"There's nothing wrong with this," I say to my punched-up pal.

He is a generous and nonjudgmental listener.

I'm just feeling so strong, so in charge of it all. I can handle it.

"It's our thing," I tell him with a brotherly head-butt.

My choice. My problem. Nobody's problem.

"You should stop thinking about it," Lloyd says, shocking me. He's seated in the kitchen when I get there, nothing but the microwave blue-light clock illuminating him.

"Jesus, Lloyd. What are you doing up? I thought you had your counselor."

"Yeah, I do."

I go to the fridge, take out the two large plastic canisters of su-perfood shake I mixed the night before. I stuff one in my gym bag and start sipping from the other.

"Don't fight, man. Arlo, just don't, okay?"

"Who are you, my big brother or something?"

"Used to be," he says.

"Well, don't worry. Anyway, you're probably just jealous be-cause I can do it if I want and you can't. I have the power and control you don't have." It's a mean jab, but I don't care. He has less than no right to talk to me about anything.

When I close the refrigerator door we are again in blue shadowy nothing.

"Power and control, big man?" he says as I head out. "How 'bout *choices*? You still have those, is the point. For now anyway."

I exit rapidly. I seem to be doing a lot of that lately. I just wish people would leave me alone. I know what I'm doing.

# DUCKIN' AND DIVIN'

"I got a thing, Jamie."

After getting so familiar with Jamie McAlpine's features, I still admire them every time, the way art students must look at great works over and over. He possesses both the world's finest mashed-potato nose and a laugh so generous I always feel like I owe him change.

"Kid," he gargles "have you never lifted your head once while you were working out here? Everybody got a *thing*. You point out one single person around here who ain't got some kinda *thing* goin' on about him and I'll show you somebody who shouldn'a oughta be here."

I can't point to any such person because I was waiting on the stoop when Jamie came to open up at five thirty.

"Hey, I don't got that kinda *thing*, Jamie," I say, following him into the gym. "I'm no gimp, or fugitive, or bottom feeder or cracks-of-society head case."

He switches on the big overhead lights, illuminating the two rings, the heavy bags, speed bags, medicine balls, kettle balls, free weights, all sort of organized into workout neighborhoods but not really. The lights come up and I can see what I was only smelling. Leather and canvas and blood and rank heroic body odor and iron and somewhere somehow always the faint whiff of drinking alcohol mixing with the rubbing alcohol, even though one of those things is banned here, and Ben-Gay and greasy meat. When I can breathe all that, anything is possible.

"We had a kid in here one time, only name he ever gave us was that—Crackso Society. Couldn't fight for shit, but he could take a punch like a crash test damn dummy."

We walk to Jamie's office, where we sit across the desk he almost certainly stole from school when he left three or four decades ago. Beige-gray metal block of a thing. He opens up his breakfast from McDonald's, aims the bag at me with a grunt of generosity.

"I ate, thanks," I say, a lie I believe any good god would forgive me for. "And I don't have that kind of a *thing*, Jamie, like I was saying."

"Like you was sayin'," he's saying while he's chewing. "I keep forgettin' you ain't like the rest of us lowly gonks around here."

"Hey," I snap. "Jamie, c'mon, you know I don't feel that way about people here. Not at all."

"Shut up, will ya. This place is my life, and even I feel it. Some of the creatures that pass through them doors, they make pond scum go *euwww*."

"Well, I don't see it. Anyway, my point is I want to fight."

"Do ya?" he says, chewing some meat McSomething.

"Yeah. I really feel it."

338

"You break up with a girl or somethin'? I love it when guys quit with a girl, especially if it was boxing that split 'em up, which it usually is. They always come in extra angry and ferocious after that."

"Not exactly."

"So, girl's gone now, and you want to take it out on somebody other than the heavy bag. Classic."

"She's not gone. I'm just kind of avoiding her a little. And lying a little when I'm not avoiding her . . ."

"Duckin' and divin'."

"That's beside the point."

"What, you suddenly come to your senses and decide this"—he gestures with the straw of his orange juice at his beautiful atrocity of a nose—"is the most attractive appendage a guy can wear outside his clothes?"

It feels like answering him just keeps getting me further away from both the beginning and the end of this conversation, so I stop.

"Okay, okay," he says. "So you want to fight. You figure you had the potential to be good. Coulda got somewhere with it if you didn't waste away your prime on football and whatnot, right?"

"Jamie, I'm not even eighteen yet."

"Old maid. Old maid. Time waits for no one, junior, don't ever forget that. Even six months at your age is a whole lot of development and experience that other people have been gaining at your expense."

"I am well aware."

"Well aware, well. Still, you could get someplace maybe, that's what you're thinkin'. That story is as old as the hills. Guys a lot older than me walking the streets carryin' that *coulda been a contenda* shit around with 'em. I seen your balance, strength, speed, reflexes. Sure, you could make a few bucks even. An undercard here and there, maybe work as a sparring partner for some dog-meat journeyman pugs."

"Sweep me off my feet, why dontcha."

"Ha," he says, rising to his feet, two-thirds of his breakfast waiting. "You want me to sweep you off your feet? You mean knock you on your ass? You're asking to spar with *me*?"

"I . . . wasn't, actually, but . . ."

He's already happy-bouncing to the nearside ring.

"You're gonna be dancin' with an expert while you're a complete novice, remember," he calls as he climbs through the ropes, pulling on a pair of big puffy practice gloves.

"I guess that's why it's good I start with an old punching bag like you," I say, following him in. I am strapping on headgear, which he's not even bothering with. "Anyway, I've been working out hard."

He actually blows raspberries at me.

"I know, I know," I say, "not the same."

"Not the same at all. Not even close."

He's maybe a little older than fifty. Nobody knows exactly because he refuses to say, and any old fight info available on him lists six different birthdates because he was always lying to suit the situation. As I watch him loosen up, however, I am reminded who he was, and is, as a fighting man. But he is smart, tough as an

**340**

angry dog, and wily. He bounces in a circle, flicking jabs, ducking phantom punches, throwing combinations that a fifty-something cannot throw.

He is doing his job. I find my body moving more in tune to what Jamie McAlpine is doing than what my own brain is telling it to do. Autopilot, glorious, abandon to the thing, autopilot is moving me around the ring.

"I'll give you three minutes," he says, gesturing up at the big clock with the orange Day-Glo sweep second hand. "That'll be a good enough test to judge where you're at without givin' my breakfast enough time to coagulate. I almost can't eat it when that thick filmy stuff starts to settle, y'know?"

"Three minutes it is," I say, smacking my gloves together.

Three seconds it is, when I realize how raw I am. Jamie wades in, peekaboo style, and right away slams two body shots into my left and right sides. Right away, my ribs ache, my organs feel the bruise. My arms come down, like body shots'll do, and he comes for my head. I block, I block. He's got me backpedaling. Cripes, he is dominating me for the first forty seconds, not beating me up but dictating where I go, where the fight goes, and at what pace. My elbows are at my sides, my hands alongside my cheeks, as I protect as much of myself as I can.

"The frickin' heavy bag puts up a better fight than you do," he says, laughing, and still coming after me.

He's too frickin' right. Look at me. Look at me, cowering. I'm not afraid to get hit. I was never afraid to get hit. What's wrong with me? I'm better than this, a lot better.

"What's wrong with ya?" he asks, in a voice that's far more irritated than concerned. He presses harder, pressuring me into the corner and hammering me with one body shot after another until I feel my hands coming lower and lower, and I know what comes next, I know it. Bring the hands down with the punishing body shots, then take the head. I know this. I know this.

Doesn't stop those hands coming, though.

He goes right after my head with a vicious leap out of his crouch.

I slip the punch almost effortlessly just as it sails by. I remember that from every fine fighter I watched on TV. Good—no, great—upper body movement. Snaky. Slick.

"Good," Jamie says as I slither out of the corner and he's left there looking a little awkward. "There it is. I was starting to wonder if there was anything there at all. . . ."

I am dancing now, on the balls of my feet. Good movement. I snap a jab, and when the jolt of connecting with his chin travels up my arm, it's like fifty thousand volts coming up and spreading right through to my torso, my heart. I hit him again with the jab, and again.

"Wonder away, old timer," I say, peppering him with the jab.

He can just manage single words now, but I can put them together for myself. "More . . . to . . . it . . . than . . ."

"Yeah," I say, getting into the rhythm, "uh-huh."

He makes a noise that sounds positive, but he's breathing heavy. I pop a left hand uppercut, then follow up instantly with a cracking straight right hand.

The voltage goes up. I feel it, *it* coming to me, and I am close to invincible.

*Bam.*

I am not invincible. I am flat on my ass.

"A slip," I say, getting right up, shaking my head, and getting after him.

"Bullshit," he wheezes.

It is mine now. No more stupid. Get cute, get overconfident, and anybody in the place will have you floored in a heartbeat. Don't be stupid, Arlo. You're not stupid.

Three minutes can be an ungodly long time.

The voltage is decreasing as I plow in, put together very nice jab-jab-cross, jab-jab-hook combinations. I have Jamie in the corner and am about to unload when, wily thing, he sneaks a choppy hard right uppercut through my gloves and to my forehead, but I am there, I am in it, answering with an uppercut of my own and another right hook, before he yells, "Time!"

There is applause from the five other guys in the gym as Jamie 'Pine and I head wheezing and sweating back toward his office.

He hasn't even stopped panting when he is already back at the breakfast. He drops into his chair, sips his juice, then chomps, pants, chomps.

I can't stop pacing around the office.

"*That's* what I have to do," I say, prowling the nine-foot-wide room like a big caged cat in a too small cage.

"Is that what you have to do?" Jamie says, grinning, wheezing, chewing.

The gym is coming alive, with the grunts of weight lifting, the thumps of heavy-bagging.

"Absolutely," I say.

"You did okay there, once you shook off that ring rust. Course anybody younger than Jack Dempsey woulda taken your head off before you got to that point."

"Yeah, yeah, but you saw. I shook it off, and I got there. Not bad for an old maid. Not bad. Better than I expected even." My heart is racing. I go to the picture window that looks out on all the activity that is McAlpine's world. "That," I say, pointing emphatically. "I want to do *that*."

I twirl back to him, and a blackness comes up like a shade pulled upside down from the floor to the ceiling. I feel like my head is baking at about 450 degrees, and the rushes of blood to the surface of my face feel like hot bloody surf.

"Jesus, Arlo, sit *down*," Jamie barks.

Somehow I manage, through flashes, to make my way to a chair.

"I'm okay," I say, leaning over with my elbows on my knees. "Bit of a head rush, you know how it is. Too much adrenaline, caught up to me. Fine now, man, fine."

"Good," Jamie says, and I hear him chewing again, which calms me some. I blink away the black flashes and the searing white till the normal midtones return. In all it's only a minute or so. To be expected, though.

I lift my head slowly to find him finishing his juice. He makes a loud burbling noise through the straw, and then looks at me, nodding, like he's finally decided to take me on.

"Um, Jamie? I have another favor that's kind of from the other end of the scale."

"That being?"

"That being . . . like you were saying earlier, about my girlfriend . . ."

"Ah, you still wanna be a sneaky lyin' sonofabitch about this."

"*Jamie.*"

"You think you invented this dodge?"

"Seen it before?"

"What do you think?"

"Okay, then you have experience. And it's not about a girlfriend, to be honest, it's about a mother. I can't be showing stuff, scuffs, cuts, swelling, that kinda thing."

"Extra padding."

"Yes," I say.

He nods. "One lying-cheating-bastard-package coming up."

"*Jamie.*"

He laughs hard and waves me out of his office. "What do you think you're gonna achieve by keepin' sayin' my name like that?"

I fold my hands and half-bow my head, giving him note-perfect altar boy that we would both know well. "Mr. McAlpine, please, sir?"

"There ya go," he says. "My guy comes in about lunchtime today. I'll have your happy hat after that, any time you wanna come in and give it a shot."

"Great," I say, full of new. That'll be the missing something. Perfect. "Great."

345

# HELMET

I'm back eight hours later.

"Is that it?" I ask Jamie as I point to the big red globe of leather sitting on his desk, which is strewn with the remains of his latest McDonalds feast.

"What else would it be?" He chucks the thing at me like a medicine ball.

It's a little heavy, though not nearly as weighty as it looks. It has a lot of padding. I slip it over my head and the first thing I notice is the reduced vision. There's protection for over and under the eyes, all the way down the nose bridge, well below the ears to the jawline and around the back of the neck. And the padding all around is probably twice the thickness of the standard headgear. It looks and feels designed more for gladiator battles with those great big pummeling bars or training giant police dogs.

All that considered, the sight lines are good.

"Arr-arr-arr," Jamie snickers as I try to get a look at myself in the window glass. "You look like one of them little kids who needs to be protected from hurting himself."

"Well," I say, turning from my awful image to his, "I guess I should just go out and hurt somebody else then."

"By all means," he says, staying at his desk.

"Anybody got a minute?" I've left his office and am yelling, over the racket of two rings. There is medium-intensity sparring going on in the boxing ring and lighter business going on in the kickboxing one. The boxers ignore me, but the two kickers come to the rope.

"What's up?" says a guy looking to be about thirty hard ones old. He must be schooling the other guy, who looks about half that. The kid suddenly notices my lunar headgear and starts laughing behind his fist.

I'm taking a risk. Extra padding will mean extra punching. It's a provocation and, frankly, an admission of some kind of weakness, fear, vulnerability. I know it looks stupid, and exposes more than a guy wants to expose in a place like this. Nobody wants to stand out as any kind of special here. Unless the specialness is fearsomeness.

It's a trade. I need to make the trade. I will endure a bit of humiliation for Ma, and the thought already makes me feel better.

"Come on up then," the guy says, and I drop my backpack and hop on up. The kid gives over his mitts, and I pull them on. I am in school clothes, but that means little as my school and reality clothes are pretty similar. Loose fitting, always ready for movement. Good, grippy shoes.

"Just really want to test out the space helmet a bit," I say. The guy nods, and we begin our little dance.

*Bob-weave-jab.* Bob weave jab. The guy moves very well. Very athletic. It suits me. I'd be good. Maybe better than I am at straight-up boxing.

*Bob-weave-jab. Bob-weave-jab.* I'm sticking him pretty good. I'm feeling other stuff now. Feeling like I have something to show, something to prove, something to achieve.

"How's the hat?" he asks, bouncing a couple of quick ones off my forehead for emphasis.

"Doin' the job," I say, instantly kind of thrilled to have something bounce off my head for a change without the echo bouncing around inside a dozen times. I lean into him, and show him some speed as I back away again with a snapping right-hand parting gift.

"What's your name, kid?"

"Arlo."

"Simon. I give lessons here for Jamie, 'cause he doesn't know squat about this."

"Pleased to meet you, Simon. Actually, been wanting to meet you."

We conduct this over the soothing rhythm of the *pop-pop-pop* of leather thwacking leather.

*Thwack.* I thwack Simon a nice one flush on the left side of his face.

"You move well," he says. "Ever thought about kickboxing?"

"Just started thinking about it."

"Good. Good to hear."

We dance a bit more, trade punches a bit more, test the various contact points of the silly important headgear, and the headgear responds well enough that getting punched has the perverse effect of making me more confident, more excited, more aggressive.

"Don't hold back, Simon," I say, feeling it now, "you can kick. I want to see how it goes."

He nods, continues to box me. Then I lean over and launch a right-foot kick that he blocks pretty easily.

"Good balance," he says. Then he sends an easy kick toward my ribs. I block with my elbow, return kick. He blocks. Then he kicks at my ribs again. I block again, kick at his head.

He doesn't even bother blocking that one. He just moves to his right, and blur-quick his right foot is smacking me sideways, landing—*Bam!*—at my temple.

Simon smiles, and I return same. The headgear is my friend.

"Taking me to school," I say happily.

"That's precisely what we're here for, young man," he says, waving his hands in such a way that I know he is lining me up with that foot again. I am certain and I am ready. . . .

For precisely the wrong thing. As I foolishly look for that foot, old Simon rocks a straight right hand that would shame any of the straight-up guys in the other ring discipline. It catches the point of my chin and does me a whiplash thing that must make it look like the back of my head and my chin are doing a dog-tail chase after one another.

It reverberates in my brain like a small fighter is continuing to kick from inside my skull.

Someone whoops like a nut job, or there's a fire engine in the house.

I backpedal until I lean way back into the ropes. I sink into them, then come out covering up.

"Kick*boxing*," Simon says, wrapping me up in a fatherly hug as I come off the ropes, the way a referee does to save some battered loser from more battering. "Never forget the two words in the title. Soon as you get infatuated with the one, the other'll lay you out."

"I'll remember," I say into his neck.

"That lesson's for free. We'll talk about next steps whenever you're ready," he says.

Scenes are flashing for me now. Like a song that's skipping, I go from Simon's neck to the kid unsmilingly taking the gloves off me without any connecting vision.

This could be a lot of things. Could be my future, or a vision of it, in which I'm the champion and Jamie is my grizzled dog-eared loyal cornerman up in the ring to greet me after the greatest championship fight of my life. The lights are here for me anyway, snapping and popping everywhere, and Jamie sure gives great grizzled. Could be a Rocky scene. Maybe they stole it from us. Maybe I'm in the scene, in the middle of it right now. Maybe I was there all along.

# CONSEQUENCES ARE CONSEQUENCES

I'm sitting on a thick, splintered oak bench as I wait for the birds to stop tweeting in my head. It's usually just a few minutes, then I'm good to go. Good to go. Good to go.

"When you're ready, come see me in the office!" Jamie yells to me from his doorway.

I don't like the sound of this. I see my brother walk out of the office behind him and hurry out of the gym. Now I really don't like this.

When I feel settled enough, I get off the bench and start walking across the concrete floor to the door of the gym. I concentrate on walking straight. I see in front of the boxing ring the fathead helmet that I guess I must have tossed there. I look back at the office. Shouldn't have done that. It's like the door jumps out at my face. Jamie's on the phone, but he's mouthing, "Wait, wait, Arlo, don't go," and I'm mouthing "Homework," and I'm gone.

It's nothing at all like a concussion. It's not even a real thing. It's subconcussive. If there is one good that's come out of Ma's nagging file of the big book of head injuries, it's that I know what I'm talking about when I talk about what *I know I do not have.*

Subconcussive. Why even bother with such a thing? It's like saying you have a brokenish hand, or a torn-like hamstring. They made up a name because these days it seems like it's all gotta be named to make it all simple and countable for people who probably just need insurance ass-cover and who *do not know shit.*

Getting your bell rung is what it is, what it always was, and what is to be expected. If you are not prepared to get your bell rung sometimes, then you should stay in your damn bed.

Because all the padded helmets in the world aren't gonna be able to save you.

# BALANCE

I walk out of McAlpine's and right into Sandy. Guilt runs hot and bloody right up under the surface of my skin all over.

"You've been avoiding me," she says.

"I haven't," I say. I have. When did I get so good at lying?

"What happened to your lip?"

"Slipped in the shower."

"Uh-huh." She is looking at me in that way, tilting her head left and right, as if to see honesty lurking somewhere way up in my nostrils. I wonder how she knew where to find me. I am glad she did. Like the criminal on the run who would never turn himself in but is happy to be caught.

I put out my hand, desperate for her to take it, to balance me, to remind me, to make me better in all the ways that can mean.

She does. God, she does. And she does and she does and she does.

She takes my hand. "Go for a run with me, then," she says as we make our way down the street.

"Don't think I'm up to it today, Sandy."

"I'm just talking about a few circuits of the track. Three miles max? Then we can walk home together? Sit on my porch for a while?"

This is the most beautiful offer I have ever had. I'm disgusted to find myself . . . For the love of . . . I'm welling up. Like a jackass, like I never used to do and now I do, and I'm more humiliated by the loss of control or sanity or whatever. I pray that the nausea takes over first.

"Honey," I say, shaking my clammy hand out of hers with some force and rushing away. "I just can't . . . feeling really sick."

"Arlo!" she calls. I turn and give her a half wave as she stands there, looking at her hand and the slick of whatever I left on it.

I almost hope she understands. I pray she doesn't.

I hit Centre Street and I feel strong enough to run, but away from Sandy rather than back to her. I start running. It's a pug run because I even run like a pug now, like a fighter runs. Right away my whole body is into it, just like boxers on TV showing off their training regimen. My shoulders get into it, juking this way and that, my fists get into it, pop-pop-popping jabs to the rhythm of my footfalls. It's a whole different breed of run and it isn't something I have to apply. It is me. The real me. I might just need to get away from Jamie, and Lloyd, and everybody else who has a preformed opinion about me, and start fresh at a new gym. Do it right and find out for real what I can give to the fight thing. Maybe that's all I need.

Several sweaty miles after I leave, I come back to a quiet house and the space to appreciate the feeling of calm and of privacy.

Feeling better after feeling scarily not better is a whole kind of joy itself.

In the bathroom I break the wrapper on a new bar of Palmolive Gold, and life is behaving itself so well at this instant it deserves some kind of prize.

The shower alone brings a smile to my face as I hold the mediciney bar of gold to my nose for the longest time, eyes closed, everything else wide open to the heat, the vapor, the wash.

After many minutes with my eyes closed, I open them up to find the strange and unhappy sense that they are still closed. I panic, putting one hand on the glass shower panel in front of me and the other on the tiled wall to my left. The bar of soap bumbles to the shower floor, slithers, and stops, and I blink over and over until the olive eyelid blackness becomes something more like camera flash and lightning, sheet lightning showing me nothing else, then bolt lightning, slashing across visions of tiles, of my hands, my feet, and pebbly, rain-dropped glass.

Sight is worse still, worse than the sight that hid from me. Rocket shots of pain and horror light slash my head inside out and I drop to my knees, crouching forward, brow to glass, hands clasped around my head, trying to hold my skull fragment continents in their places.

Of course I know what this is. Dammit. Damn it to hell.

How many times have I read the damn thing. The unfortunate fools from the NHL, NFL, pro boxing who sat in their rooms for hours and months in petrified paralyzed hell. Sometimes it seems like the Bruins have a whole extra training room full of these guys.

Thanks, File. Thanks for the info. It was always good to know what they all had that I did not have. Thanks, articles. Thanks, Ma.

Withering sensitivity to light. Nausea tides. Screaming, throbbing come-and-go headaches. Balance totally screwed, then not. Then cured. Then not. Go to hell, mercurial mood swings and volcanic rage and hide-and-seek memory and volcanic rage. Thanks for everything because it's not ever been me. Probably just the articles and the individual letters themselves forming the wicked words and the sentences that torture the inside of my eyelids that're making me so bad and mad now—and it will just go away like it usually does if I just calm the hell down.

Thanks, postconcussion syndrome. Maybe it's post-subconcussion syndrome. The junior varsity of head injury.

I stay like this, squeezing my eyes tight shut, bringing back every letter of every page of every brain-trauma article I ever read for the express purpose of convincing myself that I do not have this awful thing, heh-heh-heh, chumps. The hot rain pat-pattering my back, until I can do something else, will work fine.

As soon as I can get out of the cubicle, I switch off the light. Light is frying me. It is as if there is a direct laser line from my corneas to the upper front of my brain, and it causes me agony every time I lift the lids a fraction. I walk gingerly from the bathroom to my bedroom, using mostly wall and memory to navigate. Once there I pull the shade right down, sit on the edge of my bed in the duskiness. The dark calms me and I can finally just sit, completely empty.

My phone goes off and it has to be Sandy. When I don't answer, she calls again. Then texts. She wants to know how I am. She loves me. She rings again, texts again. I cannot pick it up, cannot even look at it, but I know it's her. When she finally gives up, I get so sad. I get so sad. Please, Sandy.

And then I sit, and sit. There is a huge hollow empty dark quiet in the space Sandy left just there, and it terrifies me for about a minute.

Then my senses are back to ridiculous. My sight, my smell, they are pulling in signals at eleven hundred and seventy times the normal rate. My nerve endings are slithering like microscopic eels throughout my body, through the skin, the fingertips, the eyebrows, the groin, slipping out, snaking out, out of me and into the atmosphere, and *feeling* the holy hell out of everything everywhere.

I cannot sit still enough. The fibers of my muscles are churning no matter how much I concentrate on shushing them. They are swinging and banging and crashing into one another, making hellacious loud, awful tormenting noises.

Stillness is my only goal now. I sit on my bed with my hands folded in the dark, and I simply try to stop feeling, sensing, anything at all.

I am aware of my father coming home. I am aware a little while later when my mother comes home. Somewhere out on the horizon of my consciousness I am aware of their nice, normal evening with dinner and low conversation and human interaction and eventually their fading off to their bedroom and their peaceful sleep.

Through it all I sit, still and safe, but the realization comes to me that my life in this room has become, to them, no different from the unpleasant, unapproachable, alien existence that Lloyd's *other* life once was just down the hall. I skulk and I hide and I sneak, and I'm sure just one more big hit will solve everything for me.

Except it won't. Not anymore.

It's done. It's really over.

# DAWN

Sleep? I suppose, but it doesn't much matter.

I am upright when the sun comes hissing in under the window shade. I take as much physical inventory as I can before moving one fiber of one muscle. I decide there's enough there to get dressed. After getting dressed, I decide there's enough for more.

"What are you doing there?" I say when I find Lloyd sitting at a kitchen chair that isn't in the kitchen. It's backed up to the back door.

"Didn't want to miss you," he says groggily.

"That's sweet," I say. "Now that you haven't missed me, could you slide out of the way?"

He slowly rises, moves the chair a couple of feet sideways, then stands up right in my face.

"You get in that ring again, and it'll be with me," he says with just enough of his old menace to be both a joke and scary to me.

"I have to tell you, big brother, you are not the force you were anymore."

He stands his ground. "Neither are you, little brother."

I lean even closer to him, hold us both there for several long seconds. Then I cup my right hand behind his skull, and kiss his cheek, finishing it off with a great smacking sound. He reaches around and thumps me on the back. I hold that gnarly nuts head of his for a few more seconds before I step around him and out.

# PORCH

I've nodded off by the time Sandy's front door slams behind me. I lift my chin off my fist but do not turn around.

"I'm sorry, Sandy," I say.

She is on my back, arms around my shoulders, warming me like a little human cape.

"You going to tell me what you're sorry for?"

"I'm going to try not to. You going to allow it?"

She sighs some deep-thought breathing right in my ear.

"For now, I suppose," she says.

"I need a tutor," I say.

"You have a tutor," she says.

"I need a better one. I need a really, really patient and understanding one. I want to learn, and I want to graduate. And I want a tutor that I want to be with all the time, all the time."

She does the extended think-breathing again.

"Wow," she says, "you really do mean patient."

I laugh, which makes my head hurt fantastically but everything else fantastically not.

"Yup," I say. "Know anybody?"

I hear her soft breathing. I could listen forever to Sandy's soft breathing, and she knows it.

"Um . . . Sandy?"

"Shhhhh," she says into the deepest part of my ear, making me tingle from there, down my spine, and all the way back up again to where her lips stay pressed to me.